HOW TO FALL IN LOVE WITH A MAN YOU THOUGHT YOU HATED

A PRIDE AND PREJUDICE VARIATION

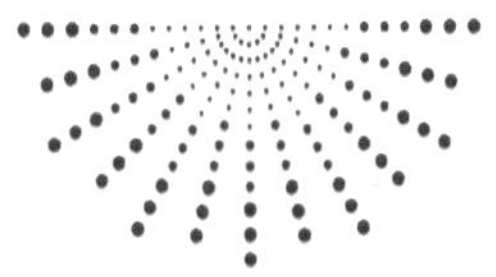

ELIZABETH ADAMS

For Jami.
Thanks for always knowing how to make a girl laugh.

I wish, as everybody else, to be perfectly happy. But like everybody else, it must be in my own way.
  Jane Austen

1

A TUESDAY AFTERNOON IN KENT

"Charlotte, you are being ridiculous!"

"One is not rendered ridiculous by simply having a different opinion from your own."

Elizabeth rolled her eyes at Charlotte's smug opinion. She sat across from her friend in the parsonage's small parlor, drinking tea and discussing the previous evening at Rosings.

"One may not be rendered ridiculous by a difference of opinion, but one is certainly rendered ridiculous by belief in the absurd." Elizabeth raised a brow triumphantly and sipped her tea.

"Only you would be proud of believing a man in love with you to be an absurd notion."

Elizabeth's mouth dropped open and she set her teacup down with a clank. Charlotte resettled herself in her chair, looking every bit the proud matron.

"Do you think it will rain today?" Charlotte looked out the window and stretched her neck to look up into the sky.

"Charlotte!"

"I suppose not. It has been rather warm lately."

Elizabeth sighed in frustration. "Very well. I will take your change of subject as a signal that you recognize the absurdity of your assumption and move on. How is Mrs. Selton? Is she feeling any better?"

Charlotte turned to face her friend. "Eliza, I know we may joke about it, but as your friend, I cannot allow you to continue to believe that a man being interested in you romantically is a ridiculous notion. *That* is ridiculous!"

Elizabeth sighed again. "It is not that I think a man finding me attractive to be impossible, but this man in particular."

"And why is that?"

"He said himself I am merely tolerable!"

"And can a person not grow in attractiveness once one knows them better?"

Elizabeth looked frustrated. "Of course, but that is hardly the case here."

"Is it not? How can you know that?"

"Because it is not!"

Charlotte took a deep breath. "What did you say the first day you met Colonel Fitzwilliam?"

Elizabeth was thrown by the change of topic, but recovered and said, "I thought him friendly and amiable."

"And handsome?"

Elizabeth opened her mouth to respond, then snapped it shut. "Well, not at first," she said slowly.

"When he left the parsonage, Maria said he was good company, but it was a shame he was not in a red coat, for it would improve his looks immensely."

Elizabeth stared silently at her friend.

"And you agreed with her."

"I was being silly! I should have held my tongue had I known you would throw it back at me this way!"

"And how do you find the colonel's looks now?"

Elizabeth was thrown again by Charlotte's question. "He is perfectly agreeable."

"Do you find him attractive?"

Elizabeth colored. "Well, I, he is," she paused and looked away, shaking her head and pursing her lips. "Yes, I find him attractive."

"And if he offered to court you tomorrow, you would accept?"

Elizabeth huffed.

"Or would you decline on the grounds of him being unattractive?"

"Of course not! What a ridiculous reason! A person cannot help their looks."

Charlotte leveled a piercing look at her friend. "Exactly."

Elizabeth rolled her eyes. "It is hardly the same thing."

"Is it not?"

"Men care much more about these things than women do."

"Do they?"

"Yes!"

"Then how is it that I am married and Jane is not?"

Elizabeth gasped and looked at Charlotte with shock and offense.

"If beauty alone were the deciding factor in marriage, Jane would have wed years ago. And if beauty alone were the deciding factor in spinsterhood, I would still be one."

"What does this have to do with Mr. Darcy?" she asked warily.

"So he found you tolerable. What of it? That was months ago. He has now come to know you better. It is entirely possible he now finds you attractive, much how you have changed in your opinion of Colonel Fitzwilliam's looks."

"I am certainly prettier than the colonel," she grumbled.

Charlotte smiled. "That you are. So you see, Mr. Darcy could very well be in love with you."

Elizabeth rolled her eyes again. "Charlotte, you have taken up an idea and run wild with it."

"Why do you say so? Has he insulted you again and I did not hear of it?"

"No."

"Does he still stare at you when you are together in company?"

"He is looking to find fault!"

"Because men so often stare at that which they dislike," said Charlotte with a look of smug disbelief.

Elizabeth huffed again. "There is nothing better to do at Rosings."

"Of course. A young man of independent means in the country of his own accord can find nothing better to do than stare at you out of boredom. I comprehend it clearly now."

"He does not speak to me!"

"He is a quiet man."

"He is rude and haughty."

"That does not mean he dislikes you."

Elizabeth sighed. "I am going for a walk."

"Very well. Stay out of the sun or you will have a red nose."

THE NEXT DAY, Charlotte and Elizabeth were walking in the village of Hunsford and stopped to look in the window of a small haberdashery.

"That is a hideous bonnet," said Elizabeth quietly.

Maria agreed. "It needs a different ribbon, and the brim should be wider."

"Yes, you are quite right. It is so ugly I cannot stop looking at it," added Charlotte.

Elizabeth turned to mock glare at her friend. "Come along, Maria," she said too brightly. "I wish to see if the library has anything new."

Charlotte sniggered to herself and followed them.

That evening, they were reading the books they had borrowed in the parlor after dinner. Mr. Collins had been called to the bedside of an elderly parishioner and the ladies sat alone. Charlotte said it happened often. It seemed to be one of her favorite things about her choice of husband.

"This book is dull," complained Maria, setting down the history she had chosen.

"Why did you choose it? It is not your usual fare," said her sister.

"It looked interesting." Maria sighed in disappointment.

"Take mine," said Charlotte as she passed her sister her book. "It is a novel, and terribly dull, but that is what makes it impossible to put down. I always find that the more I dislike a book, the more time I want to spend reading it."

Maria clearly did not know how to respond to such a speech. Elizabeth looked at her friend with pursed lips. Charlotte smiled sweetly back at her.

"Take mine," said Elizabeth, rising and depositing her book on the table next to Maria. "I have quite lost my taste for books this evening. Good night."

She left the room without a response and Maria looked about in confusion.

"What is going on?" she asked.

"Nothing to worry about, my dear. Will you read aloud while I sew? You have such a pleasant reading voice."

ELIZABETH LAY in bed long after the household had retired, unable to sleep. Why must Charlotte harp on so? It was clear to anyone with eyes that Mr. Darcy did not like her. He never spoke to her! If they were in the same room together, he never sat near her or sought her out in any way.

Well, he had spoken to her as she played the pianoforte at Rosings, but not nearly as much as the colonel. His aunt would always call him away before they had spent more than five minutes in conversation.

And why would she do that?

No! She refused to believe it. Mr. Darcy could not possibly be in love with her. It was an outrageous idea! Charlotte was now married and wished everyone around her to be married as well. There was nothing to it. Nothing at all.

Though... Charlotte had said Jane should show more affection than she felt, or at least show what affection she did feel for Mr. Bingley. He would not be brave enough to love her without encouragement, or so Charlotte had said. Well, look how that had turned out! He had left and never come back, breaking sweet Jane's heart in the process.

But why did he not come back?

The question niggled at the back of her mind until she could ignore it no longer. Elizabeth had long believed it was because of Jane's lack of fortune and connections. But what if Charlotte was correct? If Jane had encouraged him, would it have changed anything?

No, she would not think like this. It could not be! Mr. Bingley had spent hours in Jane's company. If he could not discern her feelings after that, it was his fault, not Jane's. She could not be expected to display her deepest feelings to the world with no indication of the gentleman's feelings or intentions.

For all they knew, Mr. Bingley had known exactly how Jane felt and had been talked out of proposing by his sisters and Mr. Darcy. Yes, that must be it. Charlotte was wrong. Elizabeth was certain of it.

2

A SUNNY THURSDAY MORNING

"Miss Bennet! Good day!"

"Colonel Fitzwilliam! I did not know you walked this way."

"I am making my tour of the park as I do every year and thought I would end with a call at the parsonage. But I don't want to disturb you if you would like to finish your letter." He gestured to the paper she was refolding.

"Not at all! It is the latest letter from my sister in London, but I have read it before." She deposited the letter into her reticule with a smile.

"How does Miss Bennet? Is she enjoying the Season?"

"I do not think so. Jane is the sort of person who will do all that is asked of her, and do it graciously, though she has no personal desire to do so. She does not like to disappoint others, and she will never see fault in anyone else, so if she is unhappy, she blames herself for becoming that way in the first place or refuses to acknowledge it at all."

"Is she unhappy in London then?" he asked kindly.

"Not as such—she enjoys all that Town has to offer and our aunt and uncle are keeping her well entertained. But she has recently suffered a disappointment and I'm afraid her temperament will not allow her to overcome it easily." She wondered at herself for sharing such information so easily, and with a man who did not even know her sister, but she had been worrying about Jane excessively, and she had always felt so comfortable with the colonel. No matter—it was said now. She could not take it back.

"I know a young lady in a similar situation. Even though the fault was all on his side, she insists on berating herself for all she misunderstood and what she believed of him. It has been many months now, but she is much altered by the experience."

"I am sorry for her. After seeing Jane in similar circumstances, I would not wish it on anyone. Why must men lavish attention on ladies to the exclusion of everything and everyone else, speak to them as if they are in the deepest throes of love, and then disappear without a word? It is unspeakably cruel."

He looked at her with sad eyes. "Yes, it is." Then a moment later, "It is one of the many reasons I am glad I am not a lady."

Elizabeth was surprised into laughter and gave him a mock reproachful look. "You find going to war against the French preferable to wearing bonnets and making morning calls?"

"Morning calls I do not mind, but I'm sure I would look dreadful in a bonnet."

She laughed again, and he smiled to see it.

"Jane tells me that our mother expects her to come home engaged, she does not care much to whom, and if she will not oblige her in this, which Jane certainly will not, Mama wishes her to return to Longbourn before the militia leave for the summer. If I thought Denny and Wickham could cheer her, I would agree to the plan, but Jane has never cared much either way about the officers."

Colonel Fitzwilliam's interest was piqued. "Did you say Wickham? Not George Wickham?"

"Oh, forgive me, I forgot you must be known to him. He said he grew up at Pemberley—his father was steward there."

"Yes, he did, fine lot of good it did him," he said harshly. "Miss Bennet, I must give you a friendly warning. Mr. Wickham is not to be trusted. Not with pretty young ladies, not near anyone with change in their pockets, and certainly not with credit at the local shops."

She was surprised at his vehemence, but supposed he had gotten his knowledge from Mr. Darcy, and said something vague about knowing there to be a difficult history between them.

Much to her surprise, Colonel Fitzwilliam told her that his opinion of Wickham was based on his own experience and information as well as that of his cousin. He laid out for her, in painstaking detail, how Wickham had lied and cheated his way through school, been sent down from university, caused more trouble than he could rightly tell a lady, and left a trail of debt and ruin wherever he went. In case she had felt sorry for Wickham, she should know that Mr. Darcy had long been paying his bills at various shops and had covered his debts of honor at university for some time. Darcy had cleaned up Wickham's messes of one sort or another until his father died. Then Wickham was given a thousand-pound legacy and lest she believe the cock and bull story about a living being denied him, she should know he was given three-thousand pounds in lieu of the living (that he wasn't qualified for anyway as he had never taken orders) and had signed away all rights to it while saying he wished to study the law. His knowledge was first hand as he had been one of the executors of his uncle's will.

Elizabeth stared at him, mouth agape. The colonel paced before her, furious in his recitation but controlling it with a rigidity she had not known him capable of. She grimly thought this must be how he managed on campaign and felt some sympathy for his recruits.

She felt something in her hand and looked down to see Colonel Fitzwilliam had placed his handkerchief in her palm. She looked at him in confusion and he said, "If I may?" and dabbed at the tears streaming down her cheeks.

She had not known she was crying and continued to stare at him in astonishment. George Wickham, a liar and a cheat? A gambler and seducer? He had had such truth in his looks!

"Oh, what you must think of me!" she cried. She turned from him and he spoke to her back.

"I think the same as I always have, Miss Bennet. That you are a delightful young lady whom I am glad to know."

She nearly snorted in disbelief. "I am a fool!"

Now it was her turn to pace. She went from one end of the stand of trees to the other, mumbling to herself and occasionally dashing away tears angrily. He heard something about vanity and flattery but could not make out more than that.

"Miss Bennet, please forgive me. I did not intend to distress you." He hesitated. "Was Wickham a… favorite of yours?"

She looked at him in confusion until comprehension dawned, then explained that he had been something of a favorite over the winter and they had enjoyed a friendly flirtation, but no serious feelings had been involved. Then Wickham began courting Mary King near Christmas so none of it mattered anyway.

The colonel quickly asked if Miss King had any dowry to speak of, and Elizabeth told him that she had recently inherited ten-thousand pounds and that Wickham had not seemed to notice Miss King until her inheritance became common knowledge.

At this further proof of her blindness and idiocy, Elizabeth searched in vain for somewhere to sit down. Where was a fallen log or an oddly placed bench when she needed one? Unable to find what she was looking for, she sank onto the grass from actual exhaustion and buried her face in her hands, too mortified at her past behavior to be worried about the son of an earl's opinion on her current lack of propriety.

She wept heartily for a few minutes, soaking the Colonel's handkerchief through, then mustered the courage to look up. He was kneeling before her, close enough to reach out and touch, but not close enough to make her feel crowded.

"Colonel Fitzwilliam, I beg you would pretend you never saw me like this, weeping on the ground in Lady Catherine's grove."

He smiled gently. "I will never breathe a word of it, Miss Bennet. I am sorry for distressing you."

"I have distressed myself. I have had a taste of my own vanity and the flavor is bitter. It is no fault of yours."

He nearly disagreed with her, but then said nothing and looked determinedly past her left shoulder, letting her know he was there if she needed him, but giving her the privacy she clearly desired. Eventually, his leg began to cramp, and he sat down near her, his back against a tree trunk and his legs stretched out before him.

Elizabeth was so surprised by this action that she forgot to castigate herself for a moment and nearly laughed at the fact that an earl's son was sitting beside her in the grass at Rosings.

"Colonel, just when I think I cannot be more shocked, you rise to the occasion."

He smiled and tipped his head theatrically. "I strive to please, madam."

She smiled rather sadly and said, "I have come face to face with my own shortcomings today, and I find myself rather mortified, not only at what I have found, but that you have been witness to it all."

"I beg you would not make yourself uneasy. Wickham has a talent for deception I have seldom seen duplicated. You cannot blame yourself for being taken in."

"But I can blame myself for what I did with the information I swallowed so unthinkingly." She shook her head as he looked on in worry. "I suppose I owe your cousin an apology now."

She said the last so grimly and with such an expression of dread that he could not help but smile. "Darcy will understand. His own father was taken in by Wickham. I doubt he is expecting an apology, anyhow."

She made a resigned face. "Regardless, I owe him one." A frown line appeared between her brows. "Though I hate to give him the satisfaction of thinking even worse of me than he already does. At least now he can despise me for my gullibility—I can hardly fault him for that."

"Why should you think Darcy thinks badly of you?"

"He has always disliked me."

"Has he?"

"Yes."

"What makes you think so?"

"His behavior, his expressions, his words," she said, as if explaining why the sky was blue. She let her head drop back. "And now I have given him irrefutable proof of his superiority. If I were more magnanimous, I should let him enjoy the victory."

Colonel Fitzwilliam chuckled and shook his head. "You needn't worry. Darcy thinks very highly of you."

She scoffed.

"Truly, he does. He has sung your praises more than once."

It was impossible to hide her incredulity. The idea of Mr. Darcy singing anyone's praises, let alone her own, seemed as likely as Lady Catherine allowing someone else to speak at dinner.

She leaned her head back and sighed. "Your sisters are very lucky to have such a brother."

"What makes you say that?"

"You are very patient with weeping women."

He laughed softly. "I only have one sister, and I do not believe I have ever seen her weep. She is two years my senior and spent most of our childhood ordering me about."

Elizabeth gave him a weary smile. "That is what elder sisters are for. Regardless, you have been very kind to me today, and I thank you for it."

"I am most disturbed for having distressed you. Truly, Miss Bennet. I had no wish to give you pain. If there is anything I may do for your comfort, you need only ask."

She rested her hand on his sleeve. "Thank you, Colonel. You are kinder than I deserve."

"Nonsense. I wish I could do more. Surely you know, Miss Bennet, you are deserving of every kindness?"

His expression was so sincere and his voice so gentle, she nearly burst into tears again. "You must stop, Colonel, or I shall never recover."

He smiled at this and pressed her hand. "I hope you know I will stand your friend, Miss Bennet. And should you ever need it, I shall stand as your brother."

She did cry a little at this, for she had always wished for a brother, and though she and the colonel had enjoyed a flirtation, they both knew it would be entirely fruitless. She was free to enjoy his friendship with no expectation of more. Hearing him acknowledge the same was both a relief and reassurance all at once.

"Be careful what you offer, dear Colonel. I may take you up on it."

"I am at your service."

He helped her up from the grass gently and led her to the lane as if she were an old lady who could not support herself.

"I will be well from here."

"Are you certain you do not wish me to escort you to the parsonage?"

"I am certain. Thank you, for your information and your kindness. I will not forget it."

He bowed deeply before her and watched her walk away, glad that she seemed to be mostly recovered, and relieved she had accepted his offer of friendship.

3

STILL THURSDAY

E lizabeth burst into the parsonage, her mind in great tumult and her hair a blousy mess about her face. She made directly for the stairs and she would have made it to her room unimpeded, but Charlotte stepped into the hall just as Elizabeth was reaching for the bannister.

"Eliza, whatever is the matter?" she cried.

Elizabeth opened her mouth but instead of words, a choking sob emerged. Mortified, she turned away from her friend and raced up the stairs.

Charlotte, ever practical, ordered tea, told Maria she would be indisposed until dinner, and followed Elizabeth. She rapped twice on the door and entered without waiting for a response. Elizabeth was lying on the bed, her face buried in the pillow, weeping.

Charlotte sat beside her and stroked her back. "Dearest, whatever is the matter?"

"Oh, Charlotte! It's all such a muddle!" This was followed by more sobs.

"Have you received bad news from Longbourn or from the Gardiners?"

"No, everyone is well," Elizabeth replied before noisily blowing her nose on the handkerchief her friend pressed into her hand. "I am only a very great fool who has made a goose of herself."

Charlotte resisted the urge to laugh. "Have you quarreled with one of the gentlemen? I know you often meet them on your walks."

Elizabeth shook her head, avoiding her friend's gaze.

"Eliza, you know I ordinarily would not press a confidence, but you are staying in my home and under our care. If it involves anyone from Rosings, it will affect us in some way. I must insist you tell me what has happened to leave my normally sanguine friend in such a state."

There was a knock on the door and Charlotte answered it without letting the maid come inside. She took the tea tray and was careful to close the door and lock it behind her. She quickly prepared two cups and pressed one on her friend.

"Drink this and tell me all about what is troubling you."

Elizabeth had hoped no one would ever know of her shameful idiocy, but the truth would come out sooner or later—she may as well be done with it. And perhaps seeking succor in her old friend was a wise choice.

"I met Colonel Fitzwilliam on my walk this morning."

"Yes?"

"Oh, Charlotte! I am an addlepated ninny!"

Charlotte spluttered on her tea.

"He told me the most awful things. We have been terribly deceived in the character of Mr. Wickham."

"Mr. Wickham?"

Elizabeth nodded vigorously. "Mr. Wickham. Colonel Fitzwilliam told me he was a reckless gambler—"

"That is not surprising."

"—and that he leaves debts in his wake wherever he goes."

"How could he afford to pay for anything on his income?"

"And who do you suppose discharges those debts after Wickham has left the area?"

"Who?"

"Mr. Darcy!"

"Mr. Darcy?"

"Yes!"

"But why?"

Elizabeth shrugged. "I do not know. I asked the colonel the same question and he said Mr. Darcy feels some sense of responsibility for Wickham because he had been his father's ward and a favorite of his. Colonel Fitzwilliam fears the Darcy patronage spoiled Mr. Wickham and taught him to be a monster."

"A monster?"

Elizabeth made quick work of telling Charlotte what the colonel had told her of Mr. Wickham's spending habits. Charlotte was appropriately shocked, and Elizabeth was able to forget her own stupidity for a time in the face of Mr. Wickham's villainy.

"There is more."

Charlotte leaned forward, elbows on her knees.

"He is a bald-faced liar," said Elizabeth emphatically.

Charlotte leaned back. "Have you proof of this?" she asked carefully.

Elizabeth explained about the living Wickham had supposedly been promised, and the money he had been given in exchange for relinquishing any claim to it.

"Four thousand pounds!" cried Charlotte. "A prudent man could live some time on that amount of money."

"You needn't look at me like that, Charlotte. I already think myself the greatest fool in Hertfordshire."

"We are in Kent."

"Then I am the greatest fool in two counties. How could I have believed such a man?"

"He was very charming," said Charlotte in a conciliatory fashion.

"You are too good to say you told me so, but we both know that you were not convinced by him."

"Not entirely, no. But I did not truly give him much thought."

Elizabeth fell back on the bed dramatically. "The good colonel also said there was more that was not fit for a lady's ears, but that

Wickham was not to be trusted around ladies, especially young impressionable girls."

Charlotte's eyes widened. "That is disturbing indeed."

"Indeed." Elizabeth threw her arm over her eyes. "How could I have been so blind?"

"He was a very convincing liar." Charlotte attempted to be consoling, but Elizabeth knew she was dying to tell her friend she had been a fool who should have listened to her older and wiser friend.

"Colonel Fitzwilliam said there were things he could not speak of for fear of breaking someone's confidence. He alluded to a foiled elopement of some kind. I don't know any of the particulars, but the colonel was grim when he told me of it."

"That is no small matter, Eliza. If a man elopes with a woman, there is no settlement."

"I know."

"Her dowry is completely unprotected."

"I know."

"She is utterly at his mercy. And likely socially ruined."

Elizabeth nodded miserably.

"If Wickham is such a one, then he *is* a monster."

"Yes, I think you are right."

Charlotte looked out the window, unsure of what to say to her friend. Elizabeth lay on the bed, her gaze fixed on the ceiling, tears silently running down her face.

"I am a fool. A ridiculous, vain, stupid fool."

Charlotte squeezed her hand.

"I was so sure of my judgment. He had such truth in his looks!" She guffawed. "As if looks have anything to do with a man's probity."

Charlotte could only squeeze her hand again in silent commiseration.

"He flattered me. He flirted with me. He *preferred* me. And so I believed him! Have I always been such a fickle creature, so easily swayed? I believed everything he told me of Mr. Darcy on two days' acquaintance. The impropriety of his telling me never occurred to me. Any sensible woman would have thought, 'This man is telling me intimate details of his business dealings and I only met him yesterday. Perhaps something is odd here.' Or 'What can he mean by telling such things to a near stranger?' But did I wonder anything of the sort? No! I was flattered." She laughed cynically. "I thought he trusted me. That we had made some sort of ridiculous connection and were therefore instant friends and confidants. How could I have been so stupid!"

She rolled over and buried her face in the pillow and growled into it. Charlotte stroked her hair. "Do not be too hard on yourself, my dear. You are young yet, and Wickham is a man of the world. You cannot be the first person to whom he has told such stories."

Elizabeth clenched her fists in frustration. "I should have realized! Looking back on it now, I see so many inconsistencies. Besides the impropriety of him telling me at all, he said he would not blacken the son's name for the sake of the father. But as soon as Mr. Darcy left Meryton, the whole town knew of his supposed perfidy. Wickham wasted no time spreading his lies. For that matter, he said it was for Mr. Darcy to avoid him and that he would not be frightened away from Mr. Bingley's ball, and yet he went to London instead of attending. And I defended him still! Vain girl." She shook her head.

Charlotte continued to stroke her hair, not knowing what to say.

"Mr. Darcy insulted me and I was all too happy to hate him for it. I thought myself so original, to dislike a man so many bow and scrape to. It made me feel superior. Clever." She scoffed. "I had no evidence of Mr. Darcy's lack of principle. I had not thought him as bad as all that until Wickham whispered his lies in my ear. Jane asked Mr. Bingley about it, and he said Darcy was blameless, but I ignored it, thinking Bingley was merely defending his friend. Stupid, foolish girl!"

"There, there. It could have happened to anyone."

"Not to you."

Charlotte gave her a speaking glance. Of course it would not, but then Charlotte was older and more mature, and she was not nearly as vain as Elizabeth, though she had less reason to be. "You were wrong about Mr. Wickham, but you know now. I'm certain you will be more cautious in future."

Elizabeth scoffed. She would certainly be more cautious. And distrustful and suspicious.

"It does raise a great many questions about the other officers."

"What can you mean?" replied Elizabeth.

"If they are aware of Mr. Wickham's behavior, are they of the same ilk? Or has he deceived them as well?"

Elizabeth groaned, burying her face in the pillow again.

"And of course, there is the most pressing question of all."

"What is that?"

"If you are wrong about Mr. Darcy in this matter, could you be wrong about him in other matters as well?"

Elizabeth sat up abruptly. "Such as?"

Charlotte raised a brow. "Perhaps he does not despise you as thoroughly as you have believed."

"You think he may despise me only a little?"

Charlotte shot her a look. "I suggest he may not despise you at all. I have long suspected he likes you rather well, as you know."

Elizabeth nearly groaned again, then remembered something. "You know, the colonel told me that Mr. Darcy thinks very highly of me. I confess I did not believe him at all."

"Why would he lie about such a thing?"

"I do not think he is lying, but a person may be mistaken about such a thing. It is not so difficult to believe him mistaken."

"No. What is difficult to believe is that despite evidence to the contrary and the word of two people who are older and wiser than yourself, you still insist on thinking Mr. Darcy dislikes you!"

"What evidence do you speak of?" Elizabeth asked with a doubtful look, though she had lost assurance in her own claims.

"He asked you to dance at the Netherfield ball, and only you."

"That does not prove so very much."

Charlotte rolled her eyes. "He asked you to dance at my father's party, and you refused him."

"Your father pushed him into it. He did not ask of his own volition."

Charlotte pursed her lips. "Mr. Darcy does not strike me as a man who bows to others' desires. And you have said yourself that he does not care for social niceties. You cannot have it both ways."

Elizabeth looked confused and Charlotte pressed her point.

"He has met you on your walks several times, has he not?"

"Yes, but that is merely chance!"

"Is it?"

Elizabeth was thoughtful. "I did tell him the grove was my favorite walk."

"Eliza!"

"So he could avoid it!"

"Clearly he did not understand you! He likely thought you were requesting his company."

Elizabeth's eyes widened. "Do you truly think so?"

Charlotte gave her a look that declared Elizabeth the stupidest woman to ever set foot in Hunsford.

"Oh, dear!"

"Yes!"

"What am I to do? Does Mr. Darcy think I have been *encouraging* him?"

"I cannot know. How often has he met with you?"

"I cannot recall exactly. More than three times, less than six."

"Oh, dear."

"What have I done?"

"Nothing. You have walked a path you declared your favorite. That is all. If Mr. Darcy chose to join you, that was his decision."

"But what can he mean by it?"

Charlotte had her own ideas, but in the event Mr. Darcy was not planning to propose marriage to her friend, she did not want to excite expectations that would lead to disappointment. She might tease Eliza, but this was beyond the realm of teasing now. "We cannot know for certain. It is possible he is only interested in friendship."

Elizabeth nodded her head vigorously. "Yes. Perhaps that is it. After all, there is not much entertainment in the country at present. He may simply be avoiding his aunt."

"Perhaps." Charlotte's expression showed that she believed no such thing, but Elizabeth had had enough shock for one day. She would not press her friend for useless conjecture.

"I feel a headache coming." Elizabeth rubbed her temples, wishing it was night and she could crawl under the covers until morning.

"I shall bring you something."

Elizabeth nodded and began unlacing her shoes as Charlotte left the room. She spread her shawl over herself like a blanket and lay back on the pillow. She might not be able to go to bed just yet, but she could close her eyes for a bit.

"This will help." Charlotte placed a cup of tea on the table beside the bed.

"Thank you."

Charlotte nodded and left, looking worriedly at her friend before closing the door. Soon, Elizabeth heard Mr. Collins complaining of tea at Rosings and Charlotte's soothing voice convincing him Elizabeth was ill and should stay home. A few minutes later they were gone, leaving her alone in the quiet parsonage. Elizabeth sat up and sipped the tea Charlotte had left her, barely warm now, and smacked her lips in surprise as something in it burned her throat. She quickly finished the cup and added more from the warm pot on the tray by the window. This one burned as well, but she sipped it slowly and sat down at her desk in the waning light.

She combed through her letter from Longbourn, looking for any mention of Wickham. Lydia had only written once, and it had not even been a proper letter, but a half page tacked onto Kitty's letter. She mentioned Chamberlayne and Denny, but not Wickham. Elizabeth was relieved until she remembered Denny was the one who had introduced Wickham to Meryton. He had brought him from London himself. How close were the two men? Did Denny know of Mr. Wickham's habits? She would be watchful until she could be certain.

Mary's two letters spoke of the song she was learning to play and the pig that had escaped into the garden, but nothing of the officers, unsurprisingly. Her mother's letter contained plenty of talk of the red-coated militiamen, but few were ever mentioned by name and very little of substance could be gleaned from it.

Her father's letters were as they always were—full of sarcasm and wit, but short on useful information. She must simply wait until she was home in Hertfordshire to ascertain Wickham's place in her family's social circle. With any luck, his engagement to Mary King would have removed her sisters from his sphere. But no! Miss King! She was not a close friend, but she was a perfectly nice girl, and she did not deserve to be shackled for life to a man such as Mr. Wickham. What was she to do?

She paced the small room in agitation—she always thought best while in motion—but she was frustrated by the size. Remembering she was alone in the parsonage, she pulled on her slippers and shawl and made her way to the parlor where she could pace to her heart's content.

She felt a little dizzy on the stairs, but she thought it the effect of spending the day crying. Her head was stuffy, that was all. She would be well once she reached the parlor and its level floors.

She was just inside the parlor door when the maid offered to have tea brought in.

"There is a tray in my room with a tea service. You may add more hot water to that pot." She had no desire to plow through Charlotte's tea like a countess who paid no mind to the cost. "It is still warm, I believe."

"Very well, miss."

Soon she was settled on the sofa, having paced until the tea arrived, and happily pouring out another cup. She was sipping on her second cup of tea, attempting to read the history that had so bored Maria, when the bell rang. Who would come at such an hour? Perhaps it was the colonel checking on her. He had seemed rather worried over her, dear man.

4

THE THURSDAY THAT WOULD NOT END

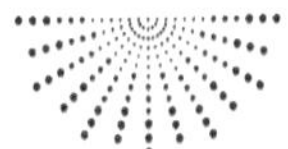

To Elizabeth's great astonishment, the man ushered into the parlor was Mr. Darcy, not the colonel.

"Mrs. Collins said you were unwell. I hope you are feeling better?"

She mumbled something about being improved and watched in fascination as he paced across the parlor.

"You will have more room if you pace this way." She gestured to the fireplace and signaled walking past it instead of across from it.

He did not seem to hear her and continued to pace the short side of the room, which he accomplished in three long strides before turning about and going back the way he had come. Finally, he stopped directly in front of her, a look of determination on his face.

"You must allow me to tell you how ardently I admire and love you."

Elizabeth gaped at him. That was the last thing she had expected he would say. Was there anything about this man that would not surprise her today? She knew her face must show her shock, just as his showed an intensity she had never seen in him before. They stared at one another for a full minute before, struck by the absurdity of it all, Elizabeth's shoulders began to shake. Mr. Darcy noticed this and took a step toward her, one hand outstretched as if to steady her.

She snorted.

He paused and lowered his hand partially, his eyes searching her expression.

She could contain her laughter no more. It burst from her, like a dam in a swollen river. Great gales of laughter, trilling from her like wind chimes.

Mr. Darcy was perplexed. Then he began to feel heat in his neck, working its way up to his cheeks. Elizabeth pressed her hand to her mouth, trying to control her mirth, and he straightened his shoulders stiffly.

"I see my feelings are amusing to you. Forgive me for disturbing you," he said curtly. He nodded stiffly and turned on his heel to leave.

His hand was on the knob when Elizabeth grabbed his arm. He stopped, hating how the sensation of her fingers wrapped about his bicep made him stupidly happy. He turned, unable to forgo all manners and simply leave her to her ridiculousness.

"Miss Bennet?" He released the knob, but he spoke to the wall above her head. He could not face her dancing eyes, not yet.

"Mr. Darcy, forgive me. Your feelings are not amusing to me, I assure you. Not in the least. I was only struck by the absurdity of the situation."

He had begun to relax until she spoke the last, and his arm stiffened again. He began to turn away from her, but she tugged him further into the room.

"Please believe me, Mr. Darcy. I mean no disrespect toward you."

He breathed deeply and closed his eyes, waiting for patience to find him. "May I ask, Miss Bennet," he began, in quiet, restrained tones, "what you find absurd about this situation?"

She looked out the window, pursed her lips, and finally made a huffing sound. "I suppose there is no avoiding it now. I must ask you to sit, sir. This may take some time."

He finally looked at her and saw her cheeks were flushed and she was nervously twisting the fingers of her left hand in the fringe on her shawl. Her right was still on his arm. She seemed to have forgotten its presence.

He nodded. "Very well."

He sat very correctly on the chair near the fire across from where Elizabeth perched on the edge of the delicate sofa, looking as if she might take flight at any moment. Had she taken laudanum for her headache? That might explain her uncontrollable laughter and the flush on her cheeks. He could not deny the relief he felt at this notion.

"Forgive me, Miss Bennet. Are you unwell? I do not mean to make you entertain visitors if you are not... prepared."

"I had a headache, but it is better now. The injury is more to my pride."

"Your pride?" he asked, confused.

"Yes. You see, I have long prided myself on my judgement. I have thought, for many years now, that I could tell the truth of a person by their expression or take the measure of a gentleman after a short acquaintance." She nervously looked to him, then returned her gaze to the fire. "I see this perplexes you."

"I own to being... curious as to your meaning."

She sighed. "I may as well come out with it as I am sure you will know the whole soon enough. Better to have it over and done with."

Now he truly was perplexed.

"I met your cousin, Colonel Fitzwilliam on a walk today. We were speaking of general things, and one of us mentioned Hertfordshire... and you." She snuck a glance at him, then looked back to the fire. "I mentioned that I had heard something of your history from an officer in the militia there. I'm certain you know of whom I speak."

"Wickham," he said lowly.

In that one word, she could feel how much Mr. Darcy hated him. She sighed. Perhaps he had good reason to.

"Yes," she said hesitantly. "Have you by chance spoken to your cousin today?"

"No, he was touring the estate and I went to Belle View on business. I barely returned in time to change for tea."

She nodded. "He can give you more details of our conversation, but suffice it to say that the good colonel informed me that Mr. Wickham is not who I believed him to be. He is a gambler, in debt to nearly every tradesman he's had the misfortune to meet, and a silver-tongued liar besides."

She had knotted her fringe hopelessly now and moved on to clenching and releasing her skirt. She could not look at Mr. Darcy. "Colonel Fitzwilliam informed me that the living Mr. Wickham says you denied him in defiance of your father's wishes was traded for the sum of three thousand pounds. A prudent man could live on such a sum for many years, but the colonel told me he returned when the living fell vacant and was quite abusive when you declined to give it to him."

Darcy was watching her carefully. Her eyes were bright and darted back and forth, like she was searching for escape. Her hands were constantly in motion, twirling the fringe on her shawl, bunching the fabric of her skirt, twisting around each other.

He reached across and clasped her hands in his, stilling their motion. He had done it instinctually, with no thought to what his next action would be but wishing to comfort her in her distress.

He rubbed his thumbs across her knuckles and spoke softly. "Dearest, is this what has overset you? That you were wrong about Wickham?" She looked at him with wide eyes. He seemed to take this as agreement. "He has fooled many before you and will likely continue to do so. He cannot open his mouth without a lie falling out. It is his way, and he is very practiced at it. Even my father was taken in by him, and he was a man of the world and decades your senior."

This seemed to mollify her somewhat and he squeezed her hands in his before releasing one and moving to sit next to her.

Elizabeth's eyes widened as she saw him moving closer and settling her right hand on his knee, clasped in his. What was happening?

She edged away from him, into the far corner of the sofa, and half-turned to face him. "Mr. Darcy," she said uneasily.

"Yes?" He smiled gently at her, his expression soft and kind, his eyes dark and full of understanding.

She looked at him then and was struck anew with how little she understood him. She felt as if she had lived weeks since this morning, not hours.

"I am afraid I do not know you at all," she said, her voice filled with dismayed wonder, her brow creased in confusion.

"Pardon me?"

"Mr. Darcy, pray forgive me. I must ask you to apply to your cousin for more details. Coherent speech is quite beyond me at the moment."

He frowned, and she found his confused expression inconveniently attractive.

"I do not understand."

She sighed. "Neither do I," she muttered. She took a deep breath and sat up straight. "Mr. Darcy, I must apologize. I believed spurious things about you in Hertfordshire, with absolutely no evidence to support them and plenty to dispute them if I had but opened my eyes. Charlotte told me not to believe him, but I did not listen. Even Jane thought there must have been some misunderstanding, that it could not be true. Mr. Bingley would not be such a close friend if such things were true. But I was so confident in my own abilities." She had not the energy to berate herself as fully as she had done that afternoon with Charlotte, and her words came out in a dejected tone. "I assure you I was much more stringent with myself earlier."

Darcy was moved by her suffering. "Do not fret over Wickham, my dear. He is not worth your distress."

"He has made a great fool of me."

"You are not the first, I am afraid."

She met his eyes and inexplicably felt tears rising to her own. "I do not like feeling foolish."

He nearly smiled. "Neither do I." He patted her cheeks dry with his handkerchief.

"I am a vain and ridiculous creature."

"We are none of us perfect."

She laughed at that, as he had intended her to do, and he smiled at her.

"You should smile more often, Mr. Darcy. You are quite handsome when you do."

He flushed. "Am I not handsome when I am not smiling?"

She appeared to consider this for a moment, then grinned at him, looking almost like her old self. "It requires further study."

"I dare not suspend any pleasure of yours."

She smiled softly at him, then yawned and tried to hide it, but he was sitting too closely to miss it.

"You are tired."

"Yes, but it is early yet. It must be the tea," she said absently. "Charlotte put something in it."

He saw her teacup on the table beside him and leaned down to smell its contents. Brandy. "Ah, I see. You should retire, Miss Bennet. We can continue our conversation another time. May I walk with you tomorrow morning?"

She nodded regally. "You may."

He grinned at her, thinking her delightful, if a little volatile, under the influence of brandy. "I will await you in the grove." He kissed her hand and held it to his lips a little longer than propriety would normally allow. "Until tomorrow, my sweet."

"Good evening."

She smiled blearily at him as he walked out the door and watched from the window as he went down the lane towards Rosings. He turned at the bend in the road and tipped his hat at her, and she waved sleepily before trudging up the stairs and falling into bed.

5

SOMEHOW, STILL THURSDAY

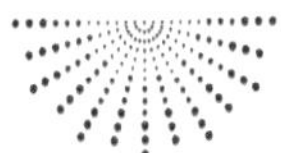

Darcy left the parsonage with a smile on his face, but by the time he arrived at Rosings, he had begun to worry. Elizabeth's words had been perplexing and even alarming. She had believed Wickham. If that were true, what had she thought of him all along? She had found him saying he loved her to be absurd. That was an odd reaction, surely? Even if she were in her cups.

He entered the house and made his way upstairs, bypassing the drawing room where his aunt sat with her guests. He had much to think about, and he could not abide company at the moment.

He had been staring at the fire in his room for nearly an hour when Colonel Fitzwilliam came in.

"Where have you been, Darcy?"

"Hmm? Oh, I did not feel like company."

"That I can easily believe. But I saw you striding across the lawn. Where were you off to?"

Darcy looked away from him.

"Checking on the welfare of a certain lady, perhaps?"

Darcy huffed.

"I saw Miss Bennet today."

Darcy abruptly turned towards his cousin and Fitzwilliam manfully withheld a smirk.

"I'm afraid I quite upset her."

"Really?" Darcy tried to appear less interested than he was, but he was burning with curiosity.

"It was unwittingly done. She mentioned a militia officer she knew by the name of Wickham, and, well, I had to warn her off him. She is a lovely girl, and I would hate to see her fall prey to the likes of him."

"Did you tell her of Georgiana?" asked Darcy, alarmed.

"No, of course not! But I did tell her that he was not to be trusted with ladies or money, and especially when the two were in the same room."

Darcy nodded. "How did she take it?"

Fitzwilliam grimaced, then laughed a little. "Not well, I'm afraid. She had swallowed his lies wholeheartedly. I think she was most angry with herself."

"Yes, she does not like to feel a fool."

Fitzwilliam looked at him shrewdly. "No, no one does. Anyroad, she is warned off him now."

Darcy debated with himself a moment, then decided he should confess to his cousin. Fitzwilliam already suspected his affection for the lady, and she had said he should speak to his cousin.

"Fitz, I went to see Miss Elizabeth this evening."

"Oh?"

"It was an interesting interview."

"How so?"

"She had been very upset earlier and Mrs. Collins had given her tea with brandy in it—quite a bit I gathered."

Fitzwilliam's eyebrows shot up his forehead. "Is that why she did not come this evening?"

"I think she was too upset to come, but she was in her cups, or very nearly, when I spoke to her in the parsonage."

Fitzwilliam could not restrain his shoulders from shaking with laughter. "Dare I ask what the lady is like while inebriated?"

Darcy glared at him. "No, you may not."

"Oh, that is how the land lies, is it?"

"Quite."

"Do you have an announcement to make?"

"Not as yet. Fitz," Darcy stood and paced away, then returned and sat again. "Miss Elizabeth suggested I ask you about your conversation earlier. She said it would help me to understand."

"Understand what?"

"Why she began laughing when I told her I loved her."

Fitzwilliam's eyes bulged comically. "She what?" He spluttered. "You told her you *love* her?"

Darcy sighed. "Please tell me of your conversation, then I shall tell you more."

"Very well." Fitzwilliam told Darcy of meeting Miss Elizabeth, their conversation, her tears and the way she berated herself, and how he offered his friendship should she ever need it. When he finished, they sat staring into the fire, sipping brandy, for some minutes until Darcy broke the silence.

"Well, that certainly explains her state of mind. She mentioned speaking to Mrs. Collins as well."

"I imagine she told her friend when she returned. They are from the same neighborhood, after all."

"Yes, they are."

Darcy continued to stare at the fire, absently twisting his glass back and forth until Fitzwilliam wanted to throttle him.

"Is that all you are going to say? Good God, man! You said you told the lady you love her! You cannot stop there!"

Darcy sighed. "Very well. I had intended to propose. That was my purpose in going there this evening."

Darcy did not notice Fitzwilliam's shock at this statement.

"She was not prepared for visitors."

"I should imagine not!"

"We spoke, and she apologized for laughing inappropriately and listening to Wickham, and she told me to speak to you."

"Is that all? You were gone an hour! I cannot believe that is all that happened."

Darcy colored. "It is all that I will tell you."

Fitzwilliam's eyebrows arched up and he leaned back in his chair. "I see. So how did you leave it with the lovely Miss Bennet?"

"I will meet her for a walk in the morning."

"And?"

"And what?"

"Will you make your proposals?"

"I had thought I would at first, but I am less certain now. She was completely surprised by my going there. She seemed..." he could not bring himself to say that at times she had seemed to be trying to get away from him, and how on reflection, that was incredibly disturbing. "I had always thought that any woman I wished to marry would be happy to accept me."

"Many would, I imagine."

"I am not certain Miss Elizabeth is one of them."

Fitzwilliam exhaled loudly. "No, I do not think she is. Though it would be damn imprudent of her. But she has done it before."

"What?" Darcy's eyes shot to his cousin's.

"She turned down her cousin, Mr. Collins. That is why he married her friend. Did you not know? You were in the neighborhood at the time."

"I heard something of it, but I thought she had put him off, or perhaps her father had."

"No, it was apparently a big to-do. Her mother wished for the match and she refused his offer. Her father stood by her. Deuced awkward at home, I can imagine. Collins is to inherit her father's estate."

"Yes, I know."

"Collins is a buffoon, and she would have been miserable with him. But she could have managed him if she had a mind to. Mrs. Collins is doing a fine job of that. If she was willing to turn him down for being a ridiculous man with good prospects, she might have refused you for being overly proud. It is unlikely, but she is young, and impetuous I think."

"Yes, she is somewhat impetuous." Darcy took a deep breath and ran his hand over his face. "Fitz, what should I do?"

"You have already spoken to the lady. Do you feel your honor is engaged?"

"Yes, though she may not remember it in the morning."

"She may not. Do you wish for her not to? It could be your escape if she does not recall your words—or if she did not wish for them."

"I know it is not the most prudent match, but I cannot imagine marrying anyone else."

"I see. Then you have only one option."

"What? Propose in the morning?"

"No! You must court her until you are certain she will say yes."

Darcy nodded thoughtfully. "You know, I had not even wondered about her answer before this evening." He stood and poked at the fire. "I had thought only my mind needed to be decided. Once I had made peace with such an unequal match, she would be mine for the taking." He stared at the flames absently. "I had not given a thought to her wishes or desires, or even her heart. I am a poor suitor indeed."

"It is not unusual that you would think a woman in her position would accept you. Most would. You are not so very uncommon. A trifle conceited perhaps…"

Darcy paid him little attention. "I have been sitting here this last hour thinking of what I would have said to her this evening. I would have spoken of my trouble in admitting my feelings, of how difficult it had been to come to the conclusion that the joy of having her as my wife was greater than the degradation of her connections and the objections of my family."

"You did not actually say her family was a degradation, did you?" asked Fitzwilliam, a look of disbelief on his face.

"No, she began laughing before I could say more than a sentence."

"Thank heaven for that! Good God, man, what were you thinking? You cannot tell a woman you love, in the middle of a *proposal*, that her family is a degradation and your relations will hate her, but it is all well and good because you are prepared to bear it for her sake!"

"What? I wanted her to know I had thought of the obstacles and was prepared to face them, for her."

Fitzwilliam sighed and pinched the bridge of his nose. "Darcy, can you truly be this stupid?"

Darcy huffed and a look of indignation came over him. "I was paying her the compliment of honesty," he said stiffly, his posture rigid and his jaw clenching.

"No, you were congratulating yourself and wounding the lady."

Shock overspread Darcy's features and Fitzwilliam gentled his tone.

"No one wishes to hear about their horrible connections. She knows it, you know it, but it is not necessary to discuss it, especially during a proposal. It is not the time."

Darcy looked at him suspiciously.

Fitzwilliam continued. "You love Miss Bennet, do you not?"

Darcy nodded warily.

"How would you like it if she said she enjoyed your company, but your aunt is overbearing, officious and a public embarrassment, and your sister had behaved so badly the previous summer that if it were to become known she would be ruined forever. Therefore, she could not consider an alliance with you."

Darcy's hands were clenched and his face was red.

"Well? Tell me, Darcy. Is that something you wish to hear from your lady love?" Fitzwilliam could see Darcy's nostrils flaring as the vein in his forehead protruded. "Or would you prefer to hear her say she enjoys your company, and that she will be pleased to marry you, and you will avoid your troublesome relations together? Hmm?"

Darcy continued to seethe as his cousin stared at him, his gaze unwavering. "It is hardly the same, Fitz," he finally bit out.

"You are correct—it is much worse. Lady Catherine has been raised to know better, but she covers her bad behavior with wealth and a title. G as well. She was young and sheltered, but we both know she knew what she was doing was wrong. She has you to thank for rescuing her. It is hardly Miss Bennet's fault that she has no brother to inherit or that her mother is silly. At least the woman means well."

Darcy huffed out a breath and paced to the window and back again. He repeated the action several times before coming to stand before his cousin. Colonel Fitzwilliam sat in the winged chair, one foot crossed over his knee, looking for all the world as if nothing of import was happening.

"It is not—"

The colonel looked at him expectantly.

"She is not, they, I—" Darcy groaned and paced off again.

Fitzwilliam was about to pick up a book from the side table when his cousin appeared before him again, his hair bedraggled from running his hands through it.

"Lady Catherine may not behave as she ought, and I am sorry for it, but she is wealthy and titled, and that allows her to be eccentric with less censure. That is the material point."

"Darcy, you either love the lady or you do not. *That* is the material point."

Darcy's mouth dropped open and he stared at his cousin a full minute before pacing off again. He continued to move about the room, occasionally mumbling to himself or tugging his cravat. His hair was completely disheveled and his cousin had read an entire chapter in his book before Darcy returned to the chair before the fire.

He sat stiffly and looked straight ahead, every ounce of dignity he possessed writ on his face. "I love her," he said solemnly.

"Wonderful! How do you wish to proceed?"

"I have no idea." Darcy slumped back in his chair as the colonel laughed and laughed until he was red in the face.

AN HOUR LATER, the cousins were still debating how best to court a lady such as Miss Bennet.

"Why cannot you acknowledge I am right?" cried the colonel.

"How can you know her better than I? I am the one in love with her, not you."

"Who has courted more ladies?"

Darcy huffed.

"And who is desired for the pleasure of his company and not the size of his coffers?"

Darcy rolled his eyes.

"Trust me, Cousin. I would not lead you astray."

Darcy gave him a doubtful look, then sighed and uncrossed his arms. "Very well. I will try it your way."

"It is not so very hard, truly. Merely think of the things you have wished to say to her, the things you hope to do together. A little affection can help move things along. Look into her eyes, kiss her hand. Stop holding yourself so rigidly! If you wish to take her hand, there is nothing saying you cannot."

"Only decorum and propriety," grumbled Darcy.

"That is why you ask to court her. She will know from the very beginning your intentions are honorable. You are not trifling with her. There is no reason to hold back all of your thoughts and wishes. How will the lady ever fall in love with you if you do not let her know you!"

Darcy huffed again. He felt he had done nothing but grumble and huff and sigh for the last two hours. He was like a horse in the stable, and Fitzwilliam the groom determined to break him. And just like the horse, everyone would be happier if he simply relented and accepted the inevitable.

"Very well. It will not be easy, but I will attempt it."

Fitzwilliam brought his hands together for one jarring clap. "Excellent! It will be easier than you think, I am sure of it. You can be pleasant and witty when you choose to be. You simply need to choose to be so with Miss Bennet."

Darcy nodded and looked out the darkened window. "What if I cannot?" he asked quietly, doubt creeping into his voice. "What if she does not come to care for me?"

Fitzwilliam squeezed his shoulder and said kindly, "She will. You know how to love well. Show her that, and she won't be able to help it."

"Are you certain?"

"I am. Miss Bennet is a warmhearted lady. She will respond to genuine affection. You just have to show it to her."

Darcy nodded. He hated how unsure and faltering he felt. It was as if they were children again and Fitzwilliam was teaching him how to aim for a bird or reload his powder. When he finally quit fighting it, he enjoyed the reversion to their childhood roles. Fitz was older and wiser, and Darcy was eager to learn. It was refreshing.

"Let us practice."

"What?" replied Darcy, aghast.

"Practice. You have admitted yourself that you are unskilled in conversing with ladies."

"How will speaking with you improve my skills?"

"I will pretend to be a lady, of course!"

Darcy stared at his cousin with mounting dread. Colonel Fitzwilliam was enjoying this entirely too much and Darcy was in no mood to be his cousin's entertainment. Finally, he rolled his eyes, sighed, and said, "How do we begin?"

"You are meeting her on a walk?"

"Yes."

"Then we shall pretend we are meeting in the grove." He moved to the window, then turned to stroll towards his cousin. "Mr. Darcy! Good morning," said the colonel, his voice pitched unnaturally high.

Darcy cringed. "Good morning, Miss Bennet."

"That will never do, Darcy! You must at least appear happy to see the lady. No one wants to look at that grumpy expression across the dinner table every night."

"I am not as good a play-actor as you, Fitz. When I look at you, I see my cousin, not Miss Bennet."

"You must use your imagination," replied the colonel with a stern look.

Darcy sighed and rubbed his hand across his eyes. "Very well. Good morning, Miss Bennet. I hope you are feeling better."

"I am quite well, thank you."

Fitzwilliam stared at his cousin, waiting for Darcy to speak next.

"Uh, may I walk with you?"

"You may."

They strolled the perimeter of Darcy's chamber before Fitzwilliam turned to his cousin in exasperation.

"Really Darcy, it is no wonder the woman was not expecting your declaration! If you cannot speak to her, how is she to know you hold her in high regard?"

Darcy huffed. "I am not like you. I do not flirt with every woman under eighty and I do not have your way with words."

"I am not suggesting you behave like me, but that you at least attempt to talk to the poor girl. She likely has no idea what to make of you."

Darcy looked at him sharply. She had said she did not know him at all…

"Did you know she thought you dislike her?"

"What? How could she think such a thing?" Darcy looked horrified.

"Because you act like this! Silent and forbidding. Did you even speak on all those walks you joined her on?"

"Of course I did!"

"Beyond basic pleasantries?" asked Fitzwilliam with a doubtful expression.

"Yes!" Darcy was indignant. "I spoke of," he hesitated, "well, we talked of Rosings, and Kent, and springtime."

"Springtime! A woman does not fall in love with a man who talks to her of the weather."

Darcy's face reddened and his lips drew in a hard line.

Colonel Fitzwilliam softened his voice. "You will have to try harder, Cousin. And unbend. She is worth it, is she not?"

Darcy sighed. "Very well. I shall try."

Fitzwilliam clapped his shoulder. "I am off to bed. Best of luck to you in the morning, Cousin. I have every faith in your success."

Darcy told him goodnight and prepared for bed, wondering what he would say to Miss Bennet in the morning, and how on earth he would go about showing her that he loved her and was utterly devoted to her without frightening or angering her. It would require delicacy, something he had never excelled at, but Fitz was right. He had to try—he had to show her how he felt, or he would lose her. And that was the worst possible outcome. He could withstand a little embarrassment if it meant having her for his own.

6

AT LAST! FRIDAY

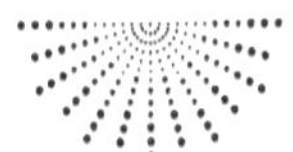

E lizabeth had had the strangest dream. She had been crying in Rosings' gardens with Colonel Fitzwilliam, then she had flirted quite brazenly with Mr. Darcy in Charlotte's parlor! Never had her dreams been so vivid, nor so full of eligible men.

She awoke shortly after dawn—for she had gone to bed at sunset—with a prodigious thirst. She felt somewhat similar to mornings after a party where she drank too much wine, but she had not had anything at all last night. In fact, she could not remember even eating dinner. Her stomach made a loud grumbling noise and she quickly dressed and put up her hair before skipping down to the kitchen. A village woman came to the parsonage to cook most days and was generally there early in the morning to bake bread. She had been very kind to Elizabeth and often packed her a scone or muffin to take with her on her walks.

"You're up early, Miss."

"I believe I went to bed rather early."

"Molly said you had an upset yesterday. I hope all is well with your family."

"Yes, everyone is well, thank you," said Elizabeth hesitantly. What upset was Mrs. Hopkins referring to?

"I'm glad to hear it, Miss." She pulled a tin of muffins from the oven and set them on the worktable to cool. "I suppose you'll be wanting to take some of those on your walk?"

"Yes, please."

Mrs. Hopkins was wrapping a few muffins when Molly came in.

"Are ya feelin' better, Miss?"

Elizabeth looked at her in confusion. "I am quite well, Molly. Why would you expect otherwise?"

"You were awful upset yesterday. And then the gentleman came to see ya and you went straight to bed before it were full dark!"

Elizabeth felt the floor tilt beneath her and grabbed the back of a chair.

"Have a care now, Miss!" cried Mrs. Hopkins. She pulled out the chair and guided Elizabeth to sit down.

"What gentleman, Molly?" she asked, dreading the answer.

"Why, Mr. Darcy, of course. Do you not remember?" asked Molly.

Elizabeth fell back in the chair and was vaguely aware of Mrs. Hopkins telling Molly to bring her a cup of tea and that good lady chafing her hands.

"There, there, dear. It's nothing that can't be solved. All will be well soon enough."

Elizabeth turned to face Mrs. Hopkins with a desolate expression. It was all coming back to her now. She *had* sat in the dirt and cried with Colonel Fitzwilliam. And she *had* flirted with Mr. Darcy in Charlotte's parlor. It had *not* been a dream. He had called her 'my sweet,' and held her hand, and looked into her eyes quite intimately.

And he was expecting her in the grove this very morning.

"I need some air," she said weakly. She moved woodenly to the table where the muffins were wrapped and grabbed the cloth, then stumbled out the door.

All the way to the grove she berated herself for her stupidity and Charlotte for whatever it was she had put in the tea.

What must Colonel Fitzwilliam think of her? She had cried through her handkerchief and his as well. He had been uncommonly kind to her, and attentive without requiring anything from her. It had been a comfort. Knowing she had such a staunch friend could only do her good.

But Mr. Darcy! Oh dear. Had he said he loved and admired her? Was she remembering correctly? And had she laughed at him? Truly? What a mess! And now they must discuss what he had said the evening before—and likely what he did not say. Did he mean to make his proposals? How would she respond?

Yesterday morning, she would have refused him and gladly sent him on his way with a bug in his ear and no guilt in her heart. But this morning, everything was different. Not only had she found out he was not half the villain she had long imagined him to be, but he had been so tender and gentle with her. He had made her laugh and been everything lovely when she had no right to expect such from him. Of all the things she knew of Mr. Darcy, the one she had been most sure of was that he was a bad-tempered man. But bad-tempered men did not speak kindly to a lady after she had laughed in his face when he declared his love.

Could she truly not know him at all?

"Good morning."

Elizabeth jumped. "Mr. Darcy! I did not see you there."

He smiled and removed his hat. "Forgive me. I did not mean to startle you."

"Would you like to walk?" she asked. Why did her voice sound so small?

He nodded and fell into step beside her. After a minute of silence, he said, "I spoke with Fitzwilliam last night."

Elizabeth sighed and closed her eyes. "I see I am to have no dignity left by the time I leave Kent."

He smiled gently and touched her elbow. "There was nothing undignified in your behavior."

"He must not have told you how I sat on the ground like a farm animal."

His brows lifted. "He left that bit out, but I'm sure you were very elegant."

She was startled into a short laugh. "You are ebullient this morning, Mr. Darcy."

"I am happy."

"Might I enquire what has made you so happy?" she asked with a grin. *Stop flirting, Lizzy!* Though it was difficult to wish to stop flirting when he was so evidently pleased by it.

"You may."

She lifted a brow in question.

"You."

"Me? I have done naught but walk beside you."

He took her hand and brought it to his mouth, kissing the back gently. "You came this morning, and very early, too, and I cannot hide my delight at seeing you."

She smiled back at him for a moment before remembering that she did not particularly like Mr. Darcy, for he was an ill-tempered, difficult man. Was he not?

She pulled away and walked on. "I am glad to know you are so easily pleased. Might you be half so happy with a muffin?" She unwrapped her bundle and held one out to him. "They are very good, I promise."

He took it, thanked her, and they were silent again as they meandered down the dim path. The sun was higher now than it had been when she rose, but the further they moved into the trees, the dimmer it became. They eventually came to a brook, and he gestured to a small bench along the bank. She sat and looked out at the water, watching a beam of sunlight dance on the surface.

She took a deep breath and said, "You said you spoke with Colonel Fitzwilliam."

He sighed.

Oh, dear.

"Yes, he told me that you had been fed a pack of lies from Wickham, which is hardly surprising, and that you were very upset."

She looked away.

"Of more interest to me was that you thought I did not like you."

"He told you that, did he?"

"Yes."

She sighed.

"I'm certain you realize by now that *dislike* could not be further from the truth."

"I have some idea, sir," she said to her shoes.

"I beg you would indulge me. Whatever has made you think I do not like you?"

She looked up at him in surprise. "Truly?"

"Truly. I would know what I have done to give you such an erroneous opinion of me."

She picked at her skirt again, then decided that the last day had been odd enough. It would be difficult for the situation to get any worse, so she may as well tell him.

"Well, it is many things really. When you were in Hertfordshire, you seemed displeased with the neighborhood overall."

"But not you specifically!"

She shot him a look.

"Forgive me. Please, carry on."

"You particularly seemed to dislike my family, you did not seem to like Mr. Bingley's preference for Jane, and you *did* say I was not handsome enough to tempt you."

"What?" he cried.

"At the assembly, before we were even introduced. You looked me right in the eye before you said it. I know you knew it was me to whom you were referring."

He colored and walked away, then paced back toward her. "But did not my attentions after that show that I felt quite the opposite?"

"What attentions?"

He had looked upset before, but now he appeared positively stricken.

"At Netherfield—"

She huffed before he could continue. "At Netherfield you argued with me each time we spoke, and you spent half an hour in the library with me without saying a word."

"And without reading a word, either." He said it with such a look, and a tilt to his mouth that was not quite a smile, that she could not help but flush scarlet. "And I asked you to dance a reel with me. You refused."

"You were in earnest?"

"Of course I was! Why else would I have asked?"

"To mock me." She said it so matter-of-factly that he could only stare at her in wide-eyed surprise.

"I do not know what sort of man asks a woman to dance only to mock her, but I can assure you, I am not such a one."

Elizabeth was about to retort when she saw an image of her father, saying something that sounded well on the surface to her mother, but when listened to more carefully, proved to be insincere and designed with nothing but his own amusement in mind. The activity was made worse by Mrs. Bennet not always understanding what her husband was doing. In a flash, Elizabeth realized that this very behavior had ruined her mother's trust in her father, and that she had expected Mr. Darcy to act as Mr. Bennet had, without accounting for how very different the two men were.

"Are you well, Miss Bennet?"

"Hmm? Oh, yes, quite well. It seems I am to be astonished and disillusioned continually on this trip. Do you think it is something in the air at Rosings?" She tried to smile at her jest, but she could tell by his expression that it fell flat.

"I am curious, but I do not want to intrude by asking what you have become disillusioned by."

"May we discuss it at another time? I need to think on it some more."

"Of course. I believe you were telling me how rude I was in Hertfordshire last autumn."

She laughed. "And you were telling me how attentive you were. Were we in the same place, do you think?"

He smiled ruefully. "I must apologize for my comment at the assembly. It was uncommonly rude of me. And patently untrue. I have no excuse other than that I was in a monstrous mood."

"I suppose it is good to know you do not say such things when you are in a good mood." He nearly rolled his eyes and she added, "Thank you. Apology accepted."

He looked around, not knowing what to say, when a loud grumble reached his ears. Elizabeth looked up at him with red cheeks and a chagrined expression.

"Was that your stomach?"

The growling was louder now and she closed her eyes in mortification. "Yes. I have not eaten since tea yesterday."

"Do not let me keep you from your meal, Miss Bennet."

He gestured to the bundle of muffins and she smiled sheepishly before taking a bite. She made quick work of the first muffin and was soon on her second. He joined her on the bench and took a bite of his own, chewing slowly as they watched the brook flow smoothly past.

"I say, this muffin is uncommonly good."

"I know! Mrs. Hopkins is a village woman Charlotte has convinced to cook at the parsonage for her. I believe she is worth every penny."

He nodded, taking another large bite.

"I shall get the receipt from her before I travel home. Would you like me to pass it on to you?" she asked.

He turned to meet her eyes and she flushed, seeing in his that if she had the receipt, he would not need it, for he wished her home and his to be one and the same. She briefly wondered how one could tell so much from only a look, but then his hand was on her cheek, tucking a curl behind her ear, and her breath became shaky.

"I like you very much, Elizabeth," he whispered.

She swallowed. "I see that."

He tilted his head and considered her for a moment, then said, "I would like to court you."

"What?"

"I would like to court you—call on you, go for walks, tell you how enchanting you are to see your blushes—"

It was maddening that she blushed when he said this.

"—and when you are ready, make my proposals."

She swallowed again and looked down, then back up tentatively. "Is that what you were going to do last night? Make your proposals?"

He considered her for a moment, then said, "Yes. I spoke with my cousin when I returned to Rosings and he convinced me you were not ready to hear what I wished to say. He also told me that I had done a poor job of courting you if you did not even realize it was happening and berated me soundly."

She chuckled. "I certainly did not realize it. Were you courting me?"

"I do not know that I thought of it in those terms, but I was paying you a great deal of attention."

Her face expressed her doubt at this assertion, but she refrained from speaking it. "So you are asking to court me now?"

"Yes."

"How do you imagine this courtship will proceed?"

"Well, I thought we could continue as we are here in Kent, only now you would know that when I join you on your walks, it is because I wish to see you."

She smiled self-consciously and he continued. "I imagine your friend Mrs. Collins might be of some assistance. She seems a discerning woman."

"She is."

He nodded. "Then I thought I might escort you to Town and call on you at your relations there."

"I am only due to be in London one week before returning to Hertfordshire. Will you call on me at Longbourn?"

She tensed as she awaited his answer. Calling on Longbourn would not be pleasant—her mother would be vulgar and loud, fussing over him when he was present and crowing about him when he was not. She did not truly wish for him to call on her there, but she *did* want him to be willing to do so if it were necessary.

"If that is where you will be, that is where I will go." He spoke firmly, with no doubt in his words or their implications, and Elizabeth could not help smiling brightly at him. "Does this please you?"

"It does. Though this is all very strange. Yesterday morning I hadn't the slightest idea this would be happening."

"Is the surprise unwelcome?"

She thought for a moment, her head tilted prettily to one side, surprised at herself that she was enjoying Mr. Darcy's attentions. He was far from being a favorite, but once she had realized he was not the villain she had thought him, she was free to see his good qualities, and she could admit that he did in fact have some. He was proving delightful to flirt with, though she would not acknowledge that she was flirting with him. But he did seem to adore her rather intently, and he was *such* a man. He was not the sort to say such things to every woman he came across. He was fastidious; exacting; scrupulous.

And he wanted *her*.

"No, it is not unwelcome," she replied, her voice soft.

He released a sigh and took her hand in his. "So I may call on you? I may court you?"

She sat up straighter and looked him in the eyes, her hand squeezing his tightly. She must not be swept up in the moment. She must *think*. "I must ask you something first."

"Very well."

"Last autumn, did Mr. Bingley care for Jane? Or was he merely amusing himself while in the country?"

Darcy looked uneasy. "He did care for her, yes."

"And was it his idea not to return to Hertfordshire?"

"No, it was not. Though he did agree to it. Eventually." He was nearly squirming he was so uncomfortable, but he could not pace away as he would wish for Elizabeth was still holding his hand.

Elizabeth looked down, her shoulders slumping in her disappointment. "Was it by your design? Did you persuade him?"

Her hand had gone lax in his and he anxiously pulled it to him and covered it with his free hand. "Elizabeth, I wish to be honest with you. Please hear me out, dearest."

"Very well."

He told her Miss Bingley had orchestrated the plan, but he had agreed to speak with Bingley. He had watched Jane at the Netherfield ball and she had seemed pleased enough with his friend, but not particularly in love. This was why he had agreed to speak to Bingley. His had been the opinion that swayed his friend, for Bingley did not have much faith in his own powers of observation. He had been led astray before and he trusted Darcy implicitly. Darcy had not liked to do it, but he had concealed Jane's presence in London from Bingley for fear his friend was not yet over her.

Elizabeth's heart sank further with each word he uttered. She was fighting tears and trembling slightly, angry and sad and disappointed. She felt a fool for thinking for even a moment that she had been wrong about Mr. Darcy—that he was not nearly as bad as she had thought him and was in fact a lovely man who might very well make a wonderful husband. She let him hold her hand and call her dearest! She had been caught up in the romance of the moment. How silly she was! She was no better than naïve Lydia or Kitty!

She tugged her hand from his and turned away, sniffling into a handkerchief. "Thank you for explaining your role in my sister's heartbreak, Mr. Darcy. I appreciate your candor. Good morning." She stood from the bench and turned to go.

"Wait!" He grabbed her arm. "Do not go. We can discuss this."

She looked at him sadly. "What is there to discuss? How could I even consider courting the man who has had a hand in ruining, perhaps forever, the happiness of a most beloved sister?"

She looked at him with tear-filled eyes and it was his undoing. "Elizabeth, my love, please, stay and talk with me. Surely we can do something!"

His voice cracked in desperation and she felt her resolve slipping. This was Mr. Darcy. The most staid and stoic man of her acquaintance, begging her to speak with him, to allow him a chance to win her. She felt her reservations crumbling, and something inside her becoming soft and open to him.

"Very well. We may talk. But I make no promises," she added with a stern glare.

"I understand."

She took a deep breath and perched on the edge of the stone bench, her eyes on the brook.

"Do you believe your sister is still in love with Mr. Bingley?"

"I should not bandy about her personal matters, but yes, I believe she is. She has tried to overcome her feelings, and she has tried to convince me she has been successful, but I know her too well to miss the melancholy notes in her letters. She is pining, but she will not admit it. She feels a fool for loving a man who only ever viewed her as a friendly acquaintance—not even enough of a friend to say goodbye to when he left the neighborhood."

Darcy winced, feeling all the reproach in her tone. "You are right—it was very badly done. At the very least, Bingley should have farewelled the neighborhood. And he would have, if we had not followed him to London."

Elizabeth nodded. He could admit when he was wrong. That was something at least.

"I believe Bingley still thinks of Miss Bennet."

Her head whipped towards him. "Truly?"

"Yes. He has been melancholy these last months. He tries to hide it, but I know him well."

She looked at him suspiciously. "Are you certain Jane is the cause of his ennui?"

"I believe she is. He speaks of her occasionally and is always wistful afterward."

"What are you getting at, Mr. Darcy?"

"I propose I speak to Bingley. If he is in fact still enamored of your sister, we bring them together. I will confess my mistake and let him know Miss Bennet would welcome a visit. The rest will be up to him."

"That seems deceptively simple."

He shrugged. "It could be quickly done. I can send him an express today."

She looked at him speculatively. "Are you doing this to please me or because it is the right thing to do?"

"Might I not wish to do both?"

"You certainly may, but I would be much prouder of you if you wished to do right even if there were no gain to yourself."

His eyes took on a new glow as he looked at her. "You have my word as a gentleman that I will make things right with Bingley, even if you never wish to see me again."

She was tempted to tease him, but something in his gaze held her back.

"Very well. Send the letter to Bingley. I shall meet you here tomorrow."

With that, she was up and walking away from him at a quick pace.

7

SATURDAY CONFESSIONS

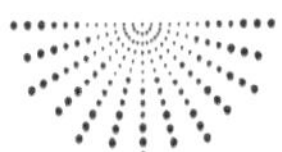

"Have you heard from Mr. Bingley?"

"Good morning, Miss Bennet. Did you have a pleasant evening?"

Elizabeth rolled her eyes and sat on the bench overlooking the brook. "My evening was as pleasant as yours, I imagine. Have you heard from your friend?"

"As a matter of fact, I have." He continued to lean against a tree with his arms across his chest, watching her.

"That was quick."

"Bingley was in when my man arrived and he waited for a response. It arrived late last night."

"It must be convenient to have men to ride all over the country for you at a moment's notice."

"It is remarkably so."

She rolled her eyes again.

"Do you care to hear his response?"

"Yes, please." She smiled and removed a muffin from her small basket as Mr. Darcy opened the letter.

"He says all the usual things, then asks me if I am sure I was mistaken about Miss Bennet, expresses surprise she is in London, tells me I am an officious oaf for presuming to know the heart of a young lady I barely knew, and says he will call on her today and beg her to forgive him." He folded the letter neatly and placed it in his pocket.

"Does he truly call you an officious oaf?"

"He used rather more colorful language, but that was the general idea."

She smirked and held out a muffin. "Are you hungry?"

"Ravenous."

She scooted over on the bench and placed the basket on her lap so Darcy could sit beside her. "I told Mrs. Hopkins I would be gone quite some time and she insisted on sending me with sustenance. There is tea if you would like some." She held out a small crockery bottle still warm from the kitchen.

"Thank you." He brought it to his lips and kept his eyes on her as he drank, then handed it back to her.

"I am glad Mr. Bingley will call on Jane. She deserves every happiness."

"Bingley has been miserable without her. To be honest, I was regretting my role in it long before today."

"Oh?"

"Yes. I do not like to practice persuasion on a friend. It is distasteful. But I truly thought it was in Bingley's best interest, so I did it. Disguise is my abhorrence, but I concealed your sister's presence in London from him. It has not sat well with me. Bingley has been so low, I have been tempted more than once to tell him she was in town and how to find her."

"What stopped you?" she asked softly.

"You." He turned to look her in the eye. "If Bingley married Miss Bennet, I would not be able to avoid seeing you, and last winter, I was foolish enough to think I could live without you and that I would be better off with a wife from the ton."

"And now?"

"Now I realize how foolish I was. I have been in society many years. If I had wanted a wife from their ranks, I could have chosen one ten times over."

"So you only changed your mind about Mr. Bingley because you changed your mind about me?"

"No, I changed my mind about Bingley because I realized I was mistaken as to Miss Bennet's feelings and having known what it is to live without the woman I love, I did not wish to inflict such a thing on my friend if happiness was within his grasp."

She flushed. "Am I that woman?"

"You know that you are."

Elizabeth was sure she resembled a September apple from how much she was blushing. Recognizing the futility of trying to overcome such a thing, she laughed breathily and shook her head a little.

"What is so funny?"

"Nothing really. I was only thinking about how I cannot stop myself from blushing even when I try."

He touched her cheek with his fingertips and traced them down to her jaw, then softly to rest below her chin and tilt her face up to his. "I like your blushes."

She smiled shyly and lowered her eyes.

"Don't do that."

"Do what?"

"Look down. I want to see your eyes."

She looked up at him, her breath coming shakily. She opened her mouth to speak, but nothing came out. Finally, she laughed a little and pulled away. "Mr. Darcy, you surprise me."

"Do I? How so?"

"You are so," she fumbled for words, "well, flirtatious!"

He smiled. "I am glad you think so. I have never spoken so freely before. I feared I might seem bumbling or vulgar."

"You are neither, though I shall tell you if you drift into vulgarity." She smiled teasingly at him, her eyes sparkling and her mouth quirked in that way he always wanted to kiss.

He was leaning towards her mouth when he remembered himself and turned away, huffing out a breath. "So shall you allow me to court you?"

Elizabeth's expression changed to one of trepidation and she looked toward the water. "I believe so, Mr. Darcy, but I must make a few things clear."

"Yes?"

"I would wish this—us—to progress slowly. It was only a few days ago I thought you disliked me heartily, and that I felt the same."

"Do you still dislike me, Miss Elizabeth?" he asked, his voice strained. It was surprisingly painful to hear that she had held him in disdain so recently. His heart hammered in his ears, but he had to know.

She looked at him anxiously, at the forest floor, then back to him. "No, Mr. Darcy, I do not dislike you. I have found that I do not know you at all. What I saw of you, what I knew of you before, was colored by my own offense. I am afraid that I cannot look back on our acquaintance without feeling quite ashamed at how constantly I baited you."

"I hope you will not quit the practice altogether."

She looked at him in surprise.

"I rather like it when you bait me. Though I can think of a more satisfying conclusion than those we were accustomed to at Netherfield."

She flamed scarlet and her mouth formed an O. After a moment, she found her tongue and said, "For a man who does not do much flirting, you are certainly making up for lost time."

He laughed. "Shall we walk?"

She took his arm when offered and they meandered down the path for some time. Finally, Elizabeth broke the silence. "May I ask you a question?"

"Of course."

"When you joined me on my walks before, it was by design, was it not?"

"Usually, yes. Though the first time had been a happy accident."

"Why did you never say anything?"

"What do you mean?"

"You went to so much trouble to walk with me, yet you hardly spoke a word! I wonder why you bothered at all."

"Is it so unusual that I would desire to simply be in your presence?"

"Yes, it is!" She laughed. "I am generally desired for my conversation, not the serenity of my presence. That is Jane's purview."

"I would not call it serene exactly." He had a teasing look on his face that she wished to know the root of.

"What would you call it?"

"I cannot know what you were feeling—likely annoyance at my lack of conversation—but I was joyful."

"Joyful?"

"Yes. And anxious upon occasion. Being with you makes me very happy, Elizabeth. And very nervous." His cheeks flushed slightly at this confession. "Surely you realize that?"

She looked down at his familiarity, the look in his eyes too much for her at the moment. But she was not a coldhearted woman. She could not hear such things and not be moved at least a little, so she brought her free hand up to his arm, squeezed it, then interlaced her fingers so she was holding his arm with both hands. He seemed inordinately pleased by this, and she felt guilty that his feelings should be so much stronger than her own.

But no matter. She had agreed to get to know him better, and she was well on her way. If stronger feelings wished to develop, she would give them leave to do so.

8

A DULL SUNDAY & AN EXCITING MONDAY

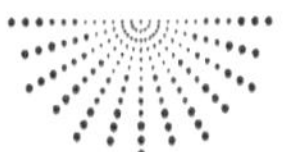

Sunday they attended church separately. The only contact between them was a quick greeting outside the church, then they were whisked away to their respective relations' homes. Darcy spent the afternoon avoiding his aunt and thinking of Elizabeth. The lady herself was not so lucky as to be left alone. After a satisfying meal, Charlotte took Elizabeth to the garden and insisted on knowing all.

"Eliza, you must tell me what has happened! It is clear there is something between you and Mr. Darcy!"

"Is it?"

Charlotte gave her a look. "Do not be coy with me, Eliza Bennet. I have known you too long to be put off by such maneuvers."

Elizabeth chuckled. "Very well. Mr. Darcy has asked to court me."

"To court you?"

"Yes."

"And you have agreed."

"Yes."

Charlotte looked both befuddled and vindicated, a combination that amused Elizabeth greatly.

"Are you terribly pleased to be proved correct in your belief of the gentleman's intentions?"

Charlotte smiled a little smugly and lifted her chin. "I am not displeased."

Elizabeth laughed. "A great understatement, I believe."

Charlotte took her hand eagerly. "You must tell me all, Eliza! What did he say? How did you respond? I confess I feared you might let your impulsiveness get the better of you and refuse him."

Elizabeth flushed a little and looked down. "You know me too well, I think. Had he asked me before my conversation with Colonel Fitzwilliam, I believe I would have refused him."

"So did your dislike rest so strongly on Mr. Wickham's report? Or is knowing he is in your power an attractive enough inducement?"

Elizabeth shifted uncomfortably. "It was many things, truly. Yes, I had thought him a villain by Mr. Wickham's information, which led me to realize my own vanity and folly. That in turn made me realize how much my dislike of Mr. Darcy was founded on his having insulted me at the assembly." She sighed. "Coming face to face with one's greatest shortcomings is not an enjoyable pastime. It is humbling."

Charlotte squeezed her hand, remembering her friend's very great distress the day of her discovery. "So you came to see him a different light, then?"

"Not immediately, but I am beginning to. At first, I thought I would merely thank him for his kindness to me that evening and be on my way. But he does seem to have sincere feelings for me, though I find them difficult to credit."

"Why should you? Is it yourself you believe undesirable? Or is it the gentleman's feelings that are lacking?"

"Both, I think." She spoke quietly, her eyes on the flowers growing next to the bench. "You know what my opinion of Mr. Darcy was. I did not think him capable of love. Affection perhaps, if the lady were of the right circles and suitably wealthy, but passionate, consuming love? I thought not." She flushed a little. "I am learning I am mistaken in that regard."

"And of yourself?" Charlotte asked gently.

"I have not found myself so very lacking, but I did not think I would catch the eye of one so high. It is simply something I never imagined. I thought I would marry a man of my father's standing, or possibly someone like my Uncle Gardiner. I never truly thought a gentleman of Mr. Darcy's position and wealth would look my way."

"You forgot to mention his intelligence and handsome countenance," Charlotte added with a teasing smile.

"And we mustn't forget his very broad shoulders," added Elizabeth, quickly entering into her friend's playful mood.

"He has no need to pad his jackets."

"And he does have a skilled tailor."

"Have you seen him ride? He has a very fine seat."

Elizabeth could not contain her laughter, and soon Charlotte joined her, giggling like girls on the bench in the garden.

"Well, I am glad for you, Eliza. He will make a very fine husband, I think."

"I am not engaged yet."

"But surely you will be? Did he not tell you his intentions are honorable?"

"He did, but I asked him to progress slowly."

Charlotte nodded. "That is sensible. It will give you time to adjust to the idea now that you have secured him."

"I have not secured him, Charlotte!"

"Have you not?" She gave Elizabeth such a look that her friend blushed and looked away.

"Charlotte, must you always know best?" she said in exasperation.

Charlotte smiled proudly. "I am glad you are coming to see the wisdom of heeding my advice."

Elizabeth laughed lightly and leaned her shoulder into her friend, nearly knocking her off the bench. "How lucky for me to have an older, wiser friend to advise me."

"You laugh now, Eliza, but remember who was right about your Mr. Darcy."

"He is not my—" she could not finish the sentence before Charlotte bumped her shoulder in return. Elizabeth had to scramble to avoid falling off the bench. "Charlotte!"

"If you do not wish to be treated like a ninny, do not say such ridiculous things!"

Elizabeth could only laugh and shake her head.

MONDAY MORNING, Elizabeth put on her yellow walking gown and a blonde straw bonnet with a periwinkle ribbon. It was simple and springlike, and she thought the color became her well. The yellow gown brought out the gold flecks in her brown eyes, and the bonnet was one of her more comfortable ones.

She stopped at the kitchen for Mrs. Hopkins muffins and a fruit tart, then skipped away to the grove. She was surprised at how happy she was to be meeting Mr. Darcy. Had she not detested the man less than a week ago? But he was so very attentive, and so kind to her, and so endearingly awkward when he was nervous that she could not help but warm to him. Her not insignificant guilt at having been so rude to him for so long played a role in her desire to please him now, though she did not care to examine it too closely. She had not liked him before, and she had been silly and vain, but that was all to be forgot. It was in the past. Now he was courting her, and she was enjoying the experience. She would not poke at it needlessly until she drove herself mad. It was a pointless exercise.

She entered the grove on quiet feet and saw him standing under a tree some distance away from her. She could not help but smile at the sight. She was not immune to masculine beauty and he was a very attractive man. Possibly the most attractive man she had ever seen. And he wished to court her! She could admit, when she allowed herself to think on it, that her initial offense at his insult had much to do with her immediate attraction to him at the assembly. That she had found his features handsome and his figure athletic was salt in the wound when he found her decidedly less so. If Mr. Collins had said he found her merely tolerable, she would not have cared two figs! But to be called tolerable by a man such as Mr. Darcy... It had stung. And immediately destroyed any attraction she had felt for him.

But now, ah now! How different things were! She was able to allow her attraction free rein. She was sensible of the possibility that she might only like Mr. Darcy now because he had disliked her in the beginning of their acquaintance, and his current infatuation somehow proved her desirability and provided vindication for her wounded vanity. But surely she was not so vain as to allow such a feeling to persist into allowing a courtship! She had felt flattered at first, but now she was coming to know him as he truly was, without her wounded pride bleeding between them. It was not just the balm to her vanity she desired, but to truly know him.

She was now within twenty feet of him, but he did not seem to hear her approach. Seized by a sudden fit of mischievousness, she set down her small basket and tiptoed to where he stood. He was taller than her, so it would be difficult, but she thought she might be able to reach around him and cover his eyes as she and her sisters often did. Alas, she was just reaching up past his shoulders when Mr. Darcy turned around quickly, his right arm on his hip, and clipped Elizabeth in the ribs, sending her toppling over sideways.

"Oof!" She was sprawled on the ground of the grove, her shawl pooled at her wrists and the lower half of her calves on display.

"Elizabeth! Are you hurt?" Mr. Darcy quickly knelt down beside her and touched her arm gently. "Forgive me. I did not see you."

Elizabeth looked up at the worried expression on Mr. Darcy's face and burst out laughing. "Forgive me, sir. It was my own fault. I should not have attempted to surprise you."

He looked adorably awkward, all concern and confusion, so she presented him with her hand and said, "Will you help me up?"

"Of course!" He reddened at not having thought to offer the service before and attempted to make up for it by picking up the trailing end of her shawl and placing it back around her shoulder. He smiled grimly when it was firmly in place and she shook her head at him.

"You must not let it spoil your morning, Mr. Darcy. Truly, I am perfectly well. It is not the first time I have taken a tumble in the grass and I doubt it shall be the last."

He reddened at the thought her words conjured and looked even more awkward than he had before.

Deciding to give him a moment to compose himself, Elizabeth went to retrieve the basket she had left under a neighboring tree. "Shall we walk to the stream?"

"There is an old folly on the hill yonder I thought you might wish to see. If you do not mind a longer walk, that is?"

"That sounds lovely!" She smiled brightly and asked him to lead the way.

The folly had been built by Sir Lewis's father and was a small round structure at the top of a hill rather distant from the house. It was a beautiful prospect, and it had a lovely view of the countryside, but she did wonder why it was built in so remote a location.

"Sir Reginald de Bourgh built it for his wife. She loved to paint landscapes, and this view was one of her favorites. She would ride her mare here with her paints and spend the afternoon. He was very fond of her, so he had this built as a gift for her thirtieth birthday."

"That is very romantic," she said softly, looking at the folly with new eyes. It was a graceful structure, with lovely simple columns, not ridiculously adorned with ornate crowns or Grecian statues. There was a tiny room in the center. Its door was locked, but she could see through the window that it contained a small chaise and a pair of chairs with a low table between them. It would have been the perfect artist's retreat. "It is charming."

"Yes, it is. My aunt is not overly fond of it, so the path leading to it has become rather overgrown. There was a wider horse path just there." He pointed to a space between the trees where the grass grew slightly shorter than its surroundings. "Only the deer use it now."

"That is rather sad."

"Yes, I have always thought so."

"What was Sir Lewis like?"

"My uncle?"

She nodded. "Growing up with such parents had to have impacted him in some way. Was he artistic like his mother? Or romantic like his father?"

"I do not know, to be honest. I was only twelve when he died. I know he was a kind man, and much older than my aunt. She was his second wife. His first had died in childbed along with the babe and he was much affected by it, or so everyone said."

"How awful!"

"Yes, it would be difficult for anyone, but his was said to be a love match, and he mourned her for nearly a decade before wedding my aunt."

Elizabeth made a noncommittal sound and turned to look over the view. It certainly painted Lady Catherine in a different light. Had she wished for a love match? Or even an affectionate marriage? Had she thought she would have it, or hoped for it with Sir Lewis, only to find he was still mourning his first wife and had only married her for an heir? She shook her head. She was being fanciful. She knew nothing of Lady Catherine's desires nor her heart. The lady may have had exactly the marriage she wished for. Sir Lewis might have been a perfectly wonderful husband to her, despite still mourning his first wife. Though, even as Elizabeth told herself this, she knew it was not true. Lady Catherine did not have the sensibility of one who had been loved. She was too cold, too shuttered to have experienced such a thing.

With a sigh, Elizabeth sat on the cold stone, letting her feet dangle over the ledge. "Are you hungry?"

"Yes. Do you have more muffins?" he asked as he lowered himself to the floor of the folly. He leaned back against a pillar, his legs stretched out before him and his eyes on Elizabeth.

"I do."

She passed him a muffin and they sat in silence while they ate, looking at the view. Well, Elizabeth was enjoying the view. Darcy was enjoying watching Elizabeth. He had never thought he would enjoy courting. It seemed a terrible waste of time and energy. If a man knew he wanted to marry a woman, why not simply ask her and be done with it? Surely the marriage itself would offer more opportunities for intimacy than a courtship would. But then he had not given the lady's feelings much consideration beyond her acceptance of his suit. To his great embarrassment, he realized he had counted on the very thing he most abhorred about society—ladies pursuing him for his wealth and position alone—to be his ally. He had expected her to accept him because it was prudent and he was a good match, yet he had also desired her affection and respect, while doing nothing to earn either. He expected a lady, Elizabeth to be precise, to fall into his arms with rapturous joy why exactly? Because he had a grand estate and a large income? It was abhorrent.

He did not know when he had last been so disgusted with himself.

"What must it have been like? To be loved like that?"

"Pardon?" With a start, Darcy realized Elizabeth had been speaking while he was lost in how own thoughts. "Forgive me, I was not attending."

Elizabeth smiled self-consciously and looked at her lap. "I was saying nothing of import. Would you like another muffin?"

"Please, continue. You were saying something about love?"

She darted her eyes to him, then back to her hands. "I was musing aloud, that is all." She met his eyes for a moment, then turned her gaze back to the trees. "I wondered what it was like, for Sir Reginald's wife. To be loved like that. For a man to build his wife a folly—he must be more than fond of her."

Darcy watched her steadily, wondering about her determination not to look at him and the pink tinge on her cheek. "A man in love would do a great deal more," he said softly.

Something about his voice, deep and low, made her turn to face him. She felt her cheeks flame before she could comprehend the look in his eyes. Her mouth dropped open slightly and her breath came faster, though she did not know why. "Would he?"

Mr. Darcy swung his legs over the folly ledge and scooted closer to her, so close she could have twitched her finger and touched him. "He would indeed, Miss Bennet."

Her breath hitched and she tried to think of something clever to say, but her mind had emptied completely. Something warm was on her hand. She could not think what it was, so lost in his gaze was she, but then she felt it moving, tracing over each finger one by one, and realized he was touching her hand. Had he removed his gloves?

Feeling overwhelmed by the intimacy of the moment, she broke his gaze and laughed nervously. "Shall we head back?" she asked. Why was her voice so breathy? Had he noticed?

"Of course." Darcy's voice was softer than usual, too. At least she was not the only one affected.

They stood and she gathered her shawl around her, careful not to look at him directly.

"Are you ready?" he asked.

"Yes." They had walked a little distance from the folly—and she had calmed considerably—when she asked, "Would anyone mind if I came here again? It is a lovely prospect."

"You are welcome to visit it as often as you choose. Though perhaps it would be wise not to mention it in front of my aunt."

"Do you think she would disapprove?"

"Not truly, but she does not like to talk of this place. I am not certain why."

"I imagine Sir Lewis visited here often with his first wife," she said unthinkingly. "It is a romantic location."

Darcy stopped and turned to face her. "Yes, it is."

He touched her cheek softly, so lightly she barely felt it, and then dropped his hand. When he withdrew, he seemed shy somehow, as if he was afraid he had offended her.

Without thinking on her actions overmuch, Elizabeth linked her arm through his and said cheerfully, "May I have your arm for the way down? You know the path better than I."

He half-smiled at her and pulled her a little closer and she rewarded him with a bright smile of her own. He seemed so very pleased when she smiled at him that she found herself doing it more and more. Making him happy gave her a rush of pleasure she did not care to examine too closely.

They were proceeding slowly. He was courting her. She knew his intentions, he knew she needed time to learn if they would suit and to develop affection for him. So far, all was proceeding as expected and

Elizabeth felt no need to question it. She had had enough self-evaluation last Thursday to last her through three courtships, and she felt no need to scrutinize their every interaction. She was getting to know him. That was all.

"HOW GOES your effort to win fair lady, Darcy?" Fitzwilliam bounded into his cousin's room after dinner where Darcy sat pretending to write a letter.

Darcy glared at the colonel for a moment for interrupting his very pleasant daydream and said, "It is going very well, I believe. I took her to the folly this morning and she was quite taken by it."

"That is progress! And have you been practicing your flirtation skills?" Fitzwilliam said with a dramatic waggle of his eyebrows.

Darcy sighed. "Yes, it is all progressing apace."

"Excellent!" He clapped his hands so loudly Darcy jumped. "I will look forward to standing up at your wedding."

"She has not accepted me yet, Cousin."

"But she will, Darcy, she will!"

Darcy looked at him suspiciously. "How can you know that? Less than a week ago you told me she was likely to refuse me."

The colonel shrugged. "Miss Bennet is an honest woman. She would not continue meeting you if she did not believe she could find her way to accepting you eventually."

A new light lit Darcy's eyes. He had not thought of it like that.

"You must be patient with her and continue to woo her. Surely it cannot be a wholly trying experience?"

He gave Darcy such a look that he blushed to the roots of his hair. "No, it is not wholly unpleasant. Not unpleasant at all, actually." He looked to the wall, a thoughtful expression on his face. "Fitz, what does it say about me that I had not even attempted to woo her before? That I had not even thought about her feelings one way or another? Shall I make a brutish husband? The sort who makes others pity his wife when they are seen together in public?"

The colonel would have laughed, but his cousin seemed genuinely distressed.

"Darcy, you will make a considerate husband, I am certain of it. Look how well you treat Georgiana!"

"She is my sister. It is different."

"Yes, you will be much closer to your wife, and receive much more from her in return."

Darcy shot him an irritated glance. Could Fitzwilliam be serious about nothing?

"Cousin, I will be the first to admit you can be overbearing and more concerned with your own comforts than the feelings of others."

Darcy's gaze leapt to his cousin.

"It is not surprising. You were raised to remember your own importance and you have the income to ensure others remember it as well."

Darcy's nostrils flared.

"But despite all that, you are a kind man, and a generous one. Your first attempt at catching Miss Bennet was deplorable, but you have seen the error of your ways and are improving with the speed of a new colt. That speaks miles for your character. There are men who would have simply walked away when told they had done wrongly. They would not have tried to make it right or cared about the opinion of a woman who was unimpressed with themselves. But you are going to great lengths to be worthy of Miss Bennet. You are a fool if you think she does not recognize that, or if you do not see what it says about you. It takes a great man to admit to his faults and correct them."

Darcy took a deep breath. He felt the best sort of pride that his cousin thought he was a good man, for he knew Colonel Fitzwilliam was among the best of men himself. But more than that, he heard the ring of truth in his cousin's words. He had been full of his own importance, and in many ways he still was. If he did not check it, he would destroy the beautiful, fragile thing that was growing between him and Elizabeth.

"I thank you, Fitzwilliam. Your opinion means a great deal to me." Darcy said softly.

They sat quietly for a few minutes before Darcy broke the silence with an irritated huff. "Am I truly so overbearing?"

"Oh, horribly so."

"And inconsiderate of others?"

"Only when they want something that does not coincide with your wishes."

"Difficult?"

"Of course."

"Officious?"

"Quite often."

"Demanding?"

"All the time."

Darcy huffed. "I wonder you travel with me at all."

"You are so spoiled you would throw a fit if I did not."

Darcy turned toward his cousin and glared at him. Colonel Fitzwilliam smiled back with his usual insouciance.

After several seconds of this they finally broke, each laughing deep, hearty chuckles. They laughed for some time, sipping their drinks, and settled back down in the stiff chairs before the fire.

"I am glad you came to Rosings, Fitz," said Darcy quietly.

"You are welcome, Cousin."

9

TUESDAY TEMPTATIONS

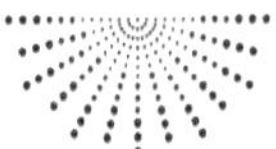

Tuesday morning, Darcy was so pleased by the events of the day before that he sought another romantic location. Luckily, his aunt had plans to visit a neighbor, so when Mrs. Collins and Elizabeth came to call on Anne, he was able to whisk her away to the rose garden. Anne was tired anyway, and with such a familiar guest as Mrs. Collins, she could entertain her in her private sitting room, which was surely preferable for Miss de Bourgh. He was doing her a service, really.

Thus he found himself strolling through Rosings's extensive rose garden—Lady Catherine believed that a country estate was only as good as its rose garden and funded it accordingly—with Elizabeth on his arm, the bright spring sunshine making rainbows on her skin, and a twitch in his hand that longed to reach out and touch those rainbows.

"How long will you remain in Kent?" asked Elizabeth.

"I had thought I would stay through the end of the week. You are departing Saturday, are you not?"

"Yes, I am. My uncle's man will accompany us."

"You will ride the stage?"

"Yes, with Miss Lucas."

He pinched his lips in a tight line.

"Why so stern-faced, Mr. Darcy?"

"I do not like the idea of you taking a stage."

"I will be accompanied by a trusted servant. I shall not be unprotected."

He continued to glare at a particularly robust rose bush.

"What do you find so offensive about this flower, sir? I see aught amiss. If you continue to glower at it so, it will wither away and die, I am certain."

He stopped the quick rejoinder that rushed to his lips. Was she referring to more than just the flower? "I am not glaring at the flower, Elizabeth, which I'm sure you know rather well."

"Will you not speak what is on your mind?"

He sighed. "I should like to escort you to Town."

Her brows rose. "Oh?"

He nodded. "We had planned to leave at that time anyhow. Fitzwilliam and I can ride alongside if the weather holds."

"And if it does not?"

"We may bring along a maid as chaperone."

Elizabeth nodded. "Why were you fretting so over telling me this?"

He exhaled a whoosh of air. "I have had it impressed upon me recently that I am selfish and do not consider well enough the desires of others."

Elizabeth bit her lip to keep herself from laughing at the comical look on his face. He did not seem pleased in the least by this latest discovery. "May I ask who impressed such things upon you?"

"I'm sure you know very well it was my cousin, Colonel Fitzwilliam. He cannot mind his own affairs."

She squeezed his arm. "Do not be too hard on the colonel. He has been very kind to me."

He pressed her hand where it rested on his. "Very well, my dear."

Elizabeth marveled at how quickly she was coming to like Mr. Darcy. Or rather, she was coming to like being courted by him. She had wondered if it was the novelty of courtship and the compliment to her vanity that she so enjoyed, or his presence in and of itself, but she was beginning to think it was the latter.

"I do not see why you should not accompany us. Your carriage is certain to be more comfortable than a public coach and I will use the money from my ticket to buy a new bonnet," she added cheekily.

He smiled down at her. "I rather like it when you do not wear a bonnet."

"Oh? Why is that, sir?"

"I'm certain you have noticed I am taller than you."

"It had caught my attention, yes."

"If you are wearing a bonnet, I cannot see your face when I look down at you."

"Which is all the time, owing to your very great stature."

Darcy rolled his eyes. "I have seen you often enough without one to know you are not enamored of them either."

"Do not let my mother hear that you have seen me without a bonnet. She will scold me heartily and insist on inspecting my apparel before I leave the house."

"Are you saying I have leverage over you?" he asked, a teasing glint in his eye.

"If you have any care for me at all, you will not dream of saying a word." They had come to a fountain near the end of the garden and she stepped up onto the low stone ledge that ran around its perimeter. "There! Now you do not need to look down at all."

Darcy watched her with a warm smile, then stepped forward so he was only a few inches from her. She was taller standing on the ledge, but he still had to look down to see her properly.

"Well, when you are this close, you are even taller, but the step helps, does it not?"

She tilted her head back and smiled coyly. Really, she was smiling at him entirely too much, but he did seem to enjoy it and she could not help but be proud of herself for pleasing him so thoroughly.

"Much better." He reached for the ribbon hanging from her bonnet and ran it between his fingers, his eyes on hers as he did so.

Oddly, she felt as if he were touching her and not her bonnet ribbons. Her breath came a little quicker, and she watched him move closer bit by bit until she could feel his breath on her cheek.

"Elizabeth," he whispered.

She closed her eyes, overcome with feelings she could not identify. "Yes, Mr. Darcy?"

He took a deep breath, then stroked her cheek with the back of his fingers. "I wish you would call me by my given name."

"Very well. What is it?"

"It is Fitzwilliam."

"Where?" she asked looking about her with a slightly alarmed expression.

Darcy almost laughed. "Not my cousin, my name."

"Oh. You wish me to call you Fitzwilliam?"

"Yes."

"Not Fitz, or William, or Wills?"

"No."

She pouted.

He tapped her nose playfully.

"It is terribly long."

"No longer than Elizabeth."

She sighed. "Very well. I suppose I cannot argue with that. Though my family calls me Lizzy."

"I have heard Mrs. Collins call you Eliza."

"She does. You may do so if you wish."

"Which do you prefer?"

"I do not know. Lizzy was the name of my childhood, so it is only natural for those who knew me as a child to employ it. When I came out, everyone began calling me Eliza."

"Do you dislike it?"

"No," she said thoughtfully, "I do not dislike it, but neither do I love it."

"And what of Elizabeth?"

"I like it very well." She would not say that she particularly liked the way he said it, in his deep voice and the slight elongation of the second syllable.

"Then I shall call you Elizabeth."

She raised a brow. "I do not believe I gave you permission to address me by my given name, Mr. Darcy."

His brow raised to match hers. He wished to tease her in return, but he could think of nothing clever to say. "Is it too familiar?"

"Not at all, but a lady does like to be asked."

Ah. "Miss Bennet, might I have permission to address you more informally?"

"You may, Mr. Darcy."

He leaned a little closer to her, and she instinctively stepped back, forgetting that the ledge of the fountain was behind her. She bumped the edge with her knees and lost her balance, prepared to fall into the fountain or gracelessly beside it in a desperate attempt to avoid a dunking, when Mr. Darcy's strong arms came about her waist and pulled her flush against him.

All her breath whooshed out of her in one long exhale as she fell into him, feeling him pressed to her from her chest to her ankles. Her wide eyes raised to meet his and she felt something she could not identify pass between them.

"Are you well?" he asked, his voice rough.

"Quite well. You?"

"Perfectly well."

They stood beside the fountain, holding one another indecorously close, until Elizabeth laughed nervously and peeled herself from him.

"I should go back to the house. Charlotte will wonder what has become of me."

He nodded and offered his arm, and they returned to the house in silence.

10

WEDNESDAYS ARE FOR SUBTERFUGE

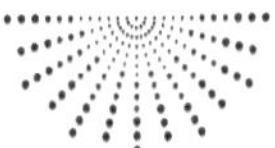

"I knew you were stupid, but I did not think you entirely devoid of sense."

"What are you on about now, Fitz?"

"You took her to the rose garden? At Rosings? Are you daft?"

Darcy looked toward the window with his lips pressed in a hard line. "Where did you hear that?"

"It is all over the house! I heard two servants speaking of it in the corridor. Apparently a gardener saw you embracing her. Really, Darcy! I thought you had more sense."

"Lady Catherine was not at home, and she came to call on our cousin with Mrs. Collins. Anne had the energy for only one guest, so I offered to show Elizabeth the garden. Nothing untoward occurred."

"So you did not embrace her by the fountain?"

"Well, I," he stumbled over his words and finally said in a rush, "she stepped back against the edge of the fountain and nearly tumbled in. I merely saved her from a dunking."

Colonel Fitzwilliam looked at him with suspicion. "Because young ladies accustomed to vigorous walks are often falling into fountains."

Darcy rolled his eyes.

"It is a wonder so many ladies survive into adulthood, what with

79

their propensity to fall into fountains. Why, they should cordon off all public fountains immediately! The danger is too great! It will be hard to enforce on private estates of course, but I'm certain if we persevere, we can keep the young ladies of Britain safe from the menace of fountains."

Darcy exhaled gruffly. "You may think what you like, Fitz, but I have told you the truth."

"Darcy, how do you not understand this yet? It does not matter what you were truly doing! It only matters that you were observed and in Lady Catherine's rose garden, of all places. She will be furious when she hears of it."

"Are you certain she has not already?"

"She has said nothing to me, but I imagine her maid will tell her."

Darcy looked at the wall calculatingly.

"I know what you are thinking! Do not even consider trying to pay her maid for her silence. That will only guarantee she goes to our aunt and it will be worse for you because of it."

Darcy pinched the bridge of his nose. "I suppose there is nothing for it. I must speak to Lady Catherine."

Colonel Fitzwilliam slapped his back. "May God go with you, Cousin!"

Darcy merely glared at him.

DARCY MARCHED to his aunt's parlor in a dark mood. He had not seen Elizabeth yet today. She had informed him after their walk yesterday that she would accompany Charlotte that morning. Mrs. Collins would be visiting some parishioners in need of assistance, and both Elizabeth and Miss Lucas would accompany her. He was disappointed, but Fitzwilliam said he would convince their aunt to invite the parsonage for tea that evening, so he could not be too dejected. But he had become accustomed to her smiles, her hand on his arm, her little flirtations, and he was quite out of sorts having been without them for more than a day now. How would he ever manage when she returned to Hertfordshire? He would simply have to follow her thither—there was nothing else for it.

Having reached the parlor, he rapped swiftly on the door and let himself in on his aunt's command.

"Darcy, there you are. I have been meaning to talk to you," said his aunt in her haughty way.

"I need to speak with you as well, Aunt. Will you not go first?"

She pointed to a seat and nodded imperiously. She really was terrifically bad-mannered. How had he not realized it before? Fitzwilliam was right—she had been raised with proper manners, but she did what she wished precisely because she knew she could get away with it.

She began speaking at length about her steward—she was certain the man was stealing from her for the rents had been lower the last quarter than they usually were, and she did not believe for a moment that nonsense about the farmer who broke his leg or the other whose field had flooded. Such things never happened at Rosings!

Darcy paid scant attention to her, planning what he would say to his aunt and how he would say it. She would be angry—no, she would be irate. She would likely march down to the parsonage and give Elizabeth a tongue lashing. She could make life very difficult for Mr. and Mrs. Collins as well. He had not thought of that before. Fitzwilliam was right—he was stupid. Taking Elizabeth to the rose garden, courting her under his aunt's very nose, had been colossally short-sighted. Now he must think quickly to remedy the situation.

He hated scenes and overblown tempers—very little was accomplished and everyone left discomposed. If no one mentioned it to her, his informing her would be pointless. Yet disguise was his abhorrence. He had no desire to live in secrets and shadows. He was doing nothing wrong! He should not have to hide like an errant child sneaking biscuits from the larder.

And he must consider how she would treat others. It would be much better to allow her time to cool before she saw Elizabeth again.

Elizabeth! She would likely be angry when she heard. If Lady Catherine knew, she would say something to Mr. Collins, who would lecture Elizabeth horribly and write to his family in Hertfordshire. She would be rightfully angry with him if that were to happen. It could destroy everything he had been working for.

There was nothing for it. He would have to tell her something. But he need not tell her *everything*.

"Lady Catherine, have the parsonage been invited to tea today?"

She stopped speaking abruptly and looked at him as if he were a talking cat. "Yes. Why do you ask?"

"I was wondering if Miss Elizabeth was feeling better."

"Better? Has she been ill?"

"I do not think she was ill, but she did nearly stumble into the fountain yesterday when we walked in the garden. She seemed a little lightheaded, but it was likely only the heat of the day."

"Falling into the fountain! How ridiculous! When I was a young lady, I never fell into any fountain, not at my father's estate, and especially not at someone else's!"

"Of course. But she did not fall in, only almost. I was able to catch her before she took a dunking."

She preened. "Well, that was good of you. She must learn not to be so reckless! I will instruct her in this when she comes to tea."

"Of course, Aunt."

She continued on about her steward, the ungrateful tenants, and the impertinent neighbor who had dared invite her to a dinner when they were so clearly beneath her.

Darcy nodded and spoke when necessary, hoping his little explanation would be enough for her if she heard something from her servants.

Elizabeth had just stepped up to Rosings's front door when she was seized by the arm.

"Pardon me, I must borrow Miss Bennet for a moment."

"Colonel Fitzwilliam!" she cried as he led her around the side of the house and into the shrubbery garden. "What are you doing?"

"Forgive me, Miss Bennet, but it was necessary." Fitzwilliam looked behind them to make sure no one had followed, then slowed his pace and led her to an enclosed area blocked from the view of anyone in the house.

"Mr. Darcy!" He stood in the center of the wall of shrubbery.

"Good evening, Elizabeth."

She looked around and saw that Colonel Fitzwilliam had disappeared. She looked back to Darcy with suspicion. "What is going on, sir?"

"When we were walking in the rose garden yesterday, we were observed."

She looked nonplussed, then her eyes widened. "You mean…?"

"Yes. I have taken the liberty of telling my aunt that you felt light-headed and nearly tipped into the fountain. She will likely inform you of the proper way to walk in a rose garden at tea. Forgive my subterfuge, but I could think of nothing else to tell her that would both explain the situation and protect your reputation. Not that you would be the first lady to… fall into a fountain, but I did not want stories spread about you."

She flushed, but immediately understood the situation. "I thank you, Mr. Darcy. I see why you chose what you did. Hopefully your explanation will mitigate any potential damage."

He nodded, looking awkward and uncomfortable. She stepped closer, unsure of her own actions, but wishing to assuage his concern as well.

She reached out and touched his arm. "I am not angry with you, Fitzwilliam."

He sighed heavily. "Truly?" He placed his hand over hers on his arm. "You are certain?"

She smiled mischievously. "I may change my mind after listening to your aunt instruct me in walking for a quarter hour, but at the moment, no, I am not angry with you."

He sighed and lifted her hand to his lips. "Thank you, Elizabeth. I do not know what I would do if I lost you now."

She was clearly surprised, but he thought she did not appear discomposed. She flushed a little and looked at the ground. He could not resist running the back of his hand down one flushed cheek. Her eyes rose to meet his, and he raised her hand to his lips again, kissing it softly, then turning it over to kiss the inside of her wrist delicately.

Her eyes widened. "You truly love me, don't you?" She flushed a deep red as soon as the words had left her mouth. She had not meant to say them aloud.

"Yes, I truly do."

She smiled tremulously, her mind emptying of all thought.

"Come," he said gently as he looped her arm through his and began to lead her back toward the house.

Elizabeth followed silently, wondering what one did with such a declaration when uttered by a man such as he. What did one do with a man like Mr. Darcy?

11

THURSDAY ONCE AGAIN

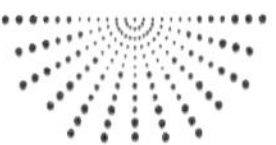

Elizabeth had gone to bed Wednesday evening with a feeling of contentment, and she woke Thursday with a smile on her face. She and Mr. Darcy had faced their first trial, albeit a small one, and come out unscathed. He had handled it with discretion and consideration, and she could not be displeased by the result. It was still possible Lady Catherine would discover what was truly happening—that Mr. Darcy was courting Elizabeth on her own estate—but she now knew that he would stand by her.

She had not admitted it even to herself, but she had feared that Mr. Darcy's love was confined to Rosings, where she was unencumbered by her inappropriate family and undesirable relations. They were in a secluded society, with little company and no real-world troubles to intrude. Would his feelings be as strong in London? Where she stayed with her relations near Cheapside and he was surrounded by his noble family? What about at Longbourn, where the company was less varied and her mother most voluble?

She had been floating along, enjoying flirting with an attractive man and being doted on with such seeming devotion, but it had not felt real, not truly, until she felt it threatened by Lady Catherine's discovery.

Now... now it was all very real. His love was genuine. His pursuit in earnest. He would not give her up the moment difficulties arose. He would chase her until he caught her. His heart was hers for the taking.

She must admit, alone in her private room at the Hunsford parsonage, that she rather enjoyed being pursued by Mr. Darcy. She liked flirting with and teasing him. She liked the way he smiled when he saw her, and how his eyes took on a particular glow when she smiled at him. She liked the feel of his lips on the back of her hand and the way his arm felt solid and steady when she walked alongside him. She liked their conversations and enjoyed his mind—he was clever and not afraid to engage her on interesting topics. He would never be one to speak to a lady of nothing other than how pretty he found her. In fact, she could not recall him ever saying he found her pretty—perhaps once, but she knew he found her pleasing by the way he looked at her, and touched her cheek, and tugged the curl that hung beside her brow.

After an evening and morning of reflection, Elizabeth came to the rather startling realization that she *liked* him. In the way a woman liked a man. She felt affection for him blooming in her heart, and knew, in the way she knew the sun would rise the next day, that she was beginning to fall in love with him.

"Did you sleep well, Eliza?" Charlotte smiled brightly as Elizabeth entered the breakfast room and began pouring her a cup of tea.

"Yes, thank you. You have made a very comfortable home here, Charlotte. I'm sure I've told you before, but it bears repeating."

Charlotte beamed at her friend. "It is a joy to run my own home. I am quite content."

Elizabeth reached over and pressed her hand. "I am glad to hear it."

Charlotte looked around the empty room to ensure they were alone. The maid was in the kitchen, Maria was still sleeping, and Mr. Collins had gone to sit with an elderly parishioner. "I know you worried for me, but it is unnecessary, you know. I am pleased with my husband, truly."

Elizabeth looked at her skeptically. She nearly nodded and changed the subject, but Charlotte seemed intent on saying her piece and Elizabeth sensed it was important for her friend to speak of this with her. "Truly, Charlotte? You are happy with your situation?"

"Immensely. I am not you like you, you know that. Mr. Collins will never be good company, but he is already improving with a little guidance, and he is not cruel, which cannot be said for all husbands."

Elizabeth nodded with a grimace. "That is true." She hesitated. "And you do not find his... company... too distasteful?" Elizabeth spoke delicately, an odd expression on her face.

Charlotte's gaze lit up with understanding. "Surprisingly, not at all."

Elizabeth's eyes widened in disbelief.

"Oh, it was awkward at first, as I believe it usually is, but he is a very considerate man, and quite complimentary. And he takes direction very well. I am well pleased with him in that respect."

Elizabeth's eyes were comically wide now. "Truly?"

Charlotte glanced at her mischievously as she sipped her tea. "Oh, yes. It would be hard to find a more satisfactory husband, in that regard."

She smiled like the cat who got the cream and Elizabeth could only stare at her, mouth open in shock, unable to speak a word. Charlotte could resist no longer and began to laugh, her shoulders shaking as Elizabeth continued to stare at her.

Mr. Collins! A wonderful lover! Of all people... She never would have believed it had not Charlotte's self-satisfied grin and a lifetime of friendship stood as witness.

Mr. Collins!

Elizabeth shook herself and laughed lightly with her friend, though she was still more than a little stunned.

"Just you wait, Eliza. Your Mr. Darcy will surprise you as well, I imagine."

Elizabeth had just taken a sip of tea and Charlotte was halfway through her second sentence when that tea came spewing out of Elizabeth's mouth, followed by a choking laugh and much coughing.

"Charlotte!"

"What? I am an old married lady now. I may speak as I find."

Elizabeth shook her head at her friend and dabbed at the tea on her wrist.

IT HAD BEEN ARRANGED the evening prior that Colonel Fitzwilliam would take the ladies to see Lullingstone Castle that afternoon. It was an ancient building that was part fortress, part house, and was famous for its garden and the view from its parapets. The ladies had declared an interest when he spoke of it the evening before and an excursion had been planned. The ladies of the parsonage were dressed and ready at the appointed time when they heard a carriage pull up outside the house. When they stepped out, they were greeted by a beaming Colonel Fitzwilliam. He leapt down from the curricle and strode over to greet them, exuding good cheer.

"Good afternoon, Colonel!" said Charlotte. "I thought we were to take the carriage?"

"Miss de Bourgh felt unwell this afternoon. With a smaller party, we may travel in style." Mr. Darcy pulled up behind him in a light phaeton. "Ah, there is my cousin. Shall we go, ladies?"

Maria Lucas was excited to be traveling in such a vehicle, for she had only ever seen them on the busy streets of London and had never dreamed she would be in one herself. She climbed up merrily into the center seat of the curricle, her sister on her other side, before they were joined by the colonel. Maria flushed at sitting so close to him, and Elizabeth and Charlotte shared an amused glance at her blushes, but Fitzwilliam was all that was gentlemanly and quickly set about putting her at ease by explaining how the reins worked and even letting her hold them for a minute while he showed her how to steer.

Elizabeth smiled at him fondly. He really was the ideal older brother. If only she had had one of her own. How might her life have been different?

"What are you thinking of?"

Darcy's low voice in her ear made her jump slightly. "Fitzwilliam, forgive me, I did not see you there."

He smiled at her easy use of his given name and stretched his arm behind her to lead her toward the smaller phaeton.

"I was thinking that your cousin is the ideal brother figure. I wish I had had a brother like him."

"I am glad to hear it. I believe he looks on you in a similar fashion. He is wonderful with my sister Georgiana as well." Darcy looked to where the colonel was preparing to depart and helped Elizabeth up into the carriage as the one bearing their friends rolled away.

"Should they not wait for us?" asked Elizabeth, settling herself into the seat. Darcy smiled, a little wickedly she thought, but it must be her imagination, for Mr. Darcy was *never* wicked.

"I told him to go a little ahead. I wished to be alone with you."

She flushed in pleasure as he moved around the phaeton to climb up the other side and settle in beside her. The vehicle was small, made more for a lady than a gentleman, and they were very close together. Feeling bold after her night of reflection, Elizabeth closed the small distance between them and looped her arm through his.

Darcy froze momentarily, afraid to move for fear of frightening her away.

"How long will it take to drive to the castle?

"Between one and two hours, depending on our speed."

"Sounds lovely."

She smiled brightly at him and he flicked the reins, feeling more than a little discombobulated.

They rode in silence for a few minutes, enjoying the new blooms of spring. Darcy wondered at her sudden comfort. When he had gotten close to her before, she had always pulled back after a moment. But here she sat, for nearly ten minutes now, her entire left side pressed to his right, and seemed to have no inclination to move.

"Have you heard from Miss Bennet?" he asked.

"I had a letter yesterday. Mr. Bingley has become a regular fixture at Gracechurch Street."

"I am glad to hear it."

"Are you truly?"

He glanced at her and saw she was curious, not accusatory. "I am. Bingley is very happy. His last letter was nearly illegible, which only happens when he is in particularly good spirits."

Elizabeth laughed, a gentle tinkling sound that washed over his senses like a fresh breeze. "Do you think he will propose soon? Or shall he take his time?"

"I imagine he will be quick about it. He will be insufferable until they are wed."

Elizabeth laughed, then sighed, a feeling of contentment coming over her. She laid her head on Mr. Darcy's shoulder for a moment, watching the scenery go by.

"Elizabeth?"

She raised her head and looked at him quizzically. "Yes?"

"Are you happy?"

"Happy? At this moment?"

"Yes."

"I am." She smiled brightly. "Can you not tell?"

"I have misread you in the past. I no longer trust my own observations."

"Fitzwilliam, I am smiling and laughing and the day is perfect. Why would you not think me happy?"

Before he could stop himself, he glanced down to where their bodies were touching and her arm looped through his. He opened his mouth, but no sound came out. Soon he was flushed and looking about for something to say but found himself completely tongue tied.

"Ah, I see. I am confusing you," Elizabeth said softly.

Darcy looked back at her, his expression still cautious. "Somewhat," he said lowly.

"Is it unwelcome?" she asked. She moved away from him and began to pull her arm from his.

"No!" He grabbed her hand with his free arm and pulled her back to him, her body crashing against his.

Elizabeth laughed merrily. "So you like it when I sit near you?"

"Yes," he answered quickly, as if he were afraid she would edge away again.

"Do you like it when I take your arm?"

"Yes."

She saw his jaw flexing now and held in her laughter. She should not tease him so, but it was in her nature. "Do you like it when I rest my head on your shoulder, or should I not crowd you so?"

Finally realizing he was being teased and recovered from his embarrassment, he raised her hand to his lips. "You may rest your head on my shoulder any time you wish."

She smiled again and he said haltingly, "Elizabeth, I must ask. Where has this new boldness come from?"

She was surprised at the directness of his question, then thought she should not be—after all, he was Mr. Darcy.

"I was reflecting on our... relationship last evening, and I came to some favorable conclusions."

"Oh? May I ask what conclusions you came to?"

She took a deep breath. "I realized that this was real."

"Real?"

"Yes. It had all had a dreamlike quality to it until yesterday. A pleasant dream, but a dream nonetheless. When you told me we had been observed in the garden, I realized I was not just flirting on a holiday." Her voice softened. "I was being pursued by an honorable man with honest intentions."

He kissed her hand again. "And that is why you are sitting so delightfully close to me now?"

Elizabeth blushed as he teased her. "Yes, it is."

"So I should gather that you are amenable to the honest intentions of an honorable man?"

"If you are the man," she said softly, eyes on her lap.

"Elizabeth, you are cruel."

Her head snapped up. "What?"

"To tell me such things when I can do nothing about it." He turned and met her eyes and her breath caught at what she saw there.

"Oh."

"Indeed."

The curricle ahead of them had just rounded a corner. Darcy looked about, saw they were alone, and drew the horses to a stop.

He turned to face Elizabeth fully. He placed one hand along the side of her face, reaching from behind her ear to beneath her chin. "Elizabeth, if you do not want me to kiss you, stop me now."

She swallowed and looked up at him, her brown eyes sparkling brightly. He leaned toward her, ever so slowly, and pressed his lips to hers. He pulled back and looked at her, and seeing her eyes half closed and a dazed expression on her face, he kissed her again, more strongly this time.

Finally, he pulled away, smiled gently at her, and set the horses to walking again. Elizabeth merely stared ahead, saying nothing. Darcy was rather smug that he had made her speechless, but his pride in his achievement shifted to wonder when she once again threaded her arm through his, then snuggled in close and rested her head on his shoulder, a soft sigh of contentment escaping her.

CHARLOTTE HAD a great interest in history, and she led them about the castle grounds, reading from a book she had found on the topic. Normally, Elizabeth would join her friend in her explorations, but she was too full of thoughts of Mr. Darcy to care about a castle in Kent, no matter how lovely it was.

They began as a group, but soon she and Darcy fell behind. He took her hand in his and guided her away from their party.

"Come."

She smiled happily and joined him, feeling a rush of excitement and intrigue. Is this what falling in love felt like? Was this romance? Was she in it at this very moment?

They rounded a corner and were in a large garden. There was a stream to one side, the castle on the other, and a maze stretching out before them.

"Shall we try the maze?" she asked gamely.

"Let's." He could think of wonderful things to do, lost in a maze with Elizabeth.

The first three turns led them to more choices, but the fourth came to a dead end. Elizabeth turned around, looking disappointed. "We should have gone left at the last crossroads. Or even straight. We will have to remember that the path to the right is a dead end."

She was about to walk past Darcy when he caught her wrist and gently pulled her back to him, a smile she had never seen before on his face. "In a moment."

He pulled her to him and kissed her, one hand still on her arm, the other stealing around her waist. Her hands came up to his chest and rested on his lapels, her chin tilted up to meet him. She was surprised by how quickly she felt comfortable kissing Mr. Darcy. She had kissed gentlemen in parlor games before, but those had been perfunctory and quick, tiny pecks that she would have given her grandfather. Mr. Darcy was the first man to kiss her like a lover.

She pulled back and smiled at him, then took his hand and pulled him back the way they had come. They reached the crossroads and turned left instead of right, Elizabeth attempting to commit the path to memory. It was difficult when every path looked like all the others, but she was determined. Darcy could not care about the maze. He would happily stay trapped in it all day if Elizabeth was with him and willing to kiss him. Each time they reached a dead end, he smiled and pulled her in for a kiss, then dutifully followed her out again. She became so accustomed to this that when they reached the fifth dead end, she turned to him and tilted her face up in anticipation.

Darcy smiled roguishly and leaned in slowly, relishing the fact that he was here with the woman he loved, and she was happy to receive his affection. He traced one finger down the side of her face, then from her shoulder down to her hand where he tangled his fingers with hers.

Elizabeth's breath came quicker, and she was sure he must hear her heart beating for how it was thundering inside her. His lips landing on hers were as light as a butterfly, his breath ghosting over her skin and sending shivers up her arms.

He kissed her again and again, first on her lips, then her forehead and cheeks, even the tip of her nose was not neglected. She squeezed his fingers between hers. "Fitzwilliam," she whispered.

Darcy was overwhelmed. He took a deep breath and pulled her closer, holding her gently in a secluded corner of a maze at a castle in Kent.

"Elizabeth, my dearest heart."

She wrapped her arms around his waist and pulled him tightly to her, snuggling closer and breathing deeply. He smelled like the forest they often walked in, and of fresh spring grass, and of leather and soap.

They stood there for some time, neither speaking. Elizabeth was filled with the wonder of romance, and Darcy was trying desperately not to ask her to marry him on the spot.

Eventually, they left their corner and found their way to the end of the maze. Darcy remembered there was a stream running beside it and they were able to use the sound of its gurgling to orientate themselves.

"Where have you been?" bellowed the colonel when they rejoined them in the gardens behind the castle.

"We got lost in the maze!" cried Elizabeth cheerily. "Thankfully, Mr. Darcy suggested we follow the stream and we eventually found our way out."

Charlotte smirked at Elizabeth, which her friend happily ignored, and Colonel Fitzwilliam looked doubtfully at Darcy.

"Did he? Darcy has always been good at finding his way about."

Darcy scowled at him, but he could not be truly irritated with his cousin. He was entirely too happy. Elizabeth took his arm and began to pull him toward the gardens.

"Come, Mr. Darcy. Maria says there is a beautiful tree blooming with cherry blossoms in the back of the garden." She turned to face Charlotte. "Shall you join us?"

Charlotte was tempted to tease her friend and say she would join them, but there was an old chapel she still wished to see. "You go ahead. I wish to see more of the castle."

They parted ways and Elizabeth released Mr. Darcy's arm and practically skipped ahead. "Isn't it beautiful?" She spun around in the center path, radiating happiness and vitality.

"Yes, it is lovely."

She skipped ahead again, wondering if she could get Mr. Darcy to chase her, but he did not seem inclined. Perhaps it was too public a location. But she could still have a little fun with him. She saw the blooming cherry tree at the end of garden and hurried to it, quickly ducking beneath its blooms. She went to the far side of the trunk and stood behind it, knowing it was not big enough to hide her entirely, but she was at least not easily visible from a distance.

"Miss Bennet?" she heard him call her name and stayed perfectly still. His footsteps grew closer and she pulled back a little more, hoping the dense blooms would conceal her a moment longer. "Elizabeth."

His voice was closer than she thought and when she looked over her left shoulder, Mr. Darcy was only a few feet away from her.

"Are you hiding from me?" he asked, an odd expression on his face.

"No," she smiled. "I am playing with you."

"Playing?"

"Yes. You are entirely too serious, Mr. Darcy. You need to learn to play."

He was directly in front of her now, sheltered beneath the canopy of pink blossoms. "Do I?"

"Luckily, I am an expert at playfulness and I can direct you accordingly."

"Can you now?" He was looming over her, her back against the tree trunk and her head tilted up to face him.

"I can."

Her eyes were sparkling in that way that drove him mad with wanting her and he could not resist ducking down and kissing her. He was just tasting her lips when Elizabeth cried out.

"Oh!"

Darcy pulled back and looked at the spot on her shoulder she was brushing with her hand. "What is it?"

"Something landed on me." She was afraid it had been bird leavings, but she did not wish to say so to her beau, so she checked her shoulder as best she could and looked around her for evidence.

A giggle came from above, then they were showered with pink and white petals, falling like rain from the tree.

"Oh!" cried Elizabeth in delight. Now seeing that what had landed on her shoulder had only been a small stick, she was free to enjoy the petals raining down on her.

"You there!"

Mr. Darcy was another matter. He was staring up into the tree and calling to someone. She followed his gaze and saw a small child, no more than nine or ten, sitting high in the tree, shaking a branch and laughing at them as the petals fell down.

"Come down here this instant!" Mr. Darcy cried.

Elizabeth could not help but laugh. Mr. Darcy was a fiercely private person, she knew, and he would not take lightly to having been spied upon in such an intimate moment. But still, it was terribly funny.

She took his hand and tugged him away from the tree. "Come away, Fitzwilliam, there is no harm done."

He looked at her as if he would ignore her for a moment, but finally he relented and followed a laughing Elizabeth back towards the castle to find their friends.

FRIDAY, FULL OF FITS AND FURY

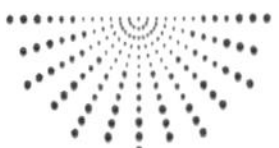

Friday morning, Elizabeth slipped out of the house early, Mrs. Hopkins's muffins in her pocket. Only a week ago, she had been dreading meeting Mr. Darcy after their humiliating confrontation. Now, she moved down the path as swiftly as possible without breaking into a run, eager to see him.

He was at the stream, seated on the bench with his back to her. Thinking she would attempt sneaking up on him again, she crept up behind him slowly and reached her hands out, covering his eyes. He immediately stiffened, and she leaned over his shoulder, whispering in his ear.

"Guess who?"

Before she knew what had happened, Mr. Darcy grabbed her and pulled her onto his lap, her legs hanging rather indecorously over his arm. She laughed gaily as he smiled down at her, and before she knew what had happened, he was kissing her as she sat sprawled across his lap.

When he pulled back, a rather satisfied look on his face, she said, "Wouldn't you feel ridiculous if it had not been me behind you?"

Darcy smirked. "I knew it was you. I could smell muffins."

Elizabeth laughed again and Darcy set her down so she could sit on the bench beside him. They ate muffins and spoke of silly nothings for a few minutes before Darcy stiffened, a grim look on his face.

"I must tell you something."

"What is it?"

"I will speak with Lady Catherine this afternoon. I must tell her I am courting you and that I will never marry Anne."

"Have you never told her that before?" she asked curiously.

"Once, a few years ago. She suddenly felt hot, and then began rambling about pains in her head and then her heart, and finally feigned a swoon. She remained in her bed for three days, pretending to be gravely ill and on her deathbed."

"Pretending? I had no idea Lady Catherine was so good an actress."

He gave her an eloquent look. "You would be surprised. I know she was perfectly well, but I have not wished to be subjected to more theatrics, so I have kept my peace. I never agree with her, and I have refused when she asks a direct question. That is probably why she has ceased asking them. Anyroad, the discussion should be had and it would be better in person. I will wait until just before dinner to minimize the chance that she may call on you at the parsonage."

"Do you think she would?"

"I do not know, but I would not put it past her. She can be intractable when she wants something, and she has refused to accept bad news before."

Elizabeth frowned in thought. "I must tell Charlotte. Lady Catherine could make life very unpleasant for them."

"Yes, she very well may. I am sorry for that."

"Do not be, Fitzwilliam. It is not your fault your aunt is a termagant."

He almost laughed, then grimaced. "We will be outside the parsonage at nine tomorrow. Will you be ready?"

"Yes, of course! I am anxious to escape Lady Catherine's wrath, though I do worry for Charlotte. Perhaps she will feel a sudden need to visit her mother!" she teased.

"It is not the worst idea. She could ride in the carriage with you and act as your chaperone."

"So that you may ride in the carriage as well?"

"Of course. Would your aunt and uncle be willing to host her?"

"I am sure that they would, though I do not know if Charlotte would wish to go. She has responsibilities here, and there is Mr. Collins to think of."

"Yes, well, it was just a thought."

"Sweet man," she said with a smile as she touched his face. "It was kind of you to consider my friend."

He caught her hand and kissed it, and they continued to talk of busy nothings, interspersed with the kisses and touches expected of the newly in love—or those rapidly falling into it.

BY THE TIME Darcy re-entered Rosings, he was in excellent spirits. He checked with his valet that his things were packed and prepared, spoke with the grooms about his horse and the carriage being ready on the morrow, then sought out his cousin.

"Fitz, would you accompany me to speak to Anne?"

"Anne?" asked Colonel Fitzwilliam incredulously. "Whatever for?"

"I intend to speak to our aunt today, and it is only courteous to speak to Anne first."

"Ah, of course. Let us bell the cat, shall we?"

Darcy rolled his eyes. "Really Fitz. She is not that bad." He led the way out the door and through the maze of Rosings's corridors.

"To you, maybe. She thinks you may be her husband one day, so she has hidden her true nature. She has no such qualms with me."

"Whatever are you talking of? Anne may be sickly, but she is hardly a harridan."

"Ha! Shows what you know!" He gave his cousin a look. "I shall not spoil the surprise for you, Cousin. You may see for yourself." He opened the door to Anne's sitting room and gestured his cousin ahead of him with a grand flourish.

Darcy looked doubtfully at the colonel as he passed him. He settled on a small sofa next to Fitzwilliam. He did not wish for Anne to attempt to sit beside him. Soon, Miss de Bourgh entered the room, followed by her companion, Mrs. Jenkinson.

"It was good of you to send for me, Cousin," she said.

Her voice was almost like a purr and it made the hair on the back of his neck stand up. Colonel Fitzwilliam smirked at him and Darcy ignored it.

"Cousin, I must speak to you about something." He scooted to the edge of the sofa, his elbows on his knees.

"Yes?" she said, her eyes taking on a gleam he could not be comfortable with.

Darcy sat up straighter. "I know your mother has often spoken of the two of us marrying, but I do not think you have ever wished it."

Colonel Fitzwilliam made a squeaking noise next to him and Anne scooted further forward in her chair, nearly falling out of it in the process. "I would not say that exactly, Cousin."

Darcy's eyes widened comically. "You wouldn't?"

Colonel Fitzwilliam elbowed him to continue.

"Well, regardless, you and I have never really spoken of it, and I thought it only right to inform you that I have begun a courtship with Miss Elizabeth Bennet."

Anne sat staring at him, her posture expectant and her eyes unblinking. "Come again?"

"I have asked Miss Bennet's permission to court her and she has given it. I will speak to her father in a week's time."

"Her father?" Her voice was eerily high.

"Yes," Darcy said slowly. "After a suitable period of courtship, I will make my proposals."

Colonel Fitzwilliam elbowed him again and Darcy looked at him in confusion. Fitzwilliam was shaking his head and clamping his lips.

"You have chosen Miss Bennet? Over me? The daughter of an insignificant country squire over the daughter of a baronet?"

Darcy continued to look confused, so Fitzwilliam shook his head and took matters into his own hands. "Anne, Darcy is pursuing Miss Bennet. He will not be proposing to you, which leaves you free to accept other proposals. Is that not good news?"

Darcy looked at him oddly. Fitzwilliam was speaking to Anne as if she were a small child, not a grown woman of five and twenty. Darcy was so preoccupied looking at Colonel Fitzwilliam that he did not realize his danger until Fitzwilliam cried out at the same time Darcy felt something sharp on his forehead.

"Good God, Anne! What are you doing?" cried the colonel.

Darcy looked about in confusion. Had she thrown something at him? He looked to the floor and saw a small porcelain vase in several pieces. Apparently, she had. He touched his head and his fingers came back wet and smeared with blood. He was turning to face her and ask what on earth she was doing when he saw something from the corner of his eye and instinctually ducked. This item was a porcelain shepherdess that grazed his shoulder.

"Look out!" cried Fitzwilliam.

Darcy ducked behind the sofa as his cousin continued throwing whatever she could get her hands on. Figurines, vases, small sculptures, even Mrs. Jenkinson's sampler, still in its hoop, were chucked at his head. The room was utter chaos. Anne was screeching unintelligible words as she threw things at him, Mrs. Jenkinson was trying to calm her to no avail, and Darcy and the colonel were crouched on the floor behind the sofa, arms over their heads.

"What the devil?!" cried Darcy.

"I told you! She is not reasonable!"

"She is not *sane*!"

"That is a definite possibility."

Mrs. Jenkinson was still trying to calm Anne and that lady was still screaming. All her words were not clear, but Darcy distinctly heard her say "give up Rosings" and "little nobody."

Colonel Fitzwilliam looked about carefully. "Come," he said to his cousin. He grabbed Darcy's arm and walked in a crouch toward the door. Darcy wondered if this was how his cousin felt on campaign and quickly followed him.

Anne saw their progress and rushed to the mantle, taking the large vase filled with flowers and throwing it hard at the door. It crashed above their heads with a loud shatter, and they were showered with dirty water and plant detritus. Before she could lob anything more, the colonel opened the door and pushed his cousin out in front of him, closing it just in time to hear something heavy thump against the heavy oak and fall to the floor.

Darcy grimaced. Whatever it was, it sounded heavy and had not broken on impact.

"That would have hurt," he said acerbically.

Colonel Fitzwilliam looked at him as if he were the stupidest man on earth and they quickly made their way down the hall.

"Should we not tell Lady Catherine? Or the housekeeper? We cannot leave Mrs. Jenkinson on her own in there!" cried Darcy.

"Darcy, have you never wondered why Mrs. Jenkinson is so very large in comparison to her charge?"

Darcy was the picture of confusion. "No, why should I? Anne is a small woman. Anyone would look large next to her."

"It might surprise you to know that Anne is not so small, you simply rarely see her standing up. She is nearly as tall as her mother."

"What?"

Colonel Fitzwilliam resisted rolling his eyes by a narrow thread. "She is very thin, and possibly frail, but a large portion of Mrs. Jenkinson's job is as Anne's enforcer."

"Enforcer? What the devil are you talking of? What exactly does she enforce?"

"Perhaps that is a bad choice of words. She is more of a minder than anything else. She monitors Anne, keeps her calm, and keeps her from hurting herself or others."

Darcy ran a hand down his face. "Are you in earnest? You are not having one of your jokes?"

"The blood on your face will tell you how earnest I am, Darcy. I have known of her temperament for years."

Darcy was incredulous. "Years? Why did you never say anything? How did you find out? Why was I not told?"

They had finally made it to the colonel's room, and he called in his man to see to Darcy's injury. "Don't worry, Tiny has plenty of experience with this sort of thing."

Tiny was the colonel's batman, so called because of his enormous size. His name was one of many things about the army Darcy did not understand. The large man came immediately, assessed the injury, and was soon cleaning Darcy up and applying a plaster to his forehead.

"Talk," said Darcy, staring darkly at his cousin. "Now."

Colonel Fitzwilliam had the gall to look perfectly unruffled. "What is there to say? Anne's temperament is uncertain, made worse by her harridan of a mother. Though I have never seen her lose her temper as badly as today."

"How did you come to learn of it?"

"Father told me. He wished me to be on my guard when we visited."

"Dare I ask how he learned of it? And did he not wish me to be on my guard as well?"

Colonel Fitzwilliam ignored his cousin's pique. "It is possible he has always known—he is her uncle. But from what I have heard, when he visited a few years ago and told Lady Catherine that Anne ought to learn how to play the pianoforte, she bit him."

"Bit him!?"

"Yes. I did not believe it myself until Father showed me the teeth marks. He left for London the day after it occurred, and I happened to be in residence in Town."

"Good God. Why was I never told?"

Fitzwilliam shrugged. "Father may have thought you knew. Or perhaps he thought it would not matter to you."

"Not matter?" roared Darcy. "How could it not matter? She just broke every item in that room because she heard something she did not like. How could such a woman ever be mistress of Pemberley?"

"Easily enough. She wouldn't. Anne comes with Rosings—you could easily marry her and bring her companion to Pemberley to manage her, or leave her at Rosings with her mother, at least part of the year. Father assumed you would take a mistress and be married in name only. Plenty of people do it."

"I need an heir!" Darcy cried, his disbelief mounting by the second. "A legitimate one!"

"Yes, I know you do, which is why I never would have let you actually marry her."

Darcy looked at him shrewdly. "You knew she would do this. You did it on purpose so I would see what she is."

Fitzwilliam shrugged. "Not entirely. But you did refuse to listen to me when I told you she was unstable."

"You never said she would do that!" he cried, pointing angrily toward the room the mayhem had occurred in.

"I did not *know* she would do that! I thought she would scream and rail at you for a while. Besides, would you have believed me if I had said it was possible?"

Darcy was about to retort when he paused and thought of what the colonel had said. "I do not know. But I will certainly remember this for the future."

"Cousin, I doubt anyone will forget what happened today."

"CHARLOTTE, MAY I SPEAK WITH YOU?" Elizabeth asked as she approached her friend in the parlor.

Charlotte was darning socks and smiled briefly at her friend. "Of course."

Elizabeth settled onto the small sofa across from her friend's chair. Charlotte looked very domestic, sitting in front of the window with her darning, a simple morning gown of pale blue bringing out similar flecks in her soft grey eyes.

"I have always envied your eyes, you know," she said absently.

"What?" Charlotte asked, disbelief in her voice. "Whatever are you talking of?"

"You know how my mother has always spoken. She went on and on about Jane's blue eyes—as blue as the sky, as blue as a cornflower." She sighed. "Kitty and Lydia also have blue eyes, and even Mary's are a soft green."

Charlotte tilted her head in understanding. "And yours are brown."

"Like shoe leather, or a dog's fur, or burned gravy," quipped Elizabeth, only partially teasing.

"Like your grandmother's," said Charlotte stringently. "Old Mrs. Bennet was a wonderful lady. She was always very kind to me. She used to buy me sweets at the shop in Meryton." She went back to her mending and added, "Besides, when has your mother's opinion ever set you on your head like this?"

Elizabeth sighed again. "I know you are right—I'm afraid I am not myself of late."

"I wonder what could be responsible for that?"

Elizabeth ignored her friend's teasing. "You know, it is funny, but I have not thought of any of this in ages. But when I saw you there, looking so pretty and contented, I couldn't help but remember."

Charlotte flushed at her friend's compliment. "Well, you should forget it as quickly. You are one of the prettiest girls in Hertfordshire, second only to Jane in Meryton, as you well know."

"But we are in Kent," she said, her usual teasing tone returned.

Charlotte shook her head and tsked at her friend. "What have you truly come to talk to me about?"

"You know me too well, my friend. Mr. Darcy told me that he is going to speak to Lady Catherine today. I am afraid she may make things rather uncomfortable for you here."

Charlotte looked thoughtful. "Yes, I fear you may be correct."

"Would you wish to accompany us to Town? There will be plenty of room in Mr. Darcy's carriage, and you may be our chaperone instead of the maid. You may stay on with me at the Gardiners' if you wish or continue on to Meryton with Maria. I'm certain Mr. Darcy would send you in the carriage if I asked him."

"Oh, he would, would he?"

Elizabeth flushed. "He is very generous."

Charlotte pinched her lips to hold in her laugh. Oh, how Elizabeth's tune had changed! "Perhaps I should. It is pleasant weather for traveling, and the more I think on it, the more I think Lady Catherine will be perfectly horrid when she hears of your engagement."

"We are not engaged, Charlotte," said Elizabeth gravely.

Charlotte waved off her concern. "It is only a formality at this point."

Elizabeth sighed, knowing her friend could not be corrected, but also knowing that Charlotte would not bandy such statements about in public, making them harmless. "So shall you accompany us to London tomorrow?"

"I believe I shall. I must prepare."

She immediately put away her darning and Elizabeth penned a note to her aunt and uncle, informing them of the change in plans. She must find a way to get it to Rosings so that Darcy could send it express for her. She was certain Mr. Collins would not go out of his way to assist her.

"Charlotte, could I find an express rider in the village?"

"Yourself?"

"Would it look too odd?"

Charlotte tilted her head thoughtfully. "Perhaps. I shall go into the village with you. That should not be so unusual."

In less than an hour, the two of them had Charlotte's trunk packed and had given instructions to the cook and maid. Charlotte penned a note to her parents, and then they were off to the village. An express rider was quickly secured at the inn and sent off to the Gardiners, and Charlotte's letter was posted to Meryton. They were on their way back from the village when Colonel Fitzwilliam came into sight on the lane.

"Good day, ladies. How do you do?"

"Very well, Colonel, thank you."

"May I escort you back to the parsonage? If that is indeed your destination?"

"I should stop and call on Mrs. Clemson before I return, but you could escort Miss Bennet," said Charlotte. She turned off at Mrs. Clemson's house and Elizabeth fell into step with the colonel.

"Have you spoken to your cousin today, Colonel Fitzwilliam?" asked Elizabeth, eager to know if Darcy had spoken to Lady Catherine yet.

"Both of them, yes." He gave her a significant look. "Darcy and I spoke to Anne not an hour past, and he is speaking with my aunt at the moment."

"Is he?" She thought her voice sounded squeaky and nervous, but perhaps it was only her perception.

"Yes, I imagine it will be a short conversation, though not a forgettable one."

She nodded, her eyes on her feet and thus missing his teasing expression.

"If I may be so bold, Miss Bennet, I believe my cousin has made a very good choice."

Her eyes snapped up to his. "You do?"

"Of course. I said I would stand your brother if necessary, and I meant it. You will see no derision from the family while I am about."

She pressed his arm. "Thank you, Colonel. That means a great deal to me."

He nodded to her and they walked in silence for a few minutes before Elizabeth broke it, saying, "I do not know when you would ever need it, but I will stand your sister, should the need arise."

A light sprung into his eyes and she wondered at it.

"I may take you up on that, Miss Bennet."

She wondered what he meant, for she could tell from his expression he had something in mind. Thinking she would not get to the bottom of it this day, she said, "And when you do, you must call me Lizzy, as my sisters do."

He smiled brightly. "I look forward to that day, Miss Bennet. And when it comes, you may call me Fitz, as my cousin does, or Richard, like my sister and brothers."

"I will." She promised. "Do you have many brothers? I know you mentioned an elder sister, but that is all I know."

"Oh, yes, we Fitzwilliams are quite prolific," he said with a grin, all traces of seriousness gone. "I am the fourth of five children."

"Oh! I had not realized we had that in common."

"Yes, one of many reasons we get on, I'm sure."

"Shall I hear about these many children or will you only taunt me with their existence and tell me nothing else about them?"

"Very well," he said with a playful huff. "If you insist. My eldest brother, Timothy, is the viscount and my father's heir and namesake. He is married to Lady Cassandra Etchley, as was, and they have a young daughter named Wilhelmina. Terrible name for a child, but they did not listen to me."

"Oh, dear!"

"Lady Cassandra is expecting my next niece or nephew this summer."

"That's exciting."

"Yes, I suppose. The birth of an earl often is."

She rolled her eyes.

"Second is my brother Harrison, named for my mother's family. We call him Harry. He is a barrister in London and making a name for himself. He is not married, but Mother is on him to get to it now that he is successful and nearing five and thirty."

"Oh! Yes, it is high time he settled down," she said primly. "He must see to it quickly before he is considered a spinster irrevocably."

"Quite so, Miss Bennet," he answered gravely. "Next is my sister Judith. She has been married to Lord Lydham more than a decade, though plain Roger Montgomery suits him better."

"Is he a dull man then?"

"He is a bit of a stick in the mud, but I must admit that I would rather have my sister married to a bore than a man about town."

"Hear, hear."

"Forgive me, Miss Bennet, I am overly familiar."

"Not at all, colonel. Please continue. I believe you have one more brother to go and we have just enough time before reaching the parsonage for you to tell me of him."

"Ah, yes. Well, there was one other sister after me. Her name was Olivia. She died when she was eleven years old and I twelve. Influenza."

She pressed his arm again, now feeling badly about teasing him. "I am sorry. Were you close?"

"Yes, we were, odd though it may be. My two elder brothers played with each other, and then were sent off to school, and sandwiched between my sisters as I was, I became caught up in their games. I attended many tea parties as a lad," he said with a nostalgic smile.

"Is this where your elder sister bossed you about?"

"Oh yes, she was terrible about it. She insisted Olivia and I do everything just as she directed. We often rebelled, which only made her angrier. She was sent off to finishing school shortly before Olivia died. It was sweet, having that time, just the two of us."

His voice was soft with remembrance and she looped her hand through his arm, offering silent support. "She sounds lovely."

"Yes, she was. You remind me of her, in some ways. She had expressive brown eyes, too, and was often laughing. She was always cheerful. Of us all, she was the last I would have imagined would have succumbed to—" he trailed off, his voice strained. "Well, anyhow, it is only Judith now."

She squeezed his arm again and he placed his hand over hers.

"My younger brother is seven years my junior. I have always thought my parents imagined Olivia was the last child. But then came Anthony. He is a curate in Shropshire at the moment. The current incumbent of the living is elderly, and Anthony is preparing to take over for him in the next year or so. He has the temperament for the church—patient, kind-natured, forgiving."

"You are all of those things, too, are you not?"

"I am flattered you think so, Miss Bennet, but I have mellowed with age. When I was four and twenty, I was not nearly so patient as my brother is. And I have always craved more adventure than Anthony. I would not have suited a quiet life in the country."

"And so your parents have one son in the law, one in the army, and one in the church, and an heir to train. How perfectly balanced."

"Yes, my father is quite pleased," said the colonel jocularly.

"Well, I for one cannot wait to meet them. I enjoy character studies and your family sounds fascinating."

"Oh, they will give you plenty to study, that is certain. Whether you will enjoy the experience is less so."

They laughed together and were soon at the gate to the parsonage. She turned to face the colonel.

"Thank you for the escort, sir. I shall see you in the morning."

He bowed more deeply than she would have expected. "Good day, Miss Bennet. Until tomorrow."

WHILE COLONEL FITZWILLIAM was walking with Elizabeth, Darcy was doing something much less agreeable—speaking with his aunt. Lady Catherine received him in the main drawing room. He was certain she had heard something of his conversation with Anne, though he could not know if she knew the contents of said conversation, and she had asked him to meet her here with the goal of intimidating him.

She would have to do better than the grandest room at Rosings if intimidation was her aim.

Kent was a perfectly agreeable county and Rosings a lovely estate, but the décor was garish, ostentatious, and not at all to his personal tastes. If she had wanted to make him feel her supposed superiority and authority, she would have done better to take him to the formal gardens. For all their over-pruning, they were excellent. But then they might remind him of the day he had walked with Elizabeth there, and that would distract him utterly from what he wished to tell his aunt.

"Darcy!"

"Yes, Aunt?"

"I have been calling you for five minutes. What are you thinking of? Standing in the middle of the room like a statue?"

He was certain it had been nowhere near five minutes, but time was not something Lady Catherine felt she needed to observe accurately.

"Forgive me, Lady Catherine." He took the seat she indicated across from herself and looked at her squarely. "Aunt, I have news."

"Oh?"

"I have asked Miss Elizabeth Bennet's permission to court her, and she has granted it."

He had originally intended to say more, but after his meeting with

Anne, he thought it best to stick to the facts and make as hasty a retreat as possible.

"You did what?"

"I have requested Miss Bennet's permission to court her."

"I heard you, I simply did not believe it. You cannot be in earnest! Jokes such as these are in terribly bad taste, Darcy. What if you were to inadvertently start a rumor? Miss Bennet may be an insignificant country girl, but she does not deserve to have her name mired in gossip for your amusement."

Darcy took a deep breath. "I am not dragging Miss Bennet's name into any ill-thought-out joke, Aunt. I have honorable intentions. I am courting Miss Elizabeth, with her permission, and intend to speak to her father as soon as I may."

Lady Catherine's face began to pale. She stared at Darcy, the color gradually leaching from her skin as she sat stone still and utterly silent.

"I wished to tell you in person out of respect. I am sorry if this upsets you in any way." She still had not spoken or moved at all, so Darcy said his last as quickly and smoothly as possible. "I will not be marrying Anne, now or ever. I wish you both good health in the future."

He rose, bowed, and made his way out of the room before she could respond. He admitted to himself he was concerned for her reaction. He had no desire to be hit with another vase, and if she was in shock, he would allow her to come to grips with his decision in private.

He made his way to the library looking for Fitzwilliam and was informed he had gone for a walk. Deciding that his cousin had the right of it, he made his way outside and soon enough his steps led him towards the parsonage. It was only polite to make a farewell call, after all. And if he happened to see Elizabeth there, all the better.

Darcy raised his hand to knock on the parsonage door and was surprised when Elizabeth opened it herself.

"Fitzwilliam, thank God you're here." She pulled the door closed behind her and pulled him off to the side of the house.

He placed his hand on her elbow and led her deeper into the garden. "What is the matter?"

She turned to face him and gasped. "Fitzwilliam! What happened to your head?"

He reached up to touch the cut along his hairline. "I'm afraid it met with a vase."

"Your head met with a vase?"

He gave her a steady look. "I promise I will tell you all soon enough, but I would like to know what is distressing you now."

She sighed and said, "Very well. Charlotte decided to travel to Town with us tomorrow, and Mr. Collins has only now returned home and been informed of it."

"And he has not taken the news well?"

She wrung her hands. "They are having a dreadful row!"

Mr. Collins's voice was heard through one of the open windows, but only the words "disgrace" and "shameful" were clear enough to comprehend.

"Is his anger about her leaving altogether, or that she is going without him?"

"What is he not angry about?" she said with exasperation. "He is angry she is going at such short notice, angry she wishes to go without him, angry she did not ask his permission first—as if she were a child!" She suddenly looked back to him with narrowed eyes. "You would never do such a thing, would you?" When he looked at her in bewilderment she added, "Force me to ask permission before going anywhere, as if I were a little girl?"

"Of course not!" he cried. He could not stop the smile from spreading across his face at the notion that she was imagining their marriage. He grasped her hand tightly in his. "Your spirit is something I love dearly, and I would not quash it for the world." He raised her hand to his lips. "I would like to be told if you are leaving the county, and I would wish you to be properly escorted, but no, Elizabeth, you would not need my permission for anything. I wish to be your husband, not your master."

She smiled brilliantly at him and raised up onto her toes to bestow a quick kiss on his lips. He looked rather dazed in response and she said, "What are we to do? I feel awful for causing trouble for Charlotte! She has been so kind to me, and this is how I repay her."

"It is not your fault—do not blame yourself. Mr. Collins would have had to learn sooner or later that his wife is not chattel."

Elizabeth looked down, chewing the inside of her lip. "That is not all they are quarreling over."

"Oh?"

She looked up at him, eyes filled with worry and a tiny bit of mischief. She took a deep breath and said, "Charlotte finally told him why you are escorting us to Town."

"I see." He straightened and his expression became harder.

"He insists that you are engaged to Miss de Bourgh, and that we must be mistaken, or that you have been allured by my wiles."

He looked back down at her at that and one side of his mouth quirked up. "Well, that part is true. You have bewitched me utterly. I don't know how you've done it. Perhaps it is witchcraft."

She smacked his arm playfully. "Oh do be serious, Fitzwilliam!"

Darcy laughed. "Very well. I will speak with Mr. Collins."

"Will you? I would greatly appreciate it."

He kissed her hand again. "Of course, my love. It is not right to allow Mrs. Collins to bear the consequences of my actions."

"Well, that is painting it a bit dark, but I agree she should not be left on her own to face Mr. Collins's displeasure when it is we who have so disappointed him."

"Quite." He led her back to the front door and into the parsonage.

Mr. Collins's voice was quieter now, but he and Charlotte were still very clearly arguing in the front parlor. The maid hovered at the back of the hallway with a tea tray, looking terrified.

"Allow me," said Darcy as he took the tray from the girl.

She scampered off to the kitchen and Elizabeth rewarded him

with a proud smile. Then she took a deep breath, rapped on the parlor door, and pushed it open.

"We've brought tea," she said brightly.

Darcy followed her in and set the tray on the table before the sofa.

"Mr. Darcy!" spluttered Mr. Collins, thoroughly shocked.

"Thank you, Mr. Darcy," said Charlotte calmly. "Do be seated."

She gestured to the sofa and Darcy sat next to Elizabeth, quickly taking her hand in his and settling it on his knee. She looked at him with surprise, but he merely gave her a look that let her know he knew what he was doing and turned to face their hosts.

"Mr. Collins, I understand there seems to be some sort of trouble."

Mr. Collins was staring at Darcy with his mouth agape, his eyes moving from Darcy's face to the hand that held Elizabeth's and back again.

After another minute of silence, Charlotte said, "Mr. Collins was not pleased to hear of my journey to Hertfordshire, Mr. Darcy."

"I assure you, Mr. Collins, the carriage is comfortable and well-sprung, and I will look after Mrs. Collins as if she were my own sister. No harm shall befall her."

Mr. Collins spluttered again, saying half-words and making less sense than usual. Darcy had trapped him neatly. He could not say he was not concerned for his wife's comfort or safety without seeming an uncaring husband.

Finally, Collins said, "I have no doubt of that, Mr. Darcy. A gentleman such as yourself could not fail to do so, but Mrs. Collins has duties here to the parishioners and to her husband. A journey at this time is ill-advised."

"Cannot a lady wish to visit her mother?" asked Mr. Darcy smoothly. "And escorting her sister and Miss Bennet to Town is a great kindness on her part."

Collins looked more flustered and said, "A maid can accompany my sister and cousin. My wife is not required. Lady Catherine may need her."

Charlotte looked to the ceiling, the closest she would come to rolling her eyes in public.

"Surely you cannot put Lady Catherine's comfort above that of your own wife!" Darcy scoffed. He looked incredulous at the very notion and Elizabeth bit her lip to keep from laughing.

"I, well, what can you mean?" Mr. Collins spluttered even more. He finally stopped speaking, took a deep breath, drew himself up to his full height and said, "Mr. Darcy, I understand my cousin may have tempted you into a declaration you now regret, but you cannot allow her wiles to ruin the union that has long been planned between you and your cousin."

Darcy sat up taller and the room became eerily still.

"Mr. Collins, I am my own man and as such, I will decide whom I will marry, not my aunt, and certainly not her parson. I have no understanding with my cousin, nor will I ever have. She is well aware of this, as is her ladyship for I told them both myself. Kindly disabuse yourself of the notion that a wedding will be forthcoming at Rosings."

Collins paled and gulped loudly enough for everyone in the room to hear it.

Elizabeth felt so proud in that moment, she would have kissed Darcy had they not been in public. She settled for squeezing his hand and gifting him a warm smile when he looked her way. He returned it as Mr. Collins continued to stare at them, utterly dumbfounded. Elizabeth thought to gloat to Mr. Collins that he had been wrong—she would receive another marriage proposal, and a significantly better one than what he had delivered in her mother's drawing room, but she refrained.

Soon Charlotte took pity on her husband and guided him into a chair.

Mr. Collins continued to gape at them another few minutes before he said, "I do not understand."

Charlotte hiccupped rather loudly and Elizabeth refused to meet her eye, knowing she would burst into laughter if she did so.

"It is simple, Mr. Collins," said Darcy patiently. "Lady Catherine wished me to marry her daughter, but I did *not* wish it. There has never been any formal arrangement of any kind and no contracts were ever signed and therefore have not been broken. I fell in love with Miss Elizabeth in Hertfordshire last autumn, and when I met her here this spring, I asked to court her. She very kindly allowed me the privilege, and I will speak to Mr. Bennet when I escort her to Longbourn."

Mr. Collins's eyes were bulging comically now. He clearly had no idea how to behave in this situation, and Elizabeth was squeezing Mr. Darcy's hand fiercely to keep her merriment in check.

Finally, Charlotte said, "We are very happy for you, Mr. Darcy. Are we not, Mr. Collins?"

"Hm? Oh, yes. Quite."

It was not much in the way of congratulations, but it was a step in the right direction.

"It is very kind of you to offer to see me to Meryton, Mr. Darcy."

"I am happy to do it, Mrs. Collins. I could do no less for such a close friend of Elizabeth's."

Mr. Darcy was very careful with propriety, so Elizabeth knew he had used her name so familiarly on purpose. Did Mr. Collins understand? Mr. Darcy would make a powerful ally and a formidable foe. It would behoove him to choose appropriately. Charlotte seemed to grasp this and was quick to make sure Mr. Darcy knew she approved of his choice.

"I shall have Mrs. Hopkins prepare a basket for the carriage in the morning. Eliza has said you are fond of her muffins."

Darcy nodded. "That I am. Thank you, Mrs. Collins. It is thoughtful of you."

And so the conversation would have ended, on a harmonious if not pleasant note, had not Lady Catherine chosen that moment to burst into the parsonage.

13

A BETTER ENDING TO A STRANGE DAY

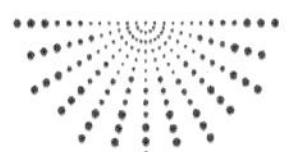

"Strumpet!"

"I beg your pardon!" retorted Elizabeth at the same time Darcy stood and said, "Aunt, you forget yourself."

"That woman," said lady Catherine, her voice low and threatening, "has come into my home and stolen that which does not belong to her."

Charlotte took this opportunity to pull Mr. Collins out of the room and into the hall before he could jump into the fray and defend his patroness. He fell onto the bench there and looked at his wife like a lost puppy. She could do aught but sit beside him and hold his hand, listening shamefully to what was being said in the parlor.

Darcy pulled his shoulders back and lifted his chin. "I am not your property, Lady Catherine. I cannot be stolen."

She sniffed. "You were set to marry Anne until *she* came along!" She pointed angrily at Elizabeth.

"I never wished to marry Anne, as you well know. I told you so years ago, but you have deluded yourself in the hopes of pawning off your undesirable daughter on someone too closely related to despise you for it."

Lady Catherine gasped. "How dare you!"

"How dare I? How dare *you?*" Darcy cried, his voice raised. "You would have saddled your own nephew with that harpy. Did you have no care for my happiness and comfort? For the continuation of the Darcy line or the succession of Pemberley? Apparently not. You have proven yourself to be without honor, decency, or family loyalty. And now you barge into a house that is not your own and berate Miss Bennet, a lady who has done nothing to you and who is of great importance to me, as well as a guest of Mrs. Collins. It seems you have no regard for anyone other than yourself!"

Elizabeth had never seen Mr. Darcy so angry. She pressed her hand into his back, reminding him she was there and offering her support as she could.

"How dare you speak to me like this?" said Lady Catherine, her voice low and shaking. "I am the daughter of the Earl of Blackburn and a member of one of the oldest families in England. You cannot say such things to me!" She banged her walking stick on the floor to emphasize her point.

"I am a Fitzwilliam as well, Aunt, if you have forgotten. My mother was the eldest daughter of the Earl of Blackburn. The current earl is my uncle, the future earl my cousin. The Darcy family is one of the oldest in England, and I am the largest landowner in Derbyshire. *You* may not speak to *me* like this."

His voice was cold and calm, and Elizabeth felt a shiver run down her spine at the venom in his words.

Lady Catherine jerked her head back as if she had been struck. "I see you are lost to every proper feeling. I take no leave of you. I do *not* wish you well." She turned with a swish of her skirts and marched out of the room.

Darcy and Elizabeth were silent for a moment, her hand still rubbing small circles on his back and his eyes staring blankly ahead. After a few more minutes of silence, Elizabeth said, "Are you well, Fitzwilliam?"

Without saying a word, he took her hand and pulled her across the parlor, through the empty hall, and out the front door. He led her around the house to the back of the garden where the foliage was thick and the road too far to see. He settled on a bench and immediately pulled Elizabeth down onto his lap. She gave a small squeak, then settled her arms around him and pressed his head to her shoulder, holding him as tightly as she could.

He returned her embrace, wrapping his arms so tightly about her his hands were resting on his elbows. She felt every shuddering breath as it ran through his body and stroked his hair soothingly, cooing sweet nothings to him.

"My very dear," she whispered into his hair. She kissed his head and stroked his hair and rubbed his back. She called him her dear and her darling and her heart. He continued to hold her so tightly she could not move, but she relished the intimacy, the chance to be the one to bring him comfort.

They stayed that way for some time, until Darcy's hold finally began to loosen, just a little. She leaned back so she could see his face, his arms still about her.

"How are you, my dear?" she asked gently.

"I am remarkably well, considering the circumstances."

She smiled and stroked his cheek.

"I do not enjoy quarrelling with my family, but I do very much enjoy being comforted by you afterwards."

"I shall be sure to be on hand any time you squabble with your cousins."

She smiled so freely at him, seated so comfortably on his lap, that his heart began to beat faster. Did she know this was where she belonged forever? It was as clear to him as the moon in the sky— luminescent and undeniable.

"Do you have any idea how much I love you, Elizabeth?"

Her smile became even softer and she gazed at him sweetly. "I am beginning to get an inkling, my darling."

"I never thought I would like being called darling, but I like it when you say it."

"Then I shall say it as often as you like, my darling. Or would you prefer sweetling?"

He made a face. "That is what my father always called Georgiana."

"Honeysuckle?"

He shook his head.

"My prince?"

He made a thoughtful face, then shook his head again.

"Hmm." She tapped her chin in an exaggerated thinking gesture. "My heart?"

His expression softened. "I like that one better."

She smiled again and rested her forehead against his. "Then I am glad we have an agreement."

"Do I, Elizabeth?"

"Do you what, my dear?"

"Do I have your heart?"

She pulled her head back from his and met his eyes. "It is less my own every day."

His lips were on hers in a flash and she was pulled impossibly closer, her heart pounding against his as he ravished her mouth, then made use of their convenient position to place kisses along the column of her neck.

"Oh, Fitzwilliam," she whispered lowly.

Her voice was like fire in his veins and he redoubled his efforts, running his hands along her back as he kissed and licked and nibbled at her skin. "Elizabeth, my love." He murmured as he kissed her. "I love you so much I cannot contain it."

Their eyes met for a moment and she said, "Then do not," and held his head in her hands as she kissed him, her tongue sliding along his lips and making him groan with pleasure.

Neither knew how long they stayed in the garden, but when Elizabeth next looked up, the sky was darkening.

"Fitzwilliam, look. It is nearly dark."

He pulled away from her long enough to take in his surroundings. He was unsurprised so much time had passed—or uncaring. He did not bother to analyze his feelings.

He could only care about Elizabeth, seated delightfully on his lap, her weight a pleasant pressure on his legs, her arms about his shoulders, her cheeks flushed and lips red from kissing.

"I am going to marry you one day," he said, looking directly into her eyes.

Her eyes grew round in response, and he placed a quick kiss on the tip of her nose before rising and escorting her back into the parsonage.

14

SATURDAY'S JOURNEY TO LONDON

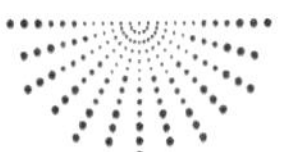

Mr. Collins wished to join them on the journey to Hertfordshire, but he did not have a horse to ride alongside and should it rain, there would not be room in the carriage. Charlotte convinced him to give his sermon as planned on Sunday, then when his curate was prepared, he could join them in a few days.

Elizabeth could spare a little pity for him. He had never been out of Lady Catherine's good graces before, and she knew enough of that great lady to know she would not make it easy on her parson. But Elizabeth could not be anything but relieved that he would not ride in the carriage with them.

They rose early on Saturday and dressed warmly in traveling clothes, then closed their trunks before sitting down for breakfast. Elizabeth bypassed the dining room and went to the kitchen to personally thank Mrs. Hopkins for the basket she had prepared for them.

"You're that welcome, Miss Bennet. And here's that receipt, like I promised."

Elizabeth took it with a smile and tucked it into her pocket. "Mr. Darcy will be pleased to have it. He is very fond of your muffins."

123

Mrs. Hopkins blushed. "I'm pleased to hear that. You tell Mr. Darcy he is welcome to them any time he is in Hunsford."

"I will." Elizabeth pressed her hand and smiled again, then skipped out of the kitchen, in too good a mood to be sedate.

Soon Darcy's coach arrived, and they were off to London. The ladies rode in the carriage while Darcy and Colonel Fitzwilliam rode alongside.

"Do quit mooning over Mr. Darcy, Eliza. You will put me off my breakfast."

Elizabeth turned sharply from the window—where she had indeed been watching Mr. Darcy—and faced her friend. "I am not mooning!"

Charlotte gave her a doubtful look and reached into the basket for a muffin. Maria giggled in the seat beside her sister and Elizabeth glared at her.

"Wait until your turn comes, Maria," she teased.

Maria's eyes widened and she leaned back into the squabs. "I do not know that I wish for a suitor."

"That is wise, since you do not have one," said Charlotte before biting into a muffin.

Elizabeth rolled her eyes. "Ignore her, Maria. You are only fifteen. It is good you do not wish for a suitor at this time. Enjoy your girl-hood while you may."

Charlotte sighed but nodded. "Yes, there is no rush. But do not leave it too long. It would be best to marry sometime between eighteen and two and twenty. Old enough to know your mind but young enough to retain your bloom."

Elizabeth laughed lightly. "Listen to your sister, Maria. She is a font of wisdom."

Charlotte mock scowled at Elizabeth before passing her a muffin. "I am glad to know you have finally learned to appreciate my judgment," she said primly.

Elizabeth and Maria laughed while Charlotte sat a little straighter and looked out the window.

DARCY RODE alongside the carriage with a light heart. He thought he heard Elizabeth's laughter coming from within, but it must be his imagination. He would never hear anything over the wheels and the horses.

"Wipe that look off your face."

Darcy started. "What look?"

"You are gazing at that carriage like a starving man looks at meat. You cannot even see her, man!"

"I am doing no such thing!" Darcy cried, affronted.

Fitzwilliam scoffed. "Whatever you say, Cousin."

Darcy pulled ahead of his cousin with a glare, though he secretly wondered if he had turned into a moon-eyed calf without realizing it. But he could not truly care. He was entirely too pleased with his life at the moment to be concerned with his cousin's opinions.

Less than an hour later, Colonel Fitzwilliam called out to his cousin and Darcy looked back at him just as he felt a large drop of water land on his face.

"It is beginning to rain!" called the colonel.

They signaled the driver to stop and climbed aboard the carriage. It all happened so quickly that the ladies looked at them in astonishment before shifting over on the bench to make more room. Elizabeth had taken the back-facing seat with Maria and Charlotte sharing the forward-facing bench. Now Colonel Fitzwilliam happily plopped down between the sisters, making Maria's eyes grow wide and Charlotte chuckle. He winked at Elizabeth as Darcy stepped in behind him and took the open seat next to Elizabeth. She blushed and smiled happily, only moving over a little to make space for him.

Before anyone could object or suggest a change in the seating arrangement, Colonel Fitzwilliam began speaking. He could be very long-winded when the mood struck him, and he regaled them with tales of marches across the peninsula and incompetent soldiers. Maria was spellbound, and he ate up her attention like a greedy pug. Charlotte gave Elizabeth a look and they shared a secret smile as they opened the basket Mrs. Hopkins had packed and passed out food to the gentlemen.

Colonel Fitzwilliam only stopped speaking long enough to take a bite of a muffin, followed by, "I say, that is an uncommonly good muffin!"

"I have the receipt if you would like a copy," said Elizabeth.

"Thank you, Miss Bennet, I may take you up on that."

And just like that, he was back in his story, Maria's eyes still wide and attentive.

They stopped at an inn to wait out the rain for an hour before climbing back aboard. The change in weather had brought a chill to the air and Darcy fetched blankets from beneath the benches for the ladies.

Colonel Fitzwilliam declared he would ride, for he preferred the open air to a closed carriage as long as he was dry. Darcy opted to ride inside. Charlotte and Maria sat on the forward-facing bench, sharing a large blanket. Maria looked sleepy and settled herself into the corner to rest as Darcy took the seat beside Elizabeth. She smiled and held open her blanket, ignoring the look Charlotte sent her.

What could they possibly get up to with their friends sitting a mere three feet away?

Darcy happily settled next to Elizabeth and within three miles, both Charlotte and Maria had drifted off to sleep. Darcy scooted a little closer to Elizabeth and reached for her hand beneath the blanket. She grasped his firmly and looked back at him with a blush.

"Are you not sleepy?" she asked in a whisper.

"Not at all. You may rest your head on my shoulder if you are tired."

She smiled and moved around until she was tucked under his arm, her head on his chest. She had intended to stay awake, but the warmth of her position combined with the motion of the carriage soon lulled her to sleep. Darcy held her tighter, making sure she did not fall forward on the seat or sit in such a way that her neck would be sore.

Unbeknownst to him, Charlotte awoke and watched him for some time. She saw how he periodically kissed Elizabeth's head, or how he stroked the hair that hung over her shoulder. He would take that one long, lazy curl and wrap it about his palm, twisting it up toward her scalp, before releasing it to fall down her back and repeating it all over again.

She saw the look in his eyes as he watched her friend sleep and the protective way that he held her. Charlotte was not romantic, but if anyone could have changed her mind, it would have been Mr. Darcy.

SOON, the carriage pulled into Gracechurch Street and Mrs. Gardiner and Jane stepped outside to meet them. Introductions were made amidst long embraces and cheerful greetings. Mrs. Gardiner invited the gentlemen inside for tea, but they declined.

Darcy would return Monday morning to escort Charlotte and Maria to Longbourn. He would also speak to Mr. Bennet when he arrived. Elizabeth had promised to have a letter ready for her father for him to deliver. He did not want to admit it, but he was nervous. He had never asked a man permission to court his daughter before. The very nature of the task meant a man would usually only do such a thing once in his life; there would be no improving with practice.

Darcy shook off his anxiety and listened to his cousin ribbing him until they reached Mayfair, then he took to his study with a brandy, claiming a need to manage his correspondence. In truth, he stared at the empty fireplace and thought of Elizabeth.

"LIZZY! YOU HAVE BEEN VERY SLY!" cried Jane. "Why did you not tell me Mr. Darcy was your beau?"

"She was in denial of it for some time herself," Charlotte quipped. Elizabeth threw her a glare. Charlotte ignored it and happily popped a piece of fruit into her mouth.

Mrs. Gardiner had set out a light luncheon for them and the ladies sat around a small table on the stone terrace behind the house. The garden was not large, but Mrs. Gardiner had a green thumb and she and her gardener had worked tirelessly to make it a beautiful oasis.

Maria was playing a game of hide and seek with the Gardiner children at the back of the garden, their laughter and shrieks of joy a pleasant backdrop to the ladies' conversation.

"Has he spoken to you of his intentions?" asked Mrs. Gardiner.

Elizabeth flushed but knew she could not avoid answering. "Yes. He has asked to court me."

Jane gasped and Mrs. Gardiner sat forward in her chair. "Has he truly? Oh, Lizzy!"

"You accepted his offer?" Jane asked, her brow crinkled in worry.

Elizabeth took her hand in hers. "Yes, I have. But not without sufficient questioning." She smiled, then seeing her sister was not assuaged, added, "There is much we did not know about Mr. Darcy, and much we were misinformed of."

She and Charlotte told them the story of Mr. Wickham and his great perfidy, and how Colonel Fitzwilliam opened Elizabeth's eyes to her gullibility.

"I have never felt so stupid in my life," lamented Elizabeth.

Jane placed a hand on her sister's knee. "Do not take it all upon yourself. All of Meryton believed him."

Elizabeth rolled her eyes. "That should have been a reason to doubt him, not trust him. Who shares such things with an entire town? With strangers!"

"I believe you have learned a valuable lesson, girls. A handsome face does not equate to a handsome nature," said Mrs. Gardiner sagely.

"That is true. Eliza and I have spoken of this at length lately." Charlotte smiled at her friend over her cup and Elizabeth resisted the urge to stick her tongue out at her.

"I will admit to being relieved to hear you are no longer enamored of Mr. Wickham, for I have received news of him," said Mrs. Gardiner.

"Oh? Why have you not said?" asked Jane. She had not thought Mr. Wickham could be so very bad and was feeling more than a little unsettled by the information she had heard.

"I have an old friend in Lambton, Mrs. Simpkins. After our last visit to Longbourn, I sent her a letter asking about Mr. Wickham's claims. I confess I was shocked by her information. Apparently, he has left debts all over Derbyshire and Mr. Darcy has discharged them. He is also considered something of a scoundrel. She personally knows of two girls who have been left increasing by him, with no support whatsoever."

Jane gasped and brought her hand to her mouth. "No!"

"Those poor girls," said Charlotte, shaking her head. "What became of them?"

"What usually becomes of them," said Elizabeth darkly.

"Actually, I was quite surprised on that count, for I assumed the same thing. Mrs. Simpkins said that Mr. Darcy provided the first girl —one of his tenants' daughters—with a dowry and another tenant's son married her. The young lad had been in love with her for years it seems, and she had been sweet on him until Mr. Wickham began whispering in her ear."

"That makes it all so much worse," said Elizabeth. "Mr. Wickham deliberately ruined her happiness for momentary pleasure." She shook her head, again chastising herself for how stupidly she had behaved toward that scoundrel.

"And the other girl?" asked Jane, afraid of the answer.

"The other girl lost her babe in childbirth. She then trained with Pemberley's cook and now has a position in the kitchen at a neighboring estate."

Elizabeth sank back into her chair. Mr. Darcy was so good! So very kind and gentlemanly and generous. How could she ever have thought him cold and bad tempered? Cold men did not put themselves out to help the victims of their former friends.

"That paints Mr. Darcy in a very generous light," said Charlotte.

"It certainly does. So I am pleased you accepted his offer of courtship, Lizzy. Such a man would make a wonderful husband."

Elizabeth smiled nervously. He would be a wonderful husband, she knew that. But there was still some place inside her, some unexplainable, rebellious place that chafed at the idea of being a wife. Whether it was being a wife in general or Mr. Darcy's in particular that unsettled her, she could not say. She had fought changing her opinion of him for so long, she wondered if she was still fighting her pride about changing her mind. Accepting Mr. Darcy meant admitting she had been horribly, blindly wrong about everything. Mr. Wickham, Darcy's nature, her own dislike of him. *Well*, she thought, *I did truly dislike him. But I also did not know him, so how true could the dislike be?*

She could go on in such a way interminably, so she put a stop to her wayward thoughts and focused on the conversation around her.

MONDAYS ARE FOR MEETINGS

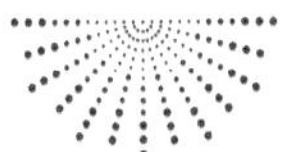

Mr. Darcy arrived early Monday morning and Elizabeth barely rose in time to see him. She and Jane had stayed up half Saturday night discussing their beaux, and Sunday had been more of the same. Elizabeth wanted to hear all about Mr. Bingley's return and how Jane had received him. Jane spared no detail—she was as much in love as she had ever been, and it made Elizabeth's heart glad to see her so happy.

Now, Elizabeth rushed down the stairs, her hair in a simple knot at the base of her neck, to see Mr. Darcy before he escorted her friends to Meryton.

She burst into the morning room to find him standing at the window all alone.

"Good morning, Mr. Darcy."

He turned and smiled at the sound of her voice. "Good morning, Miss Elizabeth." He looked around the room, and seeing no one about, quickly strode towards her and kissed her cheek. "I am glad to see you this morning."

She smiled shyly at him. "As am I." Her doubt and restlessness from the days before vanished at the sight of his smile. She had been utterly wrong about him, and she would admit it every day if it meant there would be more moments like this.

"Before I forget, do you have a letter for me?"

"Yes." She handed him the folded paper she had written for her father. "If Papa is difficult and attempts to make sport of you, which he will likely do, tell him I expected as much and that I said you are not an unwanted suitor, and remind him that he promised. That should move things along."

"He promised?"

She looked down and fidgeted with the edges of his coat. "Some months ago, he dispatched an unwanted admirer for me and told me that my choice of hu—, husband," she stumbled on the word, "was mine to make. He promised he would stand by my choice and my right to make it."

Darcy pressed her hands against his chest, longing to take her in his arms and kiss her senseless while asking if he was in fact her choice of husband. But she had asked him to progress slowly, and he wished her to be completely sure when she accepted him. She should be filled with joy, not lingering doubt.

He raised her hands to his lips one at a time and placed fervent kisses on the backs. "I am honored."

They heard Charlotte and Maria coming in from the dining room. Elizabeth quickly rose to her toes and kissed his lips for the briefest moment, then moved swiftly to the door to greet her friend.

THE JOURNEY to Meryton was uneventful and soon Darcy was standing in front of Longbourn's door. He was let in by the butler and then taken to Mr. Bennet's bookroom. By some unexpected stroke of luck, Mrs. Bennet and her two youngest daughters had gone on a call, and only Miss Mary was in the house, playing ponderously on a pianoforte somewhere out of sight.

Mr. Bennet's bookroom was aptly named. The walls were covered floor to ceiling in books. The only open space was a large window on two of the walls, and a fireplace that bore an insignia in the center and some faded script on the stone.

"Mr. Darcy, what can I do for you?"

"I have just escorted Miss Lucas and Mrs. Collins to Lucas Lodge, and I have a letter from your daughter."

He had intended to be more forthright, but as soon as he met the man's shrewd eyes and realized how very much was at stake with this interview, all coherent thought had left him. He knew only that he must leave with Mr. Bennet's consent for their courtship and eventual marriage. Elizabeth was not of age, and even if she were, he could not ask her to go against her family. He must obtain her father's consent.

Mr. Bennet took the letter Darcy held out for him with a look of surprise, then pleasure when he recognized the writing. "I did not know you were in company with Elizabeth."

"I was visiting my aunt, Lady Catherine, in Kent. Hunsford Parsonage is but a half mile up the lane."

"Ah." Mr. Bennet looked to his guest, then to his letter, then back to Mr. Darcy, clearly wondering what the man was still doing there.

"I also wished to speak with you about your daughter, Miss Elizabeth. I have asked and received her permission to court her, and now I would like your consent to the courtship and our eventual marriage." There. He had said it. He exhaled audibly and felt his shoulders drop down from his ears. The worst was over.

Mr. Bennet stared at Mr. Darcy as if he were a mule who had suddenly begun speaking.

"Forgive me, Mr. Darcy. Did you say you wish to court my Lizzy?"

"Yes."

"And she has agreed to this?" he asked, his grey brows raised nearly to his hairline.

"Yes."

Mr. Bennet's doubt was writ clearly upon his face, so Darcy added, "She did not agree immediately. There was much discussion and negotiation—"

"Negotiation?"

Darcy colored. "Miss Elizabeth requested that we progress slowly so she might have the time to come to know me." He almost added that he had confessed his error in judgement to Bingley before she would accept him, but he would keep that to himself unless absolutely necessary.

"That is a reasonable request, seeing as how she hated you when she left for Kent."

Darcy winced. It was one thing to know she had disliked him—it was another to hear it spoken of so matter-of-factly by her own father.

"I know Miss Elizabeth did not have a favorable opinion of me, but we have spoken and cleared that away. My cousin, Colonel Fitzwilliam, became friends with Miss Elizabeth and when she mentioned Wickham, he could not but warn her of the man's avarice."

Mr. Bennet's brows rose again. He had clearly not expected the conversation to take such a turn. "I think you had better begin again, Mr. Darcy."

And so Darcy told him of his history with Wickham, changing names and details to protect the privacy of the innocent, and told Mr. Bennet somewhat sparingly of his evening visit to the parsonage on the day Elizabeth had been so distressed. He did not mention the brandy or his original intent, but he gave what details he could and by the end of his recitation, Mr. Bennet looked thoroughly shocked.

"I think I had better read this letter."

He opened the seal and was surprised at its brevity.

Father,

Please do not toy with Mr. Darcy. He will be my husband one day and I wish the two of you to be friends. He has a wonderful library if such a temptation is needed to induce you to be kind to him.

I care for him, Father.

I am sure he will tell you all about our reconciliation and the information that led to it. Listen carefully and watch over my sisters. Mr. W is not to be trusted.

Charlotte likes Mr. Darcy, and if it makes you feel more assured, Aunt Gardiner thinks him a fine man, based not only on my account of him, but that of an old friend in Derbyshire who knows him away from our company. Surely two such references cannot but be in his favor?

I shall not remind you of your promise since I am sure you remember it quite clearly yourself.

I shall merely sign,
Your loving daughter,
Elizabeth Bennet

MR. BENNET LAUGHED HEARTILY when he finished the letter. "Well, Mr. Darcy, it seems I have been charged with not toying with you."

Darcy smiled uneasily, not knowing how to react to such a statement.

"Do not worry, young man, I will leave you be. Now, let us get down to business. You wish to marry my daughter?"

From there, Darcy was on firmer footing. He shared his hopes that they would be wed by the end of the year, his tentative plans for a wedding trip, and that he thought they would spend roughly eight months of the year at Pemberley, though Elizabeth might prefer something different. They spoke of settlements and pin money, entailments (Pemberley's was limited, thankfully) and wills, and their proposed living arrangements.

Georgiana would live with them as he hoped she and Elizabeth would get along, but if they did not, his sister did have her own establishment in Town that could be utilized, or she could potentially stay with another relative.

Mr. Bennet was impressed. He hated to admit it as he had long looked forward to teasing whoever Elizabeth's suitor turned out to be. In some ways, Mr. Darcy was an easy target for such endeavors, and intelligent enough to give Mr. Bennet a challenge, but he had promised Elizabeth. There would be plenty of time for fun and games in the future.

"Well, Mr. Darcy, I think that is all I need to know. If you will have the settlement drawn up, I will review it."

Darcy shook his hand and a relieved smile broke out on his face. "So I have your blessing, sir?"

Bennet drew a deep breath. "Yes, you have it, and Elizabeth as well. Tell her I expect her home within the fortnight."

"I thought she was due to return to Longbourn Saturday?"

Bennet raised one brow, much like his daughter did. "She was. I assumed you would like a little more time in Town, before being subjected to my wife's effusions. Though by all means bring her back Saturday if you prefer."

"No! A fortnight is agreeable," said Darcy quickly.

Bennet did not bother hiding his smirk. "Very well. If you can wait a moment, I will send a note for my brother with you."

DARCY'S COACH was entering London when he called out to the coachman to go to Gracechurch Street instead of his Mayfair address. Soon he was being let into the Gardiners' home and led to the drawing room.

"Mr. Darcy!" cried Mrs. Gardiner. "We did not expect to see you this evening." She smiled and stood to greet him.

"I have only just come from Hertfordshire. I have a letter for your husband from Mr. Bennet and another for Miss Elizabeth."

"How very kind of you to deliver them. Please, do be seated." She gestured him to the seat across from her and took the letters. "My husband will be home shortly. Elizabeth is with the children and their nurse, but I expect them back any moment."

Darcy nodded, not knowing how to speak to Mrs. Gardiner. She was a kind woman, and a good hostess, that much was clear, but he did not know what he could have in common with her. They shared no acquaintance, did not move in the same circles, and never attended the same events. Or did they?

"Are you fond of the theater, Mrs. Gardiner?"

"I am. I enjoy a well-performed opera and Shakespearean comedies best. What are your preferences?"

They spoke for some time on the various shows they had seen and which performers they favored.

"Of course, it is no surprise he is a favorite," said Mrs. Gardiner with a sly smile. "He is from Derbyshire."

"Are you from Derbyshire, Mrs. Gardiner?" asked Darcy with interest.

"From five years of age until I turned seventeen. My father was the doctor in Lambton until he retired and moved us to the coast."

"Your father was Mr. Holly?"

"Yes! Did you know him?"

"He set my arm when I broke it in a riding accident when I was ten."

Mrs. Gardiner made a sympathetic face. "I imagine you did not think too fondly of him after that."

"Not immediately, no," he chuckled. "But I soon learned what a service he had done me." He sipped his tea and shook his head. "Miss Elizabeth mentioned she had an aunt from Derbyshire, but I did not remember it until just now. Forgive me, Mrs. Gardiner. I am not usually so absentminded."

"That is quite all right, Mr. Darcy. It is understandable under the circumstances."

Darcy flushed under her knowing smile and laughing eyes. He cleared his throat. "Have you returned to Derbyshire often since moving away?"

"Only once, though I maintain a correspondence with a few friends there. We are taking a trip to the Lakes this summer and plan to stop in Lambton for a few days. Elizabeth shall accompany us, I believe."

"Yes, I recall her mentioning it. When you come to Lambton, I would be pleased for you all to stay at Pemberley. My sister and I generally spend the summer there—we would be delighted to have you."

"That is very generous of you, Mr. Darcy. I shall speak to my husband and let you know."

He nodded and was spared further comment by the sound of children running into the house. Their nurse scolded them into removing their outerwear before running up the stairs. Darcy took the moment of distraction to think about his impromptu invitation. Mrs. Gardiner was genteel, and Elizabeth was everything perfect, but would Mr. Gardiner be an appropriate guest for Pemberley? He was in trade and his sister was Mrs. Bennet. He felt a tiny bit of shame that the latter disturbed him more than the former.

There was nothing to be done for it now. The invitation had been given. He would just have to hope Mr. Gardiner was as genteel as his wife. He could hardly be a worse guest than Mr. Hurst, who spent the entire time he was in residence anywhere eating, drinking, or sleeping when he was not playing cards and losing money he could ill afford.

"Mr. Darcy!" Elizabeth entered the room and smiled at him brightly. "I did not expect to see you again today."

He bowed over her hand. "I hope the surprise is not unwelcome."

"Not at all. I shall have to dress for dinner soon, but would you like to take a walk while the sun is still bright?"

"I should be delighted."

Elizabeth looked to her aunt who nodded and then addressed Darcy. "I hope you will join us for dinner, Mr. Darcy. Mr. Bingley will be joining us as well, and I know my husband is anxious to meet you."

He looked to Elizabeth and saw her hopeful expression. "I would be delighted. But I have not time to return home to change."

"Do not worry about that. None of us shall faint if you are not formally attired for dinner."

Elizabeth laughed and tugged his hand. "Come!"

Mrs. Gardiner handed her niece the letter from Mr. Bennet before sending them on their way.

"I am glad your aunt did not insist on accompanying us as chaperone," he said as he pulled her arm closer and walked toward the small park a few streets over.

"My aunt is a discerning woman. She trusts my judgment and thinks highly of you. She knows we will not do anything untoward. Besides, what could we get up to on a busy city street?"

She smiled in such a way that Darcy wanted to kiss her and show her just what they could accomplish swiftly in the middle of a bustling street, but he refrained. They made it to the park and he led her to a bench.

"Would you like to read your father's letter?"

"Yes, thank you." She settled on the bench and broke the seal.

DEAR LIZZY,

VERY WELL, my dear. I have given your young man my blessing and did not toy with him overmuch in the process. I have remembered my promise, there was no need to remind me. He is not the sort of man one would refuse anyhow, but I am glad there was no need to contemplate such an action.

He is an interesting character, your Mr. Darcy. He assures me his library is very fine and that I may visit whenever I have need of your company. He is a serious young man—you must remember to tease him regularly. He is in dire need of it.

I have told Mr. Darcy you may stay another fortnight if the Gardiners will have you and have sent your uncle a note. Use your time wisely, my child, for once you are home, you will have little peace from your mother.

Your Father,

Thomas Bennet

ELIZABETH SMILED and tucked the letter into her reticule. "He likes you."

"Does he?"

"He does. I can tell." She rose and took his arm, walking slowly around the pond in the center of the park. "I am glad. I would not like the two most important men in my life to dislike one another."

Darcy could not answer such a statement and pressed his hand over hers where it rested on his arm.

~

BINGLEY ARRIVED for dinner while the ladies were still upstairs preparing. Darcy was a little nervous about how their meeting would go. Less than two weeks ago, Bingley had called him an ass and left what looked like an angry blot on the page. Darcy knew he had deserved it, but it did not make him any less apprehensive.

"Darcy!" cried Bingley. "I did not know you would be here."

"It was an impromptu decision." They asked after each other's family and health, and Darcy's concerns began to dissipate. Bingley seemed prepared to continue their friendship as it had always been— all would be well.

"How goes your courtship of Miss Bennet?" Darcy asked.

"Oh, she is an angel!"

Darcy rolled his eyes fondly and Bingley smirked at him.

"You think I refer to her beauty, which is as perfect as it ever was, but Miss Bennet is angelic because she was willing to forgive my boorish behavior. I cannot believe I ever thought I could live without her! I must have been mad."

"Yes, the heart will have its way."

Bingley nodded enthusiastically. "Yes! I would have been miserable without Jane."

"Do you have an understanding then?"

"Not as yet. I wanted to give her time to trust me again. She has not said because she is too good, but I know my abandonment was very hard on her." He leaned towards Darcy and lowered his voice. "The first time I was invited for dinner, Mr. Gardiner spoke to me privately."

Darcy's brows rose in interest.

"Told me he was inclined to think me foolish and capricious, but because Jane liked me, he would give me a chance to prove I could be worthy of her."

Darcy's brows were at his hairline now. Miss Bennet was a worthy woman, of course, but for Mr. Gardiner, a man in trade, to say such to a gentleman—it did not sit well. "What was your response?"

"I told him I had been mistaken to leave as I had and that my intentions were honorable. He hinted that Jane had been morose all winter over my leaving. Can you imagine?"

Darcy could not.

"I am usually the one with my heart blown about thither and yon. To think I did such a thing to my angel—I shall never forgive myself."

Darcy knew Bingley was likely being his usual hyperbolic self, but he could not help but think that Bingley seemed to genuinely mean it.

"When will you make your proposals?" Darcy asked.

"When I know she no longer doubts me."

Darcy nodded. He could certainly understand that.

After sitting together quietly for a few minutes, Bingley burst out with, "I did not know you were acquainted with the Gardiners, Darcy."

"I was not until yesterday when I met Mrs. Gardiner. I have yet to meet Mr. Gardiner."

Bingley's face wrinkled in confusion. "Then what are you doing here?"

Suddenly, Darcy realized he had not told Bingley he was courting Miss Elizabeth. Their most recent letters had been about Miss Bennet, and he had not written since Darcy began courting Miss Elizabeth in earnest. He had planned to tell Bingley in person, but in the activity of the last days, he had completely forgotten.

Darcy's mouth hung open for a second before the drawing room door opened and Mrs. Gardiner, Miss Bennet, and Miss Elizabeth walked in, smiling and dressed for dinner.

16

A TROUBLESOME TUESDAY

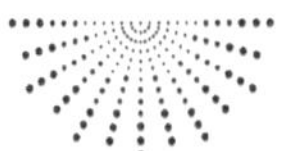

"So he discovered your courtship by watching you moon over Miss Elizabeth?" Colonel Fitzwilliam guffawed and slapped his knee. "I wish I had been there. It sounds terribly entertaining."

"You would not have thought so if you were in my position."

"But I was not and that is what makes this so amusing."

Darcy rolled his eyes. "He stared at us with an odd expression on his face all evening. As if we were mathematical equations he could not parse out."

Fitzwilliam laughed again. "Did you explain when the ladies withdrew?"

"They did not withdraw! No one saw the need for it, so we all adjourned to the drawing room together." Darcy gave his cousin a sly smile. "It was rather entertaining seeing Bingley look so befuddled when I turned Elizabeth's pages as she played."

Richard snorted. "I can imagine."

"I am to call at Gracechurch Street shortly. Will you accompany me?"

"I believe I will."

THEY HAD NOT BEEN at Gracechurch Street ten minutes before Darcy knew something was wrong. Elizabeth had greeted them civilly and introduced Colonel Fitzwilliam to her family, but she had sent him no private smiles, no longing looks. She had not teased him or said a word to him beyond a greeting since he arrived.

He sat near her and waited for a gap in her conversation, then leaned toward her and whispered, "Are you well, dearest?"

"I am in perfect health, Mr. Darcy," she answered crisply, not even sparing him a glance.

Darcy was befuddled. "Has something occurred to upset you?"

She turned a stony expression on him, then looked away again without speaking.

Well! This was not to be borne. Clearly she was angry about something, or she would not have refused to answer him. He must find a way to speak to her alone.

"The weather is fine today," he said to Mrs. Gardiner. "My cousin and I had hoped to go for a walk with the ladies."

Mrs. Gardiner smiled tightly at him. "That sounds lovely. Jane, Lizzy, fetch your things while I alert Paulson."

Mrs. Gardiner swept out of the room with her nieces before more could be said. Darcy and his cousin looked at each other oddly.

"What is going on, Darcy?"

"I have not the slightest idea."

"Something is off here. If I did not know better, I would say they wished we had not called. Did they receive bad news? Has something happened?"

"I cannot say, but I intend to find out."

Soon, they were walking down the street with a giant of a footman following along behind them. He watched the gentlemen with a wary eye, and Darcy again felt that something was terribly off. He had walked out with Elizabeth only yesterday and no one had felt the need for a chaperone. Now, even with her sister and his cousin along, her aunt had sent a footman.

"Elizabeth," Darcy ventured tentatively when they were some

distance from the house. "What is wrong? Please do not tell me it is nothing."

Elizabeth looked up at him with pursed lips and eyes that sparked with something he could not name. She looked over her shoulder at her sister walking with Colonel Fitzwilliam. Sensing her need for more privacy, Darcy quickened his pace to put more distance between the couples.

"What is going on?" he asked again.

Elizabeth sighed. "Mr. Darcy, did you enjoy dinner last night?"

"Yes, of course." Why was she speaking of dinner?

"Did you enjoy all aspects of it? Not just the food, though I know my aunt sets a good table, but also the company?"

"I always enjoy your company."

She took another deep breath. "*Everyone's* company?"

Darcy was confused. What was she getting at? "Your aunt is a skilled hostess, and you know Bingley is my friend. I do not know Miss Bennet well, but I do not mind her company."

"And?"

He looked at her in confusion. "Elizabeth, please tell me why you are upset with me, for you clearly are. These questions are not helping."

"Very well. My uncle. You barely spoke to him all evening, and when he spoke to you, you gave him such clipped answers that he was insulted in his own house."

Darcy flushed. He knew Elizabeth was not wrong. He had actively sought to avoid Mr. Gardiner's company. But he had no desire to hurt Elizabeth in the process, and it was bad manners to insult one's host in their own home.

"I admit I was not a very good guest in that regard."

"Not a good guest!" she cried. "You were nearly uncivil! I do not remember when I was last so embarrassed."

"Embarrassed!" Darcy turned to face her, shock and offense writ on his features. "You were embarrassed by me?"

"Yes! My uncle is a perfectly genial man, who did nothing but invite you into his home, offer you dinner, and attempt to be friendly toward you. Yet you treated him like he was not even worth your notice, let alone your conversation."

Darcy's mouth opened and closed, every word he thought to say dying on his tongue before he could speak it. "I, that is, I do not..."

"Please do not tell me you do not perform for strangers. This is my uncle. You were a guest in his home. The least you could have done was behave with courtesy. I have seen you be more gracious with Miss Bingley!"

That stung. Darcy looked away, unable to form a response. They had entered a little park now, and Colonel Fitzwilliam steered Miss Bennet away from Darcy and Elizabeth, leaving the footman looking back and forth between the ladies, clearly unsure whom he should follow.

"Please stay with my sister, Paulson," said Elizabeth tiredly.

Darcy thought it a good sign for a moment—she clearly felt safe with him, and perhaps she wished to be alone. But it only took a glance at the fire in her eyes to realize she was furious with him and likely wished to berate him without an audience.

He sighed and rubbed the bridge of his nose. "I am sorry I was rude to your uncle, Elizabeth. I never meant to hurt or offend you by my behavior, and I apologize for doing so."

Her arms were still crossed over her chest, but he thought he saw her stance relax a little.

"Fitzwilliam," she said hesitantly, "I would like you to answer something truthfully."

"Of course." He felt flooded with relief. She had called him by name!

"Why were you so rude to my uncle?"

He instantly flushed and he knew she saw it by the stiffening of her shoulders.

"The truth, please. Do not spare my sensibilities."

Darcy sighed. "Very well. There were a few reasons. If you will hear me out?"

She nodded.

"I spoke with Bingley briefly before you came down to dinner. He mentioned your uncle taking him aside and questioning his honor. I understand he was acting as Miss Bennet's guardian, but it did set me somewhat on edge."

She glared at him but said nothing.

"And Mr. Gardiner is your mother's brother, and I have often found her…" he paused as he searched for a word, "somewhat difficult to be in company with." He could not look at her as he said it, but she had asked for his honesty.

"Is that all? Would you not have realized a few minutes after meeting him that he is nothing like my mother?"

Darcy took a deep breath. At least she was not offended over what he said of Mrs. Bennet. "Truthfully, your uncle is in trade. I have known many such men before and they often wish for an investment of some kind, or an introduction. They often try to convince me to be part of some risky scheme that has little chance of success, and they want someone else's money to speculate with. I cannot abide it."

Elizabeth watched him thoughtfully, clearly considering everything he had said very carefully. "And you thought my uncle would be such a man? That he would vulgarly ask you for an investment, at dinner in his own home, with his wife and nieces present?"

When put in such a way, it did sound ridiculous, but he had not given it much thought. He had seen Mr. Gardiner, thought he was a tradesman with whom he wanted little to do, and focused his attention on Elizabeth.

"I can only say I was not thinking as carefully as I should have been. I had been so anxious to see you, and then I spoke with Bingley and," he paused to take a breath. "No, I am making excuses. I was abominably rude. You are correct. Mr. Gardiner was my host, and your uncle and guardian. He deserved better treatment from me. I apologize."

She watched him warily for a moment, as if she were still sketching his character. "Very well, Mr. Darcy, I accept your apology. I can understand your reasons, to an extent. Do you intend to continue in this aloof manner? Or will you make a genuine effort to get to know my Uncle Gardiner?"

He stepped closer to her, relieved to see she had uncrossed her arms and relaxed her stance. He took her hands in his and pulled her a tiny bit closer, though she was still too far away for his liking.

"I will be the opposite of aloof." He raised her hands to his lips one at a time. "I will make an effort to befriend your uncle. I can see it is important to you." He knew he had said the right thing, for her shoulders lowered and her face lost its serious lines. "I will not allow your delightful presence to distract me from what is due my hosts."

She finally smiled at him. Something seemed to loosen around his chest and he felt tension leave his body. How had he gone entire days without her smiling at him before? It felt impossible now.

"Would you like to put that to the test?" she asked slyly.

"How do you mean?"

"Come to dinner again tonight. Show my uncle you are a good man. Show me I have not been mistaken in your character." She added the last more somberly, and Darcy understood he had made a very grave misstep, and nearly collided with disaster.

"Yes, I will come to dinner this evening." She smiled at him again and he could not resist placing another kiss on her hand before tucking it beneath his and continuing their walk through the park. "That reminds me. I would like for you meet my sister while you are in town. She is currently staying with my aunt, Lady Hopewell. Will you and Miss Bennet come to dinner tomorrow evening? Mrs. Gardiner may attend as your chaperone if she likes."

Elizabeth noticed he had neatly avoided inviting her uncle, but she understood that his aunt might have more rigid ideas about society than she had, and he had apologized very prettily. It would be petty of her to hold someone else's guest list against him.

"Yes, I would be delighted to attend. I know Jane has no engagements. I will ask my aunt if she is free."

DINNER THAT NIGHT was as different from the night before as possible. Darcy spoke with Mrs. Gardiner of Lambton and Derbyshire. He talked with Mr. Gardiner of fishing, a sport they both enjoyed, and he even made an effort to get to know Miss Bennet better. She would be his sister—he ought to have made the effort before now, but he had not been thinking clearly. In truth, he had been thinking of little but Elizabeth.

He was observant enough to notice the surprise, though it was quickly hidden, on the faces of Elizabeth's aunt and uncle. They clearly had expected more of his insulting behavior from the night before, and he was filled with shame that he had behaved so to his hosts and the beloved relations of the woman he hoped to call his wife. Just before the dessert was brought out, he caught Mrs. Gardiner nodding to Elizabeth with a look of approval in her eye, and Elizabeth smiling back in relief.

He finally realized how close he had come to losing her. The thought took his breath away for a moment. As a wealthy man with a vast estate and in good health and looks as he was, he had never imagined he would be refused by any woman he would make his proposals to. Yet Elizabeth had all but told him she would have done just that. After everything they had been through, after all of the conversations and outings and all his determined wooing, after every awkward attempt to be charming he had made, the idea that he might lose her over his insufferable pride made him a little sick to his stomach.

She was worth too much to him now. He would not let her go—not for anything, and not for anyone.

"I heard you are planning a trip to The Lakes this summer and that you plan to stop in Derbyshire for some days."

"That is right," said Mr. Gardiner, thrown off by the sudden change of topic. They had been speaking of the Gardiners' oldest son attending school soon.

"I would be pleased for you to stay at Pemberley while you are in the area."

Mr. Gardiner was taken aback. "That is very generous of you, Mr. Darcy."

"Please, call me Darcy." He stole a glance at Elizabeth and saw she was watching them carefully.

"You may call me Gardiner."

Mrs. Gardiner rose then to lead the ladies out and as Elizabeth passed him, she grasped his hand for a brief moment, a beguiling smile directed solely at him.

He sighed in relief. He had fixed what was wrong, and she was his again.

17

WEDNESDAY, YOU DREADFUL DAY

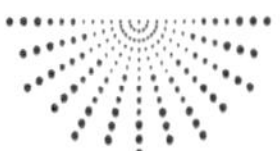

"This will not do." Elizabeth threw a pink gown onto the bed, on top of the pile of gowns already there.

"What about the green? It brings out the flecks in your eyes," suggested Jane.

"It is two years old and has been laundered more times than I care to think about. It is a favorite, but I do not think it appropriate for meeting a countess."

"I am sure we will think of something. Aunt is only a little taller than you. She has said you may borrow one of her gowns."

"I had not wanted to do so, but it may be necessary. Oh, why must you be so tall and elegant so that I cannot share in your new gowns!"

They laughed together. Jane had ordered several new things when she came to Town, as they usually did. Part of Mr. Gardiner's import business included fabric, and he was a source of quality cloth the Bennets were happy to take full advantage of. Jane would look lovely at dinner in her new blue silk evening gown, but Elizabeth was the one on trial, and she was no closer to finding something suitable than she had been a half hour ago when they began their search.

Just then, Mrs. Gardiner came bustling into the room. "Girls! You will never believe my good luck!"

"What has happened?" asked Jane.

"I stopped in at Madame Claudine's to pick up my new dress this morning, and look what I found!"

The maid behind her held up an elegant evening gown in a soft yellow, tiny crystal beads sewn onto the bodice.

"Aunt, did you have this made?"

"No, and that is the lucky part! As I was trying on my gown, Madame told me about a young lady who had had a new wardrobe made up for the Season, then at the last moment, the lady decided not to come to Town, and not to pick up her order. Madame was terribly put out, as you can imagine, and I could not help but notice that the gowns looked very near to Lizzy's size. She compared the measurements and you are surprisingly similar. With a tiny bit of adjustment, this gown will fit as if it were made for you."

"Aunt, you didn't!"

"I most certainly did! No niece of mine will go into an earl's house feeling underdressed. I am not married to the best fabric supplier in London for nothing."

Elizabeth could not help but be relieved as she touched the delicate silk of the gown. It truly was perfect. The style and cut were those she favored, and the color would be flattering on her. She had not liked to think of it, but she was nervous about meeting Mr. Darcy's family. His sister was easily the most important person in the world to him, even more than herself, and she knew he took his duty to his family very seriously. She would not like to fail such an important test.

"Aunt, you have saved me!"

"Say that after you have tried it on."

In short order, Elizabeth was taken out of her day dress and had slipped into the new gown. "I am afraid to move for fear of breaking such a delicate concoction. It is lovely."

She twisted slowly in the mirror, looking at the intricate bead work around the neckline, and the way the back fell slightly longer than the front, almost but not quite a train.

"It fits beautifully! A tiny tuck in the bodice and it will be perfect."

Elizabeth was more active than her sisters, and thus had always been a fraction slighter. She was also less well-endowed with womanly curves than Jane and Lydia. Only Kitty had a similar figure to hers, and their tastes were so different that they rarely shared clothes.

Mrs. Gardiner's maid marked the dress where it required a tuck, and Elizabeth gladly handed it over to her. She promised to have it ready in plenty of time to dress for dinner.

"I am so glad you like it, for I have something else to tell you."

She led her nieces to her dressing room.

"Oh, Aunt! You didn't!"

Mrs. Gardiner laughed delightedly. "I did! The entire wardrobe cost barely more than a few gowns. Madame was eager to be rid of it, and you know she owes me a favor. I told her we would take it all if you liked it. Oh, do not make that face, Lizzy! Your father sent your uncle funds for new gowns, and this was barely more. It is not every day one is courted by Mr. Darcy of Pemberley."

Elizabeth was wavering. She hated to think of her aunt spending so much on her, but if the clothes had truly been inexpensive, and her father had sent money for them, she could not complain. And how lucky to find gowns already made up! They had found a similar gown for Jane once several years ago, and it had felt like winning a thousand lottery tickets.

"Very well, Aunt, I accept."

Mrs. Gardiner squealed, though she would never admit to such an unladylike sound, and they began sorting through the clothing hanging in the dressing room. There were ballgowns, dinner gowns, and two more ornate gowns suitable for the theater. There were several walking dresses and those suited for morning calls. There were matching reticules, spencers, and a long pair of elegant gloves that fit perfectly. There was a cloak lined with soft satin, and more bonnets than she could count.

"I did not know Madame made bonnets," said Jane.

"She does not make them, but she adorns the forms the milliner sends her."

There were stockings, and stays and chemises, and a dressing gown so beautiful and soft that Elizabeth could not stop running her hand over it.

"Lizzy, this is …" Jane could not find the words to continue her sentence.

"I know, Jane. I cannot believe it myself. But I am so very relieved. Mr. Darcy is always so well put together. I would not like to appear dowdy beside him."

"You could never look dowdy."

Elizabeth gave her sister a look and Jane could not help but laugh. "Well, no one will dare call you dowdy now."

"No, they certainly shall not."

Elizabeth ran her hand along another gown and wondered how she would feel, adorned in such finery every day. Rather like she would feel as Mrs. Darcy, she imagined. What a wild thought!

THE GOWN WAS ready in time for dinner, just as the maid had promised. Elizabeth was bathed, dressed, and coiffed with an attention for detail she had thought only to see on her wedding day. She had never been more well put-together, and the reflection in the mirror went some way to dispelling her nerves.

Mr. Darcy was in the drawing room when she entered with Jane and her aunt, and she had the pleasure of seeing him slack-jawed and wide-eyed for a full two minutes before he said anything. Jane and Mrs. Gardiner shared knowing smiles. Elizabeth could only blush and look to the floor, then thank Mr. Darcy for his compliment. At least, she thought it was a compliment. His voice sounded rather choked and his words were not entirely clear, but she felt that he was pleased by her appearance.

Soon they were in the carriage and on the way to Lady Hopewell's townhome.

"Might you tell us a little about your family, Mr. Darcy?" asked Mrs. Gardiner as the carriage trundled through London.

"Of course. Lady Hopewell is my father's younger sister."

"Oh! I had thought we were going to the home of Colonel Fitzwilliam's parents," interjected Elizabeth.

"I apologize for the confusion. Colonel Fitzwilliam's father is Lord Blackburn. He was my mother's elder brother."

"Is he older or younger than Lady Catherine?" asked Elizabeth.

"Lady Catherine is four years his junior. My mother was the second in her family."

"I see." Though she did not. Lady Catherine was terribly bossy for someone who had no younger brothers or sisters to order about. Or perhaps that was why she was so determined to direct her environment now? Elizabeth faced the window to hide her smile at the thought of Lady Catherine as a frustrated eight-year-old, desperately trying to get her elder brother and sister to listen to her.

"Lady Hopewell was my father's second younger sister. He was the eldest in his family. Next is my aunt Helen Brigsby. She lives in Somerset with her husband—I do not know when we shall see her next. Then my aunt Lady Hopewell whom we shall see tonight. She is often in Town and is fond of entertaining. My father had a younger brother who joined the Navy. He moved to Upper Canada with his prize money when I was still at Eton and I have not seen him since."

"How adventurous! I had not realized the Darcy family was so large," said Mrs. Gardiner.

"We are not overly so. My aunts each only have two children, and it has been so long since I heard from my uncle Darcy that I cannot be certain he is even still alive, but last I heard he had three children."

"He does not write to you?" asked Elizabeth.

"He occasionally sends a letter, but I have not received one in at least three years now. His children were much younger than me, so I had not thought to write to them directly, though you make me think now I should." He smiled at Elizabeth in the darkened carriage, and she returned it, wondering if they would ever make the journey to Canada to see his family. How exciting it would be!

"Will your aunt have any other family in attendance this evening?" asked Mrs. Gardiner.

"I am not certain of the entire guest list, but she assured me it would be only family. My uncle, Lord Hopewell, will likely be there, though he is so active with Parliament that he is often out."

Elizabeth raised her brows at this. What sort of uncle would not wish to meet the woman his nephew was hoping to marry?

"My cousin Albert, Lord Winters, may make an appearance, though it is likely he will not remain for the evening. He is my aunt's only son. Her daughter Clara should be there. She is entering her third season. Now that I think of it, you are likely of an age," he said, looking to Elizabeth.

"Then perhaps we shall be friends," she replied happily.

"My great uncle may be there as well, Sir Daniel Darcy. He was a judge on the high courts. He has a dry sense of humor, but he is kind. Actually, he reminds me a little of Mr. Bennet."

Jane and Elizabeth looked at one another in surprise.

"Then we shall feel quite comfortable," said Jane, ever the peacemaker.

Elizabeth was less nervous than she had been—it helped to know who she might encounter, and she could tell by how Fitzwilliam spoke of them who he considered a friend and who he did not—but she was still walking into uncharted territory. She intended to acquit herself well, though she did not anticipate much enjoyment in the evening.

Finally, they pulled up before a large stone house, tall and stately, with lanterns lit near the door and at the posts along the street. Elizabeth let her eyes drift up, taking it all in.

Courage, Lizzy. It is only a house, she told herself.

The door was opened by a butler, and soon they had shed their outerwear and were being led into a drawing room where the tinkle of voices could be heard.

The room was as large and elegant as would be expected in such a grand house, and the furnishings were a combination of good taste and the desire to display wealth. Not as ornate as Rosings, but much showier than her aunt's home. There were roughly half a dozen people scattered throughout the room. A tall woman looked to the door as they were announced and made her way to them. She seemed to glide across the floor, she walked so smoothly. Elizabeth idly thought Caroline Bingley might like to study her; she could practice in her room for hours in an attempt to emulate her movements.

"Darcy, it is good to see you," said the gliding sylph.

She held out her hands and Darcy took them in his own, dropping a kiss on her cheek.

"Aunt, may I present Miss Elizabeth Bennet, her sister Miss Jane Bennet, and their aunt, Mrs. Gardiner. Ladies, my aunt, Lady Hopewell."

The ladies curtsied and smiled, and no one tripped on her skirts or let out an untimely burp.

First task accomplished.

"Miss Elizabeth, I am so pleased to meet you. My nephew has told me much about you. Come meet the family." She smiled and took Elizabeth's arm in hers, dragging her away from her party.

She did it so smoothly it was barely noticeable, but after meeting Lord Hopewell and their daughter Lady Clara, Elizabeth could not help but notice that her sister and aunt had been purposely left out of the introductions. She could not know why yet, but it made her wary.

Darcy's great uncle, Sir Daniel Darcy, was just as he had been described. He was a tall, thin man with a shock of white hair and rigid posture. His face was set permanently in a frown, as if he knew she had stolen her sister's bonnet and he would look at her thusly until she confessed to her crime. But just when she thought he hated her without hearing her say more than three words, she noticed a glimmer in his eye, the same telltale sparkle her father got before he teased someone. If Mr. Bennet had been free to pursue his academic interests and less inclined to laugh at everyone around him, she fancied he might have had a similar profession to Sir Daniel Darcy. She smiled at the judge and determined that she would find time to speak with him that evening.

Finally, the introduction Elizabeth had most been looking forward to was upon her. Miss Darcy was a tall girl—like all the other Darcys in the room—and on a larger scale than Elizabeth. She spoke so quietly Elizabeth could barely hear her, and she kept her eyes glued to the floor throughout the introduction and ensuing conversation. She was almost painfully shy, and Elizabeth knew it would be up to her to draw Miss Darcy out and further conversation if they were going to come to know one another at all.

Before Elizabeth could speak more than a few words to anyone, they were called in to dinner. The place settings were more elaborate than Elizabeth was used to, and she suspected they were in for at least four courses and very likely more. Lady Hopewell had placed Elizabeth on her left and Darcy on her right. Elizabeth was glad to have an ally close at hand, but she was not certain how good an ally Mr. Darcy would prove to be when the jousting was entirely verbal. She hated to admit it, but she would have felt more at ease with Colonel Fitzwilliam's jocular conversation or Charlotte's steady presence. If Mr. Darcy remained silent as his aunt questioned her about her family and accomplishments (as Elizabeth had no doubt she would), she was not sure what she would do. She knew she would be terribly disappointed in him, though. She could only hope his aunt was kind and the questions were not too invasive.

On Elizabeth's other side was Sir Daniel Darcy. She was glad to have him next to her. Mrs. Gardiner was on his other side, followed by Miss Darcy. She saw her aunt was already beginning to speak to Miss Darcy and hoped she would make progress with the younger girl.

On Mr. Darcy's other side was his cousin, Lady Clara, and then Jane. Jane was also on Lord Hopewell's left, and Elizabeth felt a knot in her stomach when she noticed it. She could foresee too many dangerous outcomes: Jane would answer questions too honestly and the experienced politician would know the whole of their family history before the second course was removed, or worse. He would be the sort of man who flirted with pretty women, and Jane was easily the most beautiful woman a man would ever see. He would not be able to resist. Or he would be an utter bore and Jane would not know how to discourage him without being impolite, and she would have an absolutely wretched evening.

The soup was brought out and Lady Hopewell began.

"So, Miss Elizabeth, you are from Hertfordshire?"

"Yes." She took a sip. The soup was delicious.

"Whereabouts exactly?"

"My father's estate is called Longbourn. It is near the market town of Meryton. It is twenty miles east of Luton, if you are familiar with that town." She took another sip. At least she would be well fed—if they let her eat.

Lady Hopewell nodded. "And your father has an estate?"

Elizabeth stifled a sigh. "Yes. It is called Longbourn." *As I said.* She glanced at Jane. Lord Hopewell was eating his food, ignoring her sister altogether.

"Do you have a large family?"

Elizabeth turned her attention back to her hostess. "At Longbourn, it is only my parents and my sisters, but we have a few Bennet cousins scattered about England. My mother's sister lives in Meryton, and her brother here in Town. It is he my sister and I are staying with."

"Oh, are you connected to the Bennets of Gilford Park? It is a lovely estate in Buckinghamshire."

"I do not believe so, ma'am."

"Oh." She took a sip of her soup, looking terribly disappointed. "How many sisters do you have?"

"There are five of us, my lady. I am the second."

Elizabeth felt as if she were back at Rosings, being questioned relentlessly by Lady Catherine, and she spared a glance for Mr. Darcy. She was trying not to laugh and thought they might share a private joke, but he did not look her way. His posture and bearing were everything they should be, but his eyes looked strained and there was a tension around his mouth only someone familiar with his expressions would notice. Was he disappointed in her answers and her manner with his aunt? She knew she was not being as deferential as she could be. Had he expected her to be? This was Darcy's family and it was important that she be respectful; it would be necessary for them to all get along. It would be even easier if they actually liked her, if for nothing but Fitzwilliam's sake.

But she was likely to marry this man. It was equally important that his family respect *her* and understand that she was not to be looked down on or talked down to simply because she was unknown to them or from a lower circle in society. She would begin as she meant to continue.

"And your sisters are all at home? None are married?" continued Lady Hopewell.

"No, none are married." She took a final sip of soup before the bowls were removed and new dishes were brought in.

In the bustle of changing courses, Elizabeth looked down the table and willed her sister to look at her. Jane seemed embarrassed that she had been ignored the entirety of the first course, but she sent a tight smile to her sister regardless. Elizabeth sent her an encouraging look and a quick exasperated expression, and Jane smiled more genuinely in response.

When the footmen stepped back and everyone began eating again, Elizabeth noticed that Jane was now talking to Lady Clara. Jane was listening attentively as Lady Clara spoke to her with great animation. Her voice was low, but Elizabeth caught enough words to let her know Clara was speaking of driving a phaeton, and how the horses had utterly refused to do as she bid. Jane seemed amused and well entertained, and Elizabeth breathed a little easier.

"Miss Elizabeth."

Elizabeth turned her head in surprise at the raspy voice beside her.

"Sir Daniel?"

He bowed his head slightly and she saw that sparkle in his eyes again. "I hope my niece hasn't been questioning you *too* much."

Elizabeth instinctively glanced back at Lady Hopewell. She was in conversation with Mr. Darcy on her other side.

"Not too much, though she does know quite a bit about me now."

He raised a brow. "I doubt that."

He took a bite of his food and Elizabeth was allowed a few bites of her own dish.

"What are you reading these days, Miss Elizabeth?"

"We have been so busy of late that I have had little time for books. I have been rereading *Lyrical Ballads* when I have a quiet half hour."

"Ah, yes. I find it soothing to read something familiar when one is in the midst of a hectic period in life."

"Just so, Sir."

He nodded again. "Shall you marry my nephew?"

Elizabeth choked on the wine she had just drunk. She coughed and spluttered as she felt her face grow red, and she could feel several pairs of eyes on her.

Sir Daniel reached out and smacked her back, a little harder than necessary, and said to the table, "Nothing to worry about. She is perfectly well."

Elizabeth glared at him, then took a shaky breath and dabbed her mouth with a napkin as the other guests returned to their conversations. She did not look at Mr. Darcy. She could not stand to see his disappointment, or worse, that he was not even looking her way.

"All better?"

She looked wryly at the judge. "Well enough, Sir."

"Good." He looked at her with narrowed eyes, and she wondered if he was trying to read her mind.

"What interests you so, Sir Daniel?"

"I have known my nephew his entire life. I have never seen him enamored of a woman, nor even mildly interested in marrying. Both are now happening at the same time and I find myself curious about the object of his affection."

Elizabeth blushed. "Is that all? Am I to be subject to another inquisition then?"

"Not at all. I would simply like to get to know you. If my nephew admires you, you must be extraordinary."

She flushed. Again. "I do not know that I am extraordinary, but I am pleased if your nephew finds me so."

"So you will marry him then?"

"Sir Daniel!"

The judge chuckled quietly as Elizabeth sat red and embarrassed. Eventually her own mirth could not be denied, and she laughed alongside him.

"You shall lower her ladyship's opinion of my manners," she teased.

"Do you care for her ladyship's opinion of your manners?"

"We are not all judges past the need to make a good impression."

"And here I thought you uncaring of popular opinion."

"I am not overly concerned about it, but I do not wish to make things awkward for Mr. Darcy. This is his family, after all."

"You care for him." It was not a question.

"I would hardly allow a man to court me if I did not."

Sir Daniel shrugged. "Many women would."

"I am not that sort of woman."

"I see that. And may I say I am glad of it."

"Thank you, Sir Daniel. I think."

They smiled at one another, she more cautiously than he, and the footmen arrived to remove their plates and serve the next course. Elizabeth took the opportunity to look down the table at Jane. She seemed to have enjoyed her conversation with Lady Clara, but now she would turn back to Lord Hopewell and his indifference.

"Do not worry overmuch. My nephew is an insufferable snob. He will come around."

Sir Daniel's quiet assurance helped her to relax, but she was still unhappy that sweet Jane was being subjected to such behavior.

"She has a very sweet nature. Such behavior will distress her," she said, just as quietly.

"Ah. It would be better if she could see the ridiculousness in it. He does not recognize his own rudeness, but we may laugh at it if we choose."

Elizabeth began to see why Mr. Darcy said Sir Daniel reminded him of Mr. Bennet.

"I suppose you are right," she said.

"We old judges often are, Miss Elizabeth."

She could not help but laugh at that. "Thank you, Sir Daniel."

"Whatever for?"

"For the good company."

He smiled and nodded, and she turned back to the countess for the next round of questioning.

"Miss Elizabeth, do you play the pianoforte?"

It would be a long evening.

DINNER WAS INTERMINABLE. Elizabeth told Lady Hopewell about her childhood—wild and country-bound; her education—indifferent and unfeminine; and her family—unconnected and untitled. Lady Hopewell was more than a little shocked by the fact that Elizabeth had neither had a governess nor gone to school. She was unimpressed by the country tutors her father had hired. She was appalled that Mr. Bennet had thought it valuable that his daughters learn to swim but had not insisted they all learn to ride.

Elizabeth did not tell her that his young cousin had drowned when she was only seven years of age and that his sister had been thrown from a horse so many times his father had been forced to sell the poor beast. Mr. Bennet had his reasons for his choices, but Elizabeth doubted Lady Hopewell would understand them. She would not debase herself or her father by justifying his decisions to someone so wholly unconnected to them.

When the courses changed—there were seven in total—she turned her attention to Sir Daniel. He was entertaining and inquisitive, and after an hour of conversation, she found his mind well-informed and his curiosity as rabid as he had claimed it to be. He asked her questions about herself, but of a different variety than his niece. He wished to know about her relationship with her father. What sort of holiday traditions she enjoyed. What kind of books she favored and whether or not she was musical.

He too had reasons for his questions. He knew his great-nephew to be fond of music and to enjoy reading, and Fitzwilliam's happiness would be greater if his wife indulged him in such things. He asked if she enjoyed the country or town more and if she was looking forward to being the mistress of an estate. He asked her about her sisters and how she spent her free time, and why her aunt and uncle in London were her favorite relations. Overall, he seemed happy with her responses, or so she thought.

"There is only one thing left to do, Miss Elizabeth."

"What is that, Sir Daniel?" She smiled brightly at him, feeling a pleasant kinship and the beginnings of familial affection for him.

"Be careful with that smile, young lady. You will fell more than one young man if you are not more judicious."

She laughed delightedly. Mr. Darcy finally looked her way, but she was too focused on his great-uncle to notice.

"You are a flatterer, Sir. I am surprised. I had thought all judges to be too stodgy for such things."

"Ah, but I am retired, my dear."

She shook her head fondly. "You must tell me what I should do now. I am all curiosity."

"Now, you must meet my daughter, Lady Hightower."

"Another lady! I had no idea Mr. Darcy's relations were all so grand."

"Well, the poor dear did not do it apurpose. She married a barrister with a modest income and was quite happy with her choice. Then his elder brother, the viscount, died and left only daughters, and her husband inherited the title." He spoke with his eyes downcast, as if a great tragedy had befallen his daughter in the form of an inheritance and a title.

"If she is anything like her father, I shall be pleased to meet her."

"Now who is the flatterer?"

Elizabeth smiled back innocently. "I speak as I find, Sir."

He shook his head. "She is in the country at present. She is only a few years older than young Fitzwilliam." She nodded towards Mr. Darcy. "I married rather late in life. She will come to Town for a few weeks at the end of the month. I will introduce you then."

"I shall look forward to it."

She was not certain how it had happened, but she knew she had just passed some sort of test and was feeling rather pleased with herself. She looked to Mr. Darcy with a smile, hoping to share in her victory. He met her gaze for what felt like the first time all evening and seemed surprised to see her looking so pleased. He returned her smile and for a minute, it was just the two of them, sharing a stolen moment.

Then the door to the dining room burst open and a loud voice cried out, "Mother, I forgot you had guests this evening."

All eyes turned to the young man standing near Lord Hopewell's chair with a mischievous grin on his face. He was wearing a bright green jacket with a garishly embroidered gold waistcoat. His hair was on the long side and fashionably disarranged, and he stood in such a way that bespoke confidence and entitlement.

Elizabeth instantly disliked him.

"Bertie, you knew perfectly well we were having Darcy's friends to dinner this evening."

"So I did. Forgive me for being late, Darcy." He looked about the table, ignoring Darcy's frown, and smiled widely. "But I am here now, so no harm done."

His eyes lit on Jane and his expression brightened. "You must be Darcy's lady love." He took her hand from where it rested on the table and kissed it after an elaborate bow. "I am very pleased to meet you." He winked at her on rising and Jane's mouth dropped open in surprise.

"Do stop your little show, Winters. You are making Miss Bennet uncomfortable," said Sir Daniel, his raspy voice suddenly strong and authoritative.

Lord Winters straightened immediately. "Forgive me, Uncle. I was only trying to be friendly."

"That is rather too friendly," said Mr. Darcy. "And I am afraid you have the wrong Miss Bennet. Miss Elizabeth is seated next to your mother. Miss Jane Bennet is her elder sister." Darcy looked to Elizabeth with an apology in his eyes for sending his cousin her way.

She tried to convey with her expression that he had done the right thing. It would be better to redirect the viscount's attention to herself instead of Jane.

"Well, in that case, I shall keep Miss Bennet company." He smiled roguishly and signaled a footman to bring him a chair. "Move over,

Clara." He unceremoniously pushed his sister over so he could fit comfortably between her and Jane.

"Bertie! You are like an ass someone has let in from the barn," huffed Clara.

"Clara, watch your language at table," corrected Lady Hopewell.

Clara gasped and looked at her mother in astonishment.

Elizabeth understood her perfectly. It seemed Mrs. Bennet was not the only mother who had a favorite child she would allow to get away with anything, no matter how egregious the action.

Dessert was brought out as soon as Lord Winters was settled, and Elizabeth could only be glad the meal was coming to a close.

"My son has high spirits, Miss Elizabeth. You mustn't mind him," declared Lady Hopewell with an indulgent smile for her son.

"I understand perfectly, my lady. My mother feels the same for my youngest sister. She is in possession of a similar disposition."

Mr. Darcy's head shot up from his study of his dessert and their eyes met for a moment. Elizabeth felt an odd desire to smirk at him, like she would have done before they were friends, before she had come to know him better. Before they were courting.

She restrained herself and focused on finishing her dessert so that they might leave this wretched dining room as soon as possible.

Finally, after what felt like an interminable amount of time to eat a fruit tart, Lady Hopewell rose to lead the ladies to the drawing room. Poor Jane was bright red and clumsy, first knocking her fork to the floor with a clatter, then catching her skirt on her chair as she turned to go. Lord Winters leaned down and released it for her, and she stammered an apology as he watched her walk away with a wide smile.

"Darcy, what on earth are you thinking?" cried Winters once the ladies had departed.

"Pardon me?" he replied coldly.

"Miss Elizabeth is lovely in her own way, I'm sure, but how can you even notice her when her sister is in the room? Have you lost your mind, man?"

"Miss Bennet is an attractive woman, but she does not suit me as Miss Elizabeth does," said Darcy succinctly.

"Attractive woman! Are you blind? She is Aphrodite herself!"

"You are drunk, Albert," said Darcy in disgust.

"I am not!" This was followed by an untimely hiccup.

"You cannot blame him for noticing a beautiful woman, Darcy," defended Lord Hopewell.

"Noticing, no, but commenting crudely and making her uncomfortable, yes."

"She was not uncomfortable!" cried Winters.

Darcy shook his head. "I believe Miss Bennet would disagree with that assessment."

"Darcy, you have little experience with women and would not know how to flirt with a lady if the fate of Pemberley depended on it."

Darcy merely looked heavenward and mentally counted to ten. There was no talking to his cousin. Why would he not go back to his apartments and leave them be? Darcy did not want him around Georgiana, and he really did not want him near Elizabeth. He might scare her away entirely.

"Gentlemen," said Sir Daniel, his sonorous voice filling the room. "Miss Bennet is here to support her sister and meet what will likely become her future family. Let us attempt to make a good impression, shall we?"

"Thank you, Uncle," said Darcy quietly.

Lord Hopewell looked away, a bored expression on his face. Lord Winters was not so easily silenced.

"Is Miss Bennet engaged?" he asked.

"No," Darcy bit out.

Winters waggled his eyebrows. "Then the field is open."

"You do not mean you would truly pursue her?" Darcy cried in frustration. "Do stop being ridiculous!"

Winters straightened his coat and pulled at his lace cuffs. "I might do." He winked at his father.

Darcy grit his teeth. "Miss Bennet is soon to be my sister and as such, you may consider her under my protection. If you harass her, you must deal with me." Darcy turned to his uncle. "And why did you not speak to her at all throughout dinner?"

"These upstarts must be made to understand their place, Darcy. I was doing you a favor," said Lord Hopewell with his nose high in the air. "They must understand they are not to importune us if you continue on this foolish path."

Darcy took in a deep breath and clenched his fists. "Miss Bennet is a gentleman's daughter and a guest in your home. Furthermore, she is a worthy lady in her own right."

Lord Hopewell looked doubtfully at Darcy. "Minor gentry, Darcy. They are hardly of the first circles."

Winters laughed, at what nobody knew, and leaned back in his chair, looking more inebriated than he had when he arrived.

"I will rejoin the ladies," said Darcy in disgust as he passed by his cousin and uncle.

THE LADIES FARED ONLY SLIGHTLY BETTER. Lady Hopewell was clearly enamored of her son, foppish boor though he was, and she insisted on regaling them with stories of his "adventures." Elizabeth rather thought they sounded like stories of a foolish young man with no regard for himself or others, but her ladyship would only see him as a hero.

Lady Clara came and sat next to Elizabeth, sighing heavily.

"He is dreadful, but Mother will not see it. She thinks everything he does is merely the high spirits of youth. He is five and twenty. His spirits must come down some day."

Elizabeth smiled. "My mother says the same of my youngest sister. She is only fifteen and I fear she cares little for rules or anything she deems not enough fun."

"She sounds like Albert. Perhaps we should introduce them?"

"Perhaps," she said with a teasing smile. "They might grow irritated with one another enough to see a reflection of their own behavior."

Lady Clara looked thoughtful for a moment. "I doubt it, but it might be fun to observe."

Elizabeth could not help the laugh that bubbled out of her at that pronouncement.

"I heard you met my cousin in Kent?"

"I did see him most recently in Kent, yes, but I met him the first time in Hertfordshire last autumn. Mr. Bingley rented an estate near my father's and Mr. Darcy was his guest."

Lady Clara nodded. "Did you meet Colonel Fitzwilliam while you were in Kent? He usually travels with Darcy."

"Yes, I did meet him. He is an amiable gentleman," Elizabeth answered with a bright smile.

"Were you in company with him often?"

Elizabeth did not have four sisters for nothing. She could recognize the signs of a lady interested in a gentleman. "Yes, I saw him nearly every day. We became quite good friends."

Lady Clara flushed and looked at her hands. "Oh. He is such good company, he is always attracting attention."

"He is excellent company, that is true. If I had had an elder brother, I would have wanted him to be just like Colonel Fitzwilliam."

Lady Clara looked up with a bright smile and Elizabeth knew she had said the right thing. Why the lady would think Elizabeth was interested romantically in the colonel when she was there as Mr. Darcy's guest she did not know, but sense and infatuation did not always travel together.

"Will you stay in Town for the remainder of the Season?" asked Lady Clara.

"No, I will return to my father's estate in less than a fortnight."

"Do you plan to attend many gatherings with the Fitzwilliam family?"

"I do not know. I imagine I will meet them at some point, and I would like to know Miss Darcy better, but I have no fixed plans at this time. The arrangements are up to Mr. Darcy."

"Of course."

Elizabeth looked to where Jane and Miss Darcy were speaking quietly across the room. She wondered if she should join them, but they seemed to be getting on well and she did not wish to leave Lady Clara on her own. Mrs. Gardiner was speaking to Lady Hopewell and the conversation did not look pleasant. From the few words Elizabeth heard, it sounded like Lady Hopewell was lecturing her aunt on how to behave with such elevated personages as herself. Heaven help them! Was Mr. Darcy's entire family comprised of Lady Catherines?

Elizabeth caught her aunt's eye and smiled gratefully at her. Mrs. Gardiner smiled tightly in return.

"Mother is not all bad," said Lady Clara. "She has a rather high opinion of herself and her title, but when she is in company with people of her own rank, she can be excellent company."

Elizabeth raised a brow, thinking it sounded very like the way Mr. Wickham had described Mr. Darcy when she first knew him—rude to the general masses, but perfectly agreeable when in company of those he considered his equals.

"Oh, I am sorry, Miss Elizabeth!" said Lady Clara. "I meant no disrespect towards you or your aunt." She seemed genuinely distressed as she wrang her hands in her lap and her cheeks flushed in mortification.

"It is all right, Lady Clara." Thinking she would speak about something the lady clearly wished to discuss, Elizabeth said, "How long have you known Colonel Fitzwilliam?"

Lady Clara's face flushed a deeper shade of red. "I met him a few times when we were children, of course, though he was much older than me. When I came out three years ago, I was so very nervous, but Colonel Fitzwilliam was very gallant. He danced with me and put me at ease, and he did not tease me when I took a wrong turn and stepped on his shoe."

Elizabeth was not surprised. She had seen him put Maria at ease in much the same manner, and Mr. Darcy had said he behaved similarly with Georgiana. "I can easily believe it of him. He has a great talent in social situations."

Lady Clara leaned towards her. "I had thought he would come to visit Georgiana, but he has not, not even once."

"He has only just returned from Kent, and he must have many demands on his time."

"Yes, of course." Lady Clara looked to her feet, clearly embarrassed. "Miss Elizabeth, if your schedule permits, would you like to come for tea later this week?"

"I would be delighted, Lady Clara," said Elizabeth with a smile. She did not know how much Lord and Lady Hopewell would like it, but she would not refuse the invitation. "And we would like to see you on Gracechurch Street if you would like to call."

Clara beamed back at her. "Thank you, Miss Elizabeth. I would like that."

It was clear that Lady Clara carried more than a small torch for Colonel Fitzwilliam. He had told Elizabeth he needed to marry with some consideration for money—surely Lady Clara had a large dowry? As the only daughter of an earl, she could hardly be penniless. She was not the most beautiful lady in Town, but she was not entirely plain, and she seemed to have a sweet disposition. Perhaps Elizabeth could help bring them together. She would never be a matchmaker in her own right, but she could assist Lady Clara with her goal if it was within her power. Of course, after this evening, she was not certain how much power she would wield.

Before Elizabeth was able to speak to Miss Darcy, whom she had been hoping to get to know, the gentlemen rejoined them, minus Lord Winters. Darcy came to stand next to Elizabeth, but before he could speak more than a greeting, Lady Hopewell entreated her daughter to play for them. When she finished, Miss Darcy shakily took to the instrument and played a beautiful concerto.

As soon as the applause died down, Mrs. Gardiner thanked Lady Hopewell for a lovely evening and said they must be returning home for they had an early appointment the following morning. Everything proper was said, and soon they were boarding Mr. Darcy's carriage and trundling toward Gracechurch Street, relief the strongest emotion by far.

18

MIDNIGHT CONFESSIONS

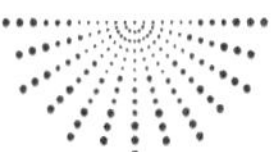

Mr. Darcy insisted on escorting the ladies back to the Gardiners', though they had assured him they did not mind if they went alone and he returned home. After all, they were only two streets away from Darcy House.

He insisted and the carriage was silent, for the ladies wished to speak of the evening but could not do so in front of Mr. Darcy, and that gentleman could not think of anything to say that would not sound as if he were defending his relations' rudeness or make the evening more awkward than it already had been, especially for Miss Jane Bennet.

Elizabeth was a jumble of mixed emotions. She had hoped to make a good impression on Darcy's family, for she thought they would soon be her own and she had no desire to cause discord. She had also wished to show that she would not be treated as the lowest person in the room simply because she was not from a grand family. If she was to take her place as Mrs. Darcy, they must respect her, as Mr. Darcy's choice or on her own merits, but the respect must be given.

This had proven a more difficult line to walk than she had anticipated.

As much as she hated to admit it, she was disappointed in Mr.

Darcy. He had behaved in the haughty manner she had first seen from him—his unwillingness to bend his neck for another's comfort, his absorption with nothing but his own concerns. He could have participated in her conversation with his aunt, or directed it to more appropriate topics, or said something that made his aunt understand she was his choice, and he would not stand for her being treated rudely. He had hardly even met her eyes across the table to show his support!

In short, she had felt abandoned by him. She had received more comfort and support from Sir Daniel, a seventy-year-old man who had been a stranger to her until tonight, than from the man who proclaimed to love her above all others.

Was this what she had to look forward to if she married him? Uncomfortable dinners with unpleasant people, Mr. Darcy silent and uncommunicative, watching the clock to see when they might politely leave? Would they keep company with dissolute people, acceptable because they were wealthy and titled, above her own dear relations? She could not help but remember how Mr. Darcy had slighted her uncle when they first met. She had not thought he valued rank above character, but tonight made her question her presuppositions. Did she wish to tie herself for life to such a man?

It was a disturbing thought, indeed.

"Mrs. Gardiner, might I walk with Miss Elizabeth in the garden? We will not be long."

Darcy's low voice in the entryway startled Elizabeth. Her fingers stopped untying the ribbons on her cloak and she looked to her aunt.

"You may, but do not tarry overlong." Mrs. Gardiner gave Mr. Darcy a hard look, and a more compassionate one to Elizabeth, before following Jane up the stairs.

Jane had not said a word since they left the drawing room at Hopewell House, and Elizabeth knew she was confused and upset at how the evening had gone. If Jane were any less kind, she would have been offended by the earl's behavior. As it was, Elizabeth was offended on her behalf. It stoked her anger anew, and she followed Darcy to the garden with heat in her steps.

"I must apologize for my family," he said simply once they reached the darkness of the garden and the door had closed soundly behind them.

"Oh?"

He ran his hand over his face, then behind his neck. She saw he was greatly agitated, but his distress was nothing to Jane's hurt, and what compassion she had for him was quickly extinguished.

"My uncle was entirely out of line. He should not have behaved as he did towards Miss Bennet. He was rude and insulting. Such behavior should have been beneath him. I will be making my apologies to your sister as well. She did not deserve such treatment. And then my cousin, in his cups..." Darcy sighed and closed his eyes for a moment. "They were utterly unseemly, in every possible way, and I cannot apologize enough. I am ashamed of their behavior."

She nodded, not knowing what to say. She walked further into the garden, occasionally looking up at the stars.

Darcy followed her. "And I am sorry my aunt harangued you so. I knew she would question you, and I imagine you expected it as well, but I had not thought it would be so..." he trailed off, lost for words.

"Thorough? Invasive? Demeaning?"

"Elizabeth," he said brokenly.

"I must admit, I was impressed she could still think of things to ask me in the sixth course. I had thought we might move on to other topics. Fashion, art, our favorite ices at Gunter's. Anything would have done."

He looked at her with such a pathetic expression she nearly relented. Then she remembered how many times she had tried to catch his eye and found him staring over her head.

"You did not have much to say for yourself."

He rubbed the back of his neck again and let his hand drop uselessly to his side. "I did not, and that is another thing for which I must apologize. You know conversation has never been a strength of mine, though I have never lamented it as much as I did tonight. You were right at Rosings when you admonished me to practice. Had I done so, I might have known how to mitigate the disaster taking place around my aunt's table."

Her heart was not so hard that she could ignore such genuine contrition. "Fitzwilliam," she said softly. His gaze met hers so hopefully that she softened a little further. "Why would you not even look at me? I thought you were angry with me, or ashamed of me."

"Of you? Never! I was ashamed, but not of you." He took her hands eagerly in his. "My aunt, though she did not display herself to advantage tonight, is generally a decent, kind woman. Her husband I could not vouch for—he is a difficult man and stuck in his ways, but he is seldom in residence, and she seems to prefer it that way. I had hoped that she would wish to know you, as she is aware of how important you are to me and we have always had a friendly relationship."

She squeezed his hand as he shook his head and looked away.

"She asked me not to interfere in her conversation with you—to allow her to speak to you unaided. When I questioned why she would wish it so, she said if you are to enter our circles, she must know that you can handle the ladies of the Ton. She said if you cannot handle a simple dinner party with my relations, how could you be expected to grace the drawing room at Pemberley. She wished to have a clear view of your character and disposition before agreeing to sponsor you in society. I stupidly gave her my word that I would absent myself from the conversation."

"Why would you agree to such a thing? Did it not sound suspicious to you? And what do you mean, sponsor me?"

"I had thought that if the ladies in my family were friendly with you, it would go some way to easing your entrance into society, and then you would not be lonely when we must be in Town. I had thought their acceptance important." He scoffed and shook his head. "I have been an utter fool! Elizabeth," he said earnestly, bringing her hands to rest on his chest, "please do not lose faith in me. I know tonight was wretched in more ways than I can enumerate, and I know it must have caused you to reconsider whether you wished for a life with me, but I promise you I will never subject you to such again, and

I will do my utmost to step in when anyone attempts to treat you as my aunt has done, regardless of my promise to them." He shook his head at himself. "I should never have made her such a promise!"

He pulled her so close their bodies were touching from knee to chest. He leaned down and rested his forehead on hers. "Please do not break with me, Elizabeth. I could not bear it."

She took a shuddering breath. "Very well, Fitzwilliam."

She could think of nothing more to say, and it was not the time to discuss how to avoid such situations in future, nor could she say that it was forgotten, for Jane's hurt, embarrassed face would not leave her mind.

They stood thus for several minutes, until the chill began to seep through her cloak.

"One good thing has come of this evening," said Darcy unexpectedly.

"What is that?"

"I got to see you looking so incredibly lovely. Is that a new gown?"

"Yes. I feel quite decadent in it," she replied with a smile.

"You look decadent in it," he said with such a look that an entire flock of butterflies set loose in her stomach.

She swallowed heavily. "Thank you, Mr. Darcy."

They walked back to the house in silence, and then Mr. Darcy left with a kiss to her hand and a lingering look.

Upstairs, Elizabeth prepared for bed as quietly as she could and dismissed the maid, then tiptoed into Jane's room through the inner door connecting their chambers. Her sister was curled on the bed and Elizabeth thought she was sleeping until Jane spoke.

"Don't stand in the door, Lizzy. Come here."

Elizabeth curled up in the bed beside her sister. "Tell me truthfully: what do you think of Mr. Darcy's family?"

Jane was silent for so long Elizabeth was afraid she had fallen asleep.

Finally, Jane said, "Lady Clara was kind to me."

"And Lady Hopewell?"

"She was very inquisitive."

Elizabeth laughed darkly. "Only you would say such a thing, Jane."

"I did not speak to him much, but Sir Daniel seemed a courteous sort of man. He was certainly taken with you."

"I do not know about that, but I think we liked on another well enough. He reminds me of Father in some ways."

"Oh?"

"Yes. He has no great esteem for titles or the rich, it seems, and he is terribly intelligent. I could have asked him questions all evening and been happy to listen to his answers to the exclusion of all else."

"That is certainly a good basis for a friendship."

"He said he wished to introduce me to his daughter, Lady High-tower. She is a viscountess, but he loves her anyway."

Jane laughed. "What an odd thing to say!"

Elizabeth shrugged. "He is an odd man, I think, but I rather liked him."

"I am glad there was someone you got on with this evening."

Elizabeth nearly teased her sister about finally saying something bordering on rude, but she was too tired to tease and squeezed Jane's hand instead.

"Yes, I am as well. I hope his daughter is as open-minded and kind as he is. It would be good to have a friend in Town. I would hate to go to parties and balls and have no one to talk to. I had not thought about that before," she added in a small voice.

Jane sat up and wrapped her arm around her younger sister. "Are you worried you will be friendless as Mr. Darcy's wife?"

"I shall not be, for you will marry Mr. Bingley and we shall be together always."

Jane looked down. "He has made no declaration, Lizzy."

"He will. He only wants time."

Jane looked toward the window, a worried expression on her face.

"Jane, you do know that Mr. Bingley is giving you time for your sake and not his own, do you not?"

Jane whipped her head around to look at her sister. "What do you mean?"

"Mr. Bingley knows he did you a great wrong when he left Hertfordshire last November. He wishes you to trust him again, and he knows that is something that can only grow with time."

"How do you know this? Has Mr. Darcy said something?"

"He has said that Mr. Bingley was miserable all winter without you, and that he moped about parties and the club like a boy who had lost his closest friend."

"Did he really?" Jane asked, her eyes bright.

"Jane Bennet! If I did not know better, I would say you are glad Mr. Bingley was so wretched without you!"

Jane looked down again and plucked at the coverlet. "I cannot be glad that Mr. Bingley was in depressed spirits, but I will admit that I am glad I was not the only one in such a position. Is that awful of me?"

Elizabeth squeezed Jane's shoulders. "No! Your feelings are natural and just. Misery loves company, you know."

Jane pushed her shoulder into her sister's. "Lizzy! That is uncharitable."

"Yes, Jane, I know. But I learned long ago that I will never be as sweet as you, so I may as well be as mischievous as myself."

Jane smiled and shook her head. "I hope you never change, Lizzy. No matter who you marry, or how you live, I hope you are always as lively and wonderful as you are now."

"I do believe I am flattered!"

Jane rolled her eyes and elbowed her sister.

"No, Jane, you know I will tease when I should be serious, but I do thank you. Yours is the most important opinion in the world to me."

"What about Mr. Darcy?"

"What about him?"

"Do you not care for his good opinion?"

"Of course I do!" She hesitated. "Well, *now* I do."

"More than my own?"

"No. Why do you ask?" asked Elizabeth suspiciously.

"A day will come when his opinion will be the most important to you—above my own, even above Father's. That is when you should accept him, Lizzy. But not before."

Elizabeth looked at her sister in surprise. "When did you become so wise, Jane?"

"I am not wise, merely older and more experienced than you," she teased.

Elizabeth smiled. "I will heed your advice, for it is sound. Is Mr. Bingley's the most important opinion to you?"

"It was."

Elizabeth looked at her sister in the moonlight, trying to understand what she saw there. "If you cannot forgive him, Jane, it is all right. If you cannot trust Mr. Bingley again, you may live with me and Mr. Darcy all your days. I would be happy to have you. I'm sure Fitzwilliam would agree. He rather likes you, you know. You are his favorite of all my sisters."

Jane gave her a look that conveyed that was not much of a compliment and said, "I thank you for the offer, Lizzy, but I have forgiven Mr. Bingley. Truly, there was not much to forgive. But I have wondered if I am being foolish."

"What do you mean?"

"Mr. Bingley's sisters do not like me. Or they do not like me as a wife for their brother. They will likely not be welcoming even were we to wed. I can hope for civility, but not much more. What would our life be like? You saw how the earl treated me this evening. He did not even look at me! I would hate to feel that way in my own husband's family."

"It might be better if Miss Bingley did not notice you."

"Do be serious, Lizzy!"

"Very well. I understand what you are saying, and I agree it is not an ideal situation. You will simply have to tell Mr. Bingley that his sisters must treat you with respect or you do not wish to be around them. Surely he would not stand for any mistreatment of you."

"Would he not?"

Elizabeth looked at Jane as if seeing her for the first time. "I think we have both changed very much since last winter," she said slowly.

Jane could only nod, her eyes glassy in the moonlight. "I have learned a great deal. Some things I will admit I did not wish to know, but I cannot remain innocent forever. The world is full of those who will be cruel for the most ridiculous of reasons. I wish it were not so, but I cannot ignore it any longer."

Elizabeth squeezed her shoulders again. "I am sorry it has come to this, Jane. But at least now you can decide what you wish to do about Mr. Bingley with your eyes fully open to his character and situation."

Jane nodded.

"I do not think he travels in very exalted circles. He has not even met most of Mr. Darcy's family, if that is any consolation."

"Oh, Lizzy! I am being selfish. You must be so upset about Mr. Darcy's relations. Was Lady Hopewell very awful? Every time I looked toward you, she seemed to be holding an inquisition!"

"She was not gentle, but neither was she more than I could handle. Do not misunderstand me—I did not enjoy the evening, and I am in no hurry to repeat it anytime soon, but it was manageable."

"Poor Mr. Darcy. He must be so embarrassed."

"Yes," said Elizabeth quietly. "I believe he was."

Elizabeth lay back beside her sister, wondering if she and Mr. Darcy might have just levelled the disparity between them.

Darcy sat in his private sitting room, a warm robe around his nightshirt and a brandy in his hand. He stared at the flames, wondering how on earth he had gotten into this situation. He had thought he was offering Elizabeth all the advantages in their union. He would elevate her station, enrich her situation, and increase her consequence. She would go from a maiden to a wife; from an insignificant family to one of the oldest in England; from a confined country neighborhood to his exalted society.

What a fool he had been!

He had never considered, not even for a moment, that the transition would be uncommonly difficult for her, and that the advantages might not be worth the effort. Seeing how his family treated her, he could not in good conscience blame her if she chose to end their courtship. He would certainly not wish to deal with all that she would have to manage in the coming months.

Yet he had begged her not to break with him, to give him a chance to prove he was worth all the trouble he was putting her through. He must now prove himself worthy of the faith she was placing in him.

He had realized he was in trouble before they left his aunt's home. The look on Mrs. Gardiner's face—utterly unimpressed with his grand family and their atrocious manners, and Miss Bennet's wounded feelings had alerted him to the danger he was in. But nothing was as frightening as the utter indifference he saw in Elizabeth's eyes when she looked at him. They had begun the evening with smiles and affectionate glances. By the time they entered the carriage to depart, she had looked as if she did not care whether or not she ever saw him again.

It had scared him more than he liked to admit.

"How was dinner with the Hopewells?"

Darcy jumped forward so quickly his brandy sloshed out of the glass. "Fitz! What are you doing here?"

"Forgive me for startling you. I did knock, but there was no answer and I thought you may have fallen asleep before blowing out your candles again."

Darcy rolled his eyes. "That was one time, and I was eleven."

Fitz shrugged. "Fire is no laughing matter, Cousin."

Darcy sat back in his seat and took a sip of his brandy. "Dinner was a disaster."

"Truly? Was Winters a boor?"

"Worse. He arrived two hours late and in his cups, then proceeded to make a cake of himself flirting with Miss Bennet. She practically ran out of the room when the ladies withdrew."

Fitzwilliam winced. "Did Lord Hopewell not intervene?"

Darcy laughed cynically. "He was even worse! Miss Bennet was seated on his left and he did not speak a word to her the entire evening."

"Truly?"

"Not one word."

"They ate in silence?"

"Through seven courses."

Fitzwilliam grimaced. "Miss Bennet must be terribly offended."

"I am sure she would be if she thought about herself at all, but I am afraid she is the kind to take things too much on herself. She will be upset she did not manage the situation better."

"I cannot imagine what that's like," said Fitzwilliam with a pointed look to his cousin.

"I am not like Miss Bennet!"

"Not at first glance, I grant you, but you must admit there are similarities."

Darcy looked at him skeptically. "How so?"

"You are both reserved and prefer to keep your feelings to yourself. You both prefer to listen rather than speak, and you both rely on your more verbose relations in social situations. You take responsibility for things no other person would dream of claiming, and you are both drawn to lively, cheerful personalities. Need I go on?"

Darcy sat staring at his cousin, shock all over his face. Was he truly so much like Miss Bennet? It would certainly explain why Elizabeth seemed to understand him so well, and why Bingley felt so comfortable with Miss Bennet, but it painted him in a less favorable light. If Miss Bennet was as reserved as he himself was, she would feel more than she showed. Significantly more. Which meant that when he separated Bingley from her, he had broken her heart. Aghast, he looked up into the shrewd eyes of his cousin.

"Stop right there, Darcy. I can see you taking on more responsibility as you sit there."

Darcy glared at him. "I am doing no such thing."

"No? You are not heaping an extra helping of blame on yourself for your role in separating Bingley from Miss Jane Bennet?"

Darcy opened his mouth, then closed it with a snap.

"I thought so."

"How do you know so much about Miss Bennet, anyhow? You only met her two days ago."

"Miss Elizabeth told me."

Darcy's eyes widened at this.

"And if you ever listened to Bingley when he is waxing on about his angel instead of composing letters in your mind, you would know a great deal more about the lady."

Darcy looked away and exhaled heavily. His cousin was right, but he did not have to like it.

"Come now, do not sulk," chided Fitzwilliam.

"I am not sulking."

"Of course not. You are merely sitting sullenly in your banyan, drinking brandy, and staring into the fire."

Darcy glared at him. "You were not there, Fitz. You did not see how awful it was."

Colonel Fitzwilliam softened his voice and looked at his cousin with compassion. "What shall you do to remedy the situation?"

"For starters, I will apologize to the ladies. Aunt was terribly rude to Mrs. Gardiner on top of the inquisition she levelled at Elizabeth."

Fitzwilliam shook his head. "Did no one acquit themselves well?"

"Sir Daniel was kind to Elizabeth. She seems to have won him over."

"That is not surprising. More than anyone else in the family, he values character over connections."

"Yes. And Lady Clara was welcoming to both Miss Bennet and Elizabeth, but I do not know if it will be enough to counteract the rudeness of her parents and brother."

Fitzwilliam grimaced. "You have an uphill climb, that is certain."

"Might your family receive them better, do you think?"

"I cannot say. I would normally say yes, but then I would have thought Lady Hopewell would behave better towards the lady you hope to wed."

"I had thought so, too." He pinched the bridge of his nose and closed his eyes against the approaching headache. "I have never been so ashamed of my family in my life."

Fitzwilliam smiled sadly. "I am sorry, Cousin. How did you leave it with Elizabeth?"

"Begging her not to break with me."

Fitzwilliam spluttered on his brandy. "Truly?"

Darcy levelled serious eyes at him. "I am in earnest."

Fitzwilliam sank back into his chair. "I am sorry, Darcy."

Darcy pinched his nose again. "As am I, Fitz."

They drank together in silence until Darcy shook himself a little and said, "Enough of this. Let us speak of something else. Is your mother still throwing ladies at you like a cricket bowler?"

Fitzwilliam chuckled darkly. "Yes. I do wish she would stop. Harry should wed before me—he is four years older and has a house."

"That your parents gifted him last year. I had thought it might be because he had found someone he wished to wed, but no announcement has been forthcoming."

"No, Harry has proven even more reluctant to wed than I am. I had thought he might settle down last autumn, but the lady he was paying attention to went back to the country and he has said nothing more about it. But we have never been particularly close. I do not expect him to confide such things to me."

"Would it be so terrible if he never wed? Timothy is married and his wife is fecund, and your father has two other younger sons to inherit if needed. It is hardly necessary for Harry to continue the line."

"True, but you know Mother has always had a soft spot for him. She would like to see grandchildren before she is much older."

"She has five grandchildren and another due in summer!"

"Ah, but they are not Harry's children," replied Fitzwilliam with a knowing smile.

Darcy rolled his eyes. "I will never understand my aunts. Your mother has Timothy and Judith's children to dote on, yet she will not be happy until Harry has his own. Lady Clara is a perfectly good daughter, doing just as she ought, but Lady Hopewell does nothing but criticize her while letting Winters get away with anything and everything."

"Impossible women."

Darcy stared darkly into his brandy. "I am thinking of speaking to your mother tomorrow."

"Oh?"

"I want to ask her to be kind to Elizabeth. If she cannot do that, I think it best if we forego introductions until we are wed."

Fitzwilliam sat up straighter. "Truly? Mother will be furious if you hide your bride from her."

"I will be furious if I lose the woman I love to my family's bad manners."

Fitzwilliam winced. "Do you really think Elizabeth would break with you over such a thing?"

"She does not love me, Fitz."

His cousin's brows shot up at the easy admission.

"She has been nothing but honest with me from the beginning. She wishes to progress slowly so that she could come to know me and care for me. She does not wish for a marriage without affection."

"You are in love with her. That is the opposite of without affection."

"I know that, but I can hardly complain when she says she hopes to fall in love with me."

Fitzwilliam nodded. "That is hard to argue with."

"But she is not in love with me yet, and my family treating her like a milkmaid who wandered into the house will hardly encourage her."

Fitzwilliam stifled a laugh. He knew it was not funny, not truly, but his cousin was so rarely out of sorts, it was somewhat amusing. "I will put in a good word with my parents."

"Thank you, Fitz." Darcy leaned back into his chair and rubbed his forehead tiredly. "Whatever happened to the lady you were so enamored of? What was her name? Miss Corning? Cartwright?"

"Emma Covington." Fitzwilliam took a large swallow of his brandy.

"Yes, Miss Covington. Whatever happened to her? You seemed quite mad about her."

"That was nearly two years ago, Darcy. Much has changed." Fitzwilliam's voice lowered and his expression darkened.

Darcy's curiosity was piqued. "What has changed? Did the lady marry and I did not hear of it?"

"No, nothing like that." Fitzwilliam stared at the fire, then finally turned back to face his cousin. "Her father invested unwisely. When he realized the investment was failing, he attempted to gamble his way out."

"Oh, Fitz," Darcy said compassionately. Financial ruin was one of the worst things that could happen to a family. He would not wish it on anyone. "Is all lost then?"

"The estate was not entailed, so they were able to sell it and recoup their losses. Her father died not a month afterward—he could not stand the shame of it."

"I can imagine."

"Her brother has let out the house in Town and they have been staying with Mrs. Partridge, their mother's sister."

"Is their mother still alive?"

"Yes, but she rarely goes out and has not been seen in some time. It is hardly surprising."

"It was only Miss Covington and her brother, was it not?"

"Yes, thankfully. As I understand it, the sale of their home was enough to recoup some of the mother's settlement and Miss Covington's dowry, but nowhere near all."

"Do you know what her dowry is now?"

"I had heard it was near ten thousand pounds, but I am not certain."

"That is not insignificant."

"No, but hardly enough to live on if one were to have a family."

"It would not be easy, but with some assistance from your father, and your pay—"

"Darcy, Miss Bennet has turned you into a romantic! If we had had this conversation three months ago, you would have told me it was an unlucky turn and that I would find another lady I could tolerate enough to marry."

Darcy looked at him with a wry grin. "I know. I have changed my tune rather spectacularly, have I not?"

Fitzwilliam chuckled. "That is a gross understatement. Father will not recognize you."

"I hardly think that!"

"Think what you will, but you do smile an inordinate amount these days."

"Elizabeth makes me happy," he shrugged nonchalantly.

Fitzwilliam sighed. "May we all be so lucky, Cousin."

Darcy looked at him with sympathy. "Is there no way to make it work with Miss Covington?"

"You know my situation. Unlike you, I am dependent on my father's approval for my future prospects."

"I thought your father had decided to settle some property on you."

"He has. But it is not without conditions."

"Ah."

"Exactly."

"He would not approve of Miss Covington? She was acceptable two years ago. Has she not maintained some connections?"

"I am sure she has, but Father is notoriously difficult to please, you know that."

"Surely he would not withhold your birthright if you wished to marry," said Darcy.

"If I married a woman he approved of, he would not. The irony, of course, if that if I married an heiress, I would not need my legacy."

"That is ludicrous! Lord Blackburn's investments are doing well, his eldest son is not a spendthrift or a gambler, and the harvest has been strong several years in a row now. He could well afford to give you a small estate in Staffordshire."

"Unfortunately, what he *can* afford and what he *will* afford are two different things."

Darcy shook his head. "If there is anything I can do, promise you will tell me."

"I promise, but I doubt there is much you can do besides convince Father I have not lost my head entirely."

19

WHAT IS IT ABOUT THURSDAYS?

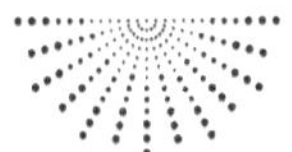

Mrs. Gardiner came to Elizabeth's room the next morning as she was putting up her hair.

"I would speak to you, my dear."

"Yes, Aunt?"

"I assume you have spoken to Jane?"

Elizabeth sighed. "Yes. She is in low spirits, but she will recover. Mr. Darcy is embarrassed and has said he will apologize to Jane himself."

"Lizzy, I do not wish to overstep my place, but I must caution you. Indeed, I would be remiss if I did not. Many in the upper circles are accustomed to behaving however they please, regardless of who they hurt in the process. I know Mr. Darcy is a fine match, and he may be all that is worthy himself—"

"He is, Aunt," interrupted Elizabeth.

Mrs. Gardiner looked at her sympathetically. "I am sure you are right. But he cannot be divorced from his situation any more than you can. As much as I hate to say it, what occurred last evening was not so very unusual."

Elizabeth's eyes widened.

"Perhaps it was odd that a guest in the earl's own home was treated so infamously, but the upper classes have long been in the habit of doing exactly what they wish, whenever they wish it. If you are to enter these circles, you will see this for yourself. Jane will as well if she marries Mr. Bingley, though perhaps to a lesser extent due to Mr. Bingley's lower status."

"Have you experienced such things yourself, Aunt?"

"I have sat on committees with wealthy ladies and been ignored as if I were not even in the room. I have been talked over and cut in front of at the haberdasher's and the modiste, because I could not possibly be as important as a grand lady. You saw this behavior in Miss Bingley last autumn. She is not the rule, but neither is she the exception."

Elizabeth was awash in confusion. "Are you suggesting I not marry Mr. Darcy? Only a few days ago you were saying what a fine thing it was to be courted by him!"

Mrs. Gardiner sighed. "I did indeed say that, when I believed Mr. Darcy had his family's approval and would not stand for any disparagement if he did not. But if last night was indicative of how his family would behave in the future, and how Mr. Darcy will react to it, I do not want to think about how society at large will treat you. If his family does not support the match, it may cause a great many difficulties for you as his wife as well as a rift in his family. I would not want him to come to resent you for that."

"What are you saying, Aunt?"

"I'm saying that you must consider very carefully what you want your life to look like going forward. Could you live with a husband who stood idly by while his family insulted your sisters and interrogated you? Do you want to have relations who suffer your presence with ill-concealed disdain and expect you to be grateful for it?

"Mr. Darcy lives in a very different world from that which you have grown up in. There will be many advantages to your elevation in society, but there will also be complications and troubles, and this is one of those. In Hertfordshire, you were a daughter of one of the most prominent families. Your name and rank protected you and gave you respect wherever you were known. If you move into Mr. Darcy's sphere, you will join his world, and while the Darcy name is respected, it is not titled and there are wealthier and certainly more self-important people who inhabit it. You must prepare yourself for what you may face."

"Surely not all of the ton is like Lord and Lady Hopewell!"

"They are not, but enough of them are that you will likely face a difficult road, especially if Mr. Darcy's family does not support your union. It will be particularly hard if Mr. Darcy allows what happened last night to continue. I would not be acting in your best interests if I did not caution you to consider very carefully what you would be committing yourself to if you were to accept Mr. Darcy."

"Would there not be a great scandal if I were to break with Mr. Darcy? It is well enough known that we are courting."

"I cannot lie to you, there may be a scandal. Some would say you were mad to let such a wonderful catch get away, others would believe he found you wanting and escaped while he could. There may be no scandal at all. But you know you are always welcome with us, and if you would like, your uncle might introduce you to some eligible business acquaintances of his. Some of them are quite genteel, and you might like the busy life of the wife of a tradesman."

Elizabeth was reeling. Give up Mr. Darcy! She had thought about it the night before, when he was so distant, but now that she was faced with the thought in the cold light of day, discussing it with her aunt as if it were as clear cut a decision as which gown to wear to dinner, she felt as if there was not enough air in the room.

"Breathe, my dear. Shh."

Her aunt's voice came from her side where Mrs. Gardiner stood rubbing her back in slow, soothing circles. She felt a strange sensation on her cheek and reached up only to find her fingers came away wet. She was crying. When had that happened?

"Lizzy," said Mrs. Gardiner carefully, "are you in love with Mr. Darcy?"

Elizabeth looked at her with a lost expression. "I do not know, Aunt. Can one go from hating a man to loving him in a fortnight? It is not logical!"

"Love seldom is, my dear."

~

AN HOUR LATER, they were seated at a late breakfast when a footman brought in a large bouquet of flowers, all light shades of pink and blue and white. It was very delicate and sweet looking, and Jane smiled happily when it was announced that they were for her. She plucked the card from the top and frowned.

"They are from Mr. Darcy."

"Mr. Darcy? Are they not for Lizzy?" asked Mrs. Gardiner.

"He is apologizing for his relations."

Jane passed the card to Elizabeth, who read it aloud.

DEAR MISS BENNET,

I CANNOT APOLOGIZE ENOUGH for the behavior of my uncle and then my cousin last evening. Their actions were unacceptable and I will do my utmost to see that you are never put in such a situation again.

You were graciousness itself last evening, and I know you only endured them in the hope of your sister's acceptance by my family. I thank you for bearing such rudeness for our sake, but please believe me when I say it is not necessary that you do so, now or in the future. If someone had treated Georgiana in such a way, I would have been appalled.

I know you have no brother of your own, so I offer myself humbly to that position. Should you ever have need of a champion, I would be honored to assist you in whatever way I may.

YOURS WITH GRATITUDE,
  Fitzwilliam Darcy

"WELL!" cried Mrs. Gardiner. "The man can certainly apologize!"

The footman entered with a potted purple hyacinth for Mrs. Gardiner.

Her brows immediately raised, knowing the flower to be a symbol of contrition and a request for forgiveness. The note for her was more succinct, but the apology was sincere, and Mrs. Gardiner felt a trifle guilty for encouraging her niece away from such a suitor.

Elizabeth received a smaller bouquet of pink roses, signaling gentle, hopeful love, and appreciation for the recipient, or so her aunt explained, in addition to a larger wrapped parcel. Everyone looked to Elizabeth with expectant eyes when it was set before her.

"Open it, Lizzy!" cried Jane.

Elizabeth pulled back the strings and lifted the top from the box. Inside was an intricately patterned shawl, a combination of colors in reds, corals, and pinks, with a light fringe around the edge.

"How exquisite! Is it made in India? It certainly looks it," said Mrs. Gardiner.

Elizabeth picked up the card and read silently while her aunt and sister opened the shawl and examined it more fully.

My dearest Elizabeth,

I hope this morning finds you rested and restored from last night's exertions. I do not intend to revisit unpleasant events, but I know it was not enjoyable for you, and I hope this token offers some consolation and further evidence of my contrition.

I thought you might prefer not to see me today, so I do not intend to call, but if I am wrong, and you would like a visit, please send word and I will be with you in a trice.

I would like to take you for a drive in the curricle tomorrow or the day after, if you and the weather are amenable. Bingley has suggested we take a drive together to Kew Gardens and make a day of it. I do not know if your aunt would approve such an excursion, but I second his idea if you would enjoy the outing.

I hope you are well, dearest. Know that you are in my thoughts and ever present in my heart. I remain yours,

 FD

"Is the man who delivered the packages still here?" she asked the footman.

"Yes, miss. He is watering his horse in the mews."

"Could you please ask him to wait and take a response to Mr. Darcy?"

"Feeling any better this morning, Darcy?" Colonel Fitzwilliam asked when he joined his cousin at the breakfast table.

"Much, thank you. I have sent a message to your mother. She will receive me in an hour. Will you accompany me?"

"Of course. Do you have a plan?"

"I shall tell her an abridged version of last night's events and throw myself on her mercy."

"You are becoming desperate!"

"Not desperate, Fitz. Determined. Half measures will not do."

"Very well, I will assist as I may. But do not be surprised if Mother thinks you are half mad."

"I will take my chances."

Blackburn House was around the corner from Darcy's townhouse, so the men elected to walk. Darcy handed his hat to the footman at the door and took a deep breath.

"Once more unto the breach, Cousin," whispered Colonel Fitzwilliam over his shoulder.

Darcy glared at him and followed the servant to his aunt's favorite parlor at the back of the house. He thought it was a good sign that he was being received so informally.

"Darcy! And Richard! What a pleasant surprise." She turned her cheek towards her son to receive a kiss and gestured for them to sit on the sofa directly across from her. "What has prompted this call, Darcy? Is Georgiana well?"

"Yes, she is, thank you. She is looking forward to returning next week."

Lady Blackburn nodded as if she were completely unsurprised by this information. Who would not want to stay at her house? It was magnificent.

"I wished to speak to you on another matter."

"Oh?"

Darcy shifted in his seat. "Yes. I have recently entered into a courtship with Miss Elizabeth Bennet."

"Miss Bennet? Do I know her?" Lady Blackburn had heard a rumor that her nephew had been seen with a young lady, but she had refused to believe it.

"I do not believe so. Her father owns an estate in Hertfordshire. I met her last autumn when I was visiting my friend Bingley nearby."

"I see." Lady Blackburn was not a fan of the Bingleys. Charles Bingley was a nice enough young man, but he was young and green still, and Miss Bingley was positively horrid. He had another sister who had done relatively well for herself in marriage, but both she and her husband were such dreadful bores that any gains they had made in fortune or status were mitigated by their awful personalities.

"We attended dinner last evening at Hopewell House."

Lady Blackburn's chin tilted fractionally higher.

"The dinner was not a success."

Now her brow raised to mirror her chin. Darcy gritted his teeth as he composed responses to all the statements his aunt was not speaking aloud.

"We had hoped that you might make a better emissary for Miss Elizabeth than Lady Hopewell," said Colonel Fitzwilliam.

Darcy looked at his cousin gratefully, then turned back to his aunt.

"Just so, Aunt. If I may be frank," she nodded her permission and he continued, "last night's dinner did not show the family to advantage. I care very deeply for Miss Bennet, and I would not want to lose her over such a thing."

Lady Blackburn's eyebrows were near her hairline now, but still, she said nothing.

"If you can see your way to coming to know her and support her, I would be very grateful."

"I can assure you, Mother, that Miss Elizabeth is an excellent choice for Darcy. She is witty, well-read, and lively by nature. She is also young and pretty and in excellent health."

Darcy glared at his cousin. Elizabeth was not a mare at Tattersall's!

"Most importantly," continued Fitzwilliam, "she will keep Darcy interested and on his best behavior. Truly, she has worked wonders on him already."

Darcy made a face at his cousin. It was true that Miss Elizabeth had had a softening effect on his nature and he certainly felt she was making him a better man, but he did not like to hear himself spoken of as if he were a dog being trained.

"I think if you came to know her, you would like her on her own merits," added Darcy.

Lady Blackburn held up her hand to silence the gentlemen. "Boys, I think you had better tell me everything."

Darcy and Fitzwilliam looked at each other, then they launched into the story of how they had come to this point. Darcy told her how he had met Miss Bennet in Hertfordshire and rather inconveniently insulted her before falling in love with her. He had tried to forget her, failed, and then met her again in Kent. Fitzwilliam told his mother how Darcy had been stupidly silent in front of Miss Bennet for how nervous she made him, and then how he had come to respect the lady on his own and consider her a friend.

Darcy explained that his reasons for hesitating had been her unruly younger sisters, vulgar mother, and lack of connections, but now that he knew the Gardiners, he knew they were worthy, genteel people—and rather financially successful—and in comparison to his own family, Mrs. Bennet and Lydia seemed rather mild. The eldest Miss Bennet was likely to be engaged to Bingley soon, and with improved connections, it was probable the other sisters would marry and not become a burden on Darcy's coffers.

He held nothing back, explaining how Elizabeth had requested time during their courtship and how he was determined to give it to her, and how he was impressed by her integrity. He told her how awful his family had behaved at dinner the night before, and how worried he was that it would make Elizabeth rethink the idea of marrying him altogether.

Lady Blackburn listened attentively throughout, silently shocked that Darcy—Darcy!—would be so enamored of a woman he would risk his entire family for her. She had to admit that she was impressed that Miss Bennet had not immediately encouraged her nephew to propose, and it showed wisdom that the young lady recognized that this life may not be the most likely to make her happy.

But she could not like that her family would be what cost Darcy his greatest desire, nor that Miss Bennet might decide against him, rather than the other way around. She liked to consider herself a modern woman with a broad view of the world, but she was still a product of her environment, and the idea of a young country miss throwing over *her* nephew did not sit well.

On the other hand, she knew the Darcy family enough to know that Lord Hopewell was a snob of the first water, and his son was utterly useless. She and Lady Hopewell had been friendly when they were younger, and they were social acquaintances often included on one another's guest lists, but she would not have called her a friend. No, she was too much in competition with Lady Hopewell to be her friend, though her nephew and son did not know that. They likely only saw two women who spoke to each other with smiles and compliments and assumed they must be friends.

Lady Blackburn shook her head. Men would never understand how female friendships worked.

"I must meet this Miss Bennet for myself," she declared.

Darcy sat up, anxiety writ on his features. "Are you certain, Aunt?"

"I am. Do you think she is available today?"

Darcy turned to his cousin, then back towards his aunt, opening and closing his mouth twice before saying, "I will ask her, my lady."

"Very good. Find out if she can receive me at two o'clock today and we will make the call."

"Aunt, I mean no disrespect, but I can only introduce you to Elizabeth if you are planning to be kind to her. I cannot have a repeat of last night's performance. I simply cannot."

"Of course, Darcy. What do you take me for?" She smiled and rose, signaling an end to their interview. "When you have your answer, send me an address and I will meet you at Miss Bennet's uncle's home."

"I would be happy to escort you, Mother."

"Very well, but you must leave with Darcy for I will attend Lady Mayberry afterward."

Darcy and Fitzwilliam thanked her and bowed, then swiftly walked back to Darcy House.

"Well that was unusual," said Fitzwilliam.

"I am surprised she agreed to it. Do you think it will work?"

"Do you mean will she convince Miss Bennet your entire family is not determined to chase her off?"

Darcy nodded.

"I can only hope so."

There was a note awaiting Darcy when he stepped into his house. "Thank you, Parker. Were the flowers well received?"

"I believe so, sir. The maids were going on about how happy the ladies were."

"Wonderful. Thank you, that will be all."

Darcy led the way to his favorite sitting room overlooking the garden and opened his note.

FITZWILLIAM,

. . .

It is sweet of you to offer to stay away while I regain my equilibrium, and likely wise as well, but I find that I am already missing you. It is terribly ungentlemanly of you to cause such feelings in a lady and not assuage them, so I must ask you to wait on me at your earliest convenience. I have offered to walk in the park with my cousins. I would be happy for you to join us if you like.

Thank you for the flowers—they are lovely and smell delightful. My aunt and sister send their thanks as well. The shawl is particularly pretty. If you join me at the park today, you shall see me wearing it.

I hope to see you soon.

Yours,

Elizabeth

DARCY FOLDED the letter and put it in his breast pocket with a smile. "Care for a walk in the park, Fitz?"

ELIZABETH WAS HIDING behind a large oak tree, one hand over her eyes as she counted aloud. The breeze caught on her shawl and raised the fringe up to tickle her skin. She raised her voice as she came to the last three numbers, then shouted, "Here I come!"

The Gardiners' nurse sat on a nearby bench with eighteen-month-old Sarah Gardiner on her lap, but the three older children were nowhere to be seen. The nurse gestured towards a copse of trees a few yards away and Elizabeth nodded and made her way thither. She studied the trees, looking for the flutter of a skirt or the bright blue of her cousin's jacket. Seeing something behind a small tree, she picked her way to it and was nearly close enough to reach out and tag young John when she stepped on a twig and the snap echoed off the trees.

John took off like a shot, running for the oak they had deemed as home base, and Elizabeth tore after him. He ran across the small meadow, darting around his nurse on the bench, and up the short hill toward the tree. Elizabeth knew his destination and cut him off just before he reached the tree, grabbing his arm in her outstretched hand. The motion made young John spin around until he smacked into Elizabeth and the two of them fell to the ground in a heap. They panted for breath between gasping laughs, until John yelled for his brother and sister to come out of hiding, for he had been caught.

Elizabeth smiled and closed her eyes, enjoying the feeling of the grass along her back and the sunshine on her face.

"You certainly look comfortable."

Elizabeth's eyes flew open to behold Mr. Darcy and Colonel Fitzwilliam standing over her, smirking. John scrambled up and ran to join his brother near the pond. Elizabeth shook her head and held her hand up to Mr. Darcy.

"Be a gentleman and help me up."

He grasped her hand with a smile and pulled her up so forcefully she smacked into his chest and said, "Oh!"

Fitzwilliam rolled his eyes. "Let her go, Darcy. We are in a public park."

Darcy smiled and released her. "No one is here to see us. It is only children and their nurses out today."

"That is precisely why I chose this time to come out. Parks are for being enjoyed, not strolling around like peacocks," said Elizabeth as she brushed the grass off her skirt.

"I must confess I did not know you could run so fast, Miss Elizabeth," said Fitzwilliam.

"Oh, I am very fleet of foot, Colonel. I shall have to race you sometime."

"I will take you up on that," he replied.

They turned towards the pond and Darcy offered Elizabeth his arm. She took it with a smile, then playfully took Colonel Fitzwilliam's arm with her other hand.

"Pardon me for saying so, gentlemen, but you have the look of mischievous boys about you. Dare I ask what you have been getting up to this morning?"

The men caught each other's eyes over her head, and Colonel Fitzwilliam said, "We visited my mother, actually."

"Oh? Is she well?"

"Very well. In fact, she would like to meet you this afternoon if you are amenable."

Elizabeth's eyes widened and she looked towards Mr. Darcy.

"You do not have to meet her if you would prefer not to, Elizabeth. But she would like to know you."

"My mother is powerful in her own way, but she is a kind woman, and she is fond of Darcy."

Elizabeth understood they were saying Lady Blackburn would not antagonize her, but she was unsure if she should meet her today.

"Are you asking me to accompany you to call on her?"

"She wished to call on you and your aunt, if you are home to callers."

"I see." She thought for a moment, then looked from one to the other before saying, "Very well. I will ask my aunt."

They rounded up the children and made their way back to Gracechurch Street, where Elizabeth quickly closeted herself with her aunt. Jane was visiting a neighbor, but they decided she would likely be back in time to receive her ladyship.

"I can only assume this is some sort of test," said Mrs. Gardiner.

"I thought so as well, but Colonel Fitzwilliam assures me his mother is fond of Mr. Darcy and genuinely wants to know me."

Mrs. Gardiner looked skeptical. "I hope he is right."

They told the gentlemen they would receive Lady Blackburn that afternoon, and Colonel Fitzwilliam left to deliver the message to his mother and escort her to Gracechurch Street.

Elizabeth could only hope the meeting would go well. She had thought the name Blackburn sounded menacing when she heard it, but then Lord and Lady Hopewell had a lovely name and had turned out to be un-lovely people, so perhaps Lady Blackburn would be the opposite of her name as well. One could hope.

Lady Blackburn came to Gracechurch Street with all the pomp and circumstance of a countess in a crested coach that was polished to a shine. She approached the door like a queen, her gloves spotless, her gown new, her hat perched perfectly on her head.

Colonel Fitzwilliam had always thought of this show as her armor, the things she put between herself and everyone else to maintain her position, protect herself, and keep those dear to her safe. They were more alike than different, he and his mother.

They were led into the drawing room where Darcy stood near the door, Elizabeth slightly behind him, as if he would protect her with his own body, and Miss Bennet and Mrs. Gardiner just on the other side of the room. They were announced and Darcy took it upon himself to introduce his aunt to their hostess and the Miss Bennets.

Lady Blackburn looked Elizabeth up and down, taking in the fabric of her dress, the price of the trimmings, the style chosen and what it said about its wearer, and Elizabeth's face and figure. She seemed to consider the younger lady for some time before she nodded slightly and moved to sit near Elizabeth.

Elizabeth took a deep breath. She had not known what to expect. The lady was neither as false nor imposing as Lady Hopewell, nor was she as jovial as Colonel Fitzwilliam. Lady Blackburn's shrewd eyes took in every detail of Elizabeth's person until she felt as if she were an animal displayed in the menagerie. But then she had noticed it. The slight tick around the countess's mouth, the crinkle beside one eye that said she was holding in a smile.

Elizabeth thought she just might like Lady Blackburn.

"Would you care for some tea, my lady?" offered Mrs. Gardiner.

"I had hoped Miss Elizabeth Bennet might be willing to accompany me on a walk? I saw a pretty little park not far from here."

The party looked at each other, eyes darting from person to person, until Elizabeth stood and said, "I'll just get my things."

Darcy was uncomfortable, Colonel Fitzwilliam was suspicious, and Lady Blackburn was self-satisfied. Jane looked worried and Mrs. Gardiner pursed her lips in disapproval.

Elizabeth had a spirit that could not bear to be crushed at the will of others, and she relied on it now. She accompanied Lady Blackburn outside, and once they had entered the little park, the older woman said, "My son holds you in high esteem, Miss Elizabeth."

"As I hold him, my lady."

"He spoke of you in such a way that I thought for a moment that he had an interest in you himself, and only the barrier of fortune had kept him from declaring himself."

Elizabeth had expected many things from Lady Blackburn, but not that.

"Do not be alarmed, Miss Elizabeth. My son does not view you in that light. I must say I am glad of it. He and Darcy have always been close. It would have torn them apart to be in love with the same woman."

"I can imagine," said Elizabeth weakly.

"I am sure you can. After further conversation, I realized Richard looked on you as another sister. I imagine you remind him of someone."

"Of Olivia?"

The countess turned to her sharply. "He told you of my daughter?"

"Yes. I am very sorry for your loss, my lady. I cannot imagine how difficult that was."

Lady Blackburn looked away, swallowing thickly. "It was many years ago now." She straightened her shoulders and looked ahead. "Richard has told me enough about you that I see no reason to question you further. I only wish to know one thing. Do you care for my nephew?"

Elizabeth studied her shoes for a moment. "Yes. Though sometimes I wish I did not."

Lady Blackburn smiled wryly. "I can imagine. Darcy is not an easy man to come to know. I would imagine he is not easy to fall in love with either."

"Easier than I would have thought," said Elizabeth without thinking. Her eyes widened and she looked at Lady Blackburn with her mouth agape.

That lady smirked back at her. "Just so." She walked on, causing

Elizabeth to rush to catch up to her. "Regardless of the difficulty involved in having a relationship with a man such as my nephew, I believe it is worth the effort in the end. He is fiercely loyal, and there is nothing he would not do for those he cares for."

Elizabeth looked intrigued, so the lady continued.

"You should have heard him this morning warning me off you. He insisted I not meet you at all if I could not be kind." She chortled. "I would have been insulted had it not been so amusing."

Elizabeth flushed and looked toward the meadow where children were running with a hoop. It was gratifying to know Mr. Darcy had fought so hard for her; that her equanimity was valuable to him.

"I am not displeased to hear it," she said quietly.

"No, I imagine you are not."

Elizabeth refused to blush further under the lady's scrutiny.

"I will support you as best I can, Miss Bennet."

"You will?"

"Of course. Darcy is very dear to me, and Richard values you. And he is right—you do have Olivia's way about you." She gave Elizabeth a wistful smile and the younger woman returned it.

"I am grateful for your support, my lady."

"You are welcome to it. And it will drive Lady Hopewell mad, which can only be an added inducement."

Elizabeth laughed.

When they returned to Gracechurch Street, they were met by four pairs of anxious eyes. Elizabeth smiled brightly at the room and asked if they might have some tea for the walk had left her quite thirsty. She prepared a cup for Lady Blackburn and winked when she delivered it.

That lady smiled and said, "Thank you, my dear," and Darcy nearly fell off his chair.

Lady Blackburn began a conversation with Mrs. Gardiner. They had both grown up in the Peak District and they had a lively conversation on the beauties of the area. The call ended with Lady Blackburn inviting Mrs. Gardiner to call on her and join in a charity effort she was part of. She kissed the cheeks of Darcy and her son and patted Miss Elizabeth's hand with a warm smile.

Everyone stared blankly at one another for more than a minute after the door had closed behind her.

"Well," said Jane, a little breathless.

"Indeed," added Darcy.

"You have worked your magic on my mother, Miss Elizabeth," said the colonel. "Not that I ever doubted you."

"That was in large part due to your efforts, Colonel. I must thank you for the glowing recommendation."

He bowed slightly. "I am always happy to assist a lady."

Darcy still looked rather gobsmacked and did not join the conversation until Elizabeth surreptitiously took his hand and squeezed it. He looked at her in surprise, and seeing that she was truly not distressed, he smiled weakly and made an effort to converse.

Elizabeth could only be glad she had now met both sides of Mr. Darcy's family and come out of it unscathed and with the support of someone as powerful as Lady Blackburn.

20

MISCHIEF IN MERYTON

While Elizabeth was being courted in London, Charlotte was holding court in Meryton. She had been carted around by her mother to various teas and functions, and made to repeatedly describe Rosings, her parsonage, and how Lady Catherine allowed them to walk in the gardens whenever they wished.

Charlotte found it all tedious, but it made her mother happy. She was happy to see her old friends again, and she could not help but notice the change in attitudes around her. Her entire life in Meryton, people had known her as the eldest Lucas girl. Pleasant, but not handsome, and with a dowry as small as hers, she had needed to be handsome.

She had been declared a spinster in the making at fifteen, and by two and twenty she was a spinster in truth. No one had ever thought she would marry, and she had occupied a strange place in society. She was respected as the eldest daughter of one of Meryton's most prominent members, as well as for her own good nature—she hoped. Yet she was pitied as well. Her fate was to live at Lucas Lodge all her days, assuming her father lived into old age and her brother did not force her out. The people of the town had thought to watch her grow upward in years and downward in consequence until one day she was simply forgotten. Charlotte had expected it as well.

And then Mr. Collins came to Longbourn. He was a bumbling fool and said the most ridiculous things, but he was respectable, had good prospects, and he was not a cruel man. She knew she could do a great deal worse, and she had long wished to have a family and home of her own. She leapt at the chance to cease being the Spinster of Lucas Lodge and instead take up the mantle of Mistress of Hunsford Parsonage.

Being a vicar's wife suited her. She felt useful in the community, and she truly thought she was helping the parishioners with their concerns. She listened when an ear was needed and sat with the bedridden and the elderly so they would not grow lonely. She mended and sewed and consoled as she could, and she thrived on the busyness and the joy of running her own home. It had given her a confidence she had never before possessed, and she idly wondered if this was how Elizabeth felt all the time and subsequently why she was willing to take risks Charlotte never would have imagined.

Thinking of Elizabeth made Charlotte think about all she had learned with her friend in Hunsford. Chiefly, what they had learned about Mr. Wickham. Even now, he was flirting with Miss Long on the other side of the room, acting for all the world as if his engagement to Miss Mary King had not ended only a week ago. He was certainly not heartbroken, nor did he even have the decency to act as if he cared about her departure.

Charlotte shook her head. She could only think Mary King had made a lucky escape. Such a man would only make his wife miserable.

She was incensed when she thought about how Mr. Wickham was free to move about, charming as he pleased, where he pleased, with no consequences for his actions. She knew such was the way of the world —men were granted freedoms women could only dream of—but women were not without their own form of power. She knew there were ways to stop someone of Mr. Wickham's ilk. She would begin tomorrow.

SHE WAS DRINKING tea with her mother and her friends in the parlor when Charlotte began her first maneuver.

"Do you know, I heard the most awful thing in Kent."

Four pairs of eyes moved to her instantly.

"What was that, dear?" asked Mrs. Lucas, thinking it could not be so very interesting as Charlotte had been home three days already and had said nothing of it.

"It was about one of the officers in the militia here."

Now Lady Lucas perked up. "One of the officers? Which one?"

"I heard the most dreadful things. He is a liar and a gambler, leaving debts everywhere he goes." She waited until they were watching her carefully and added, "And he is a seducer!"

They gasped in unison, just as she had planned.

"Who is it?" asked Mrs. Long.

"It must be that Mr. Saunderson. I have always wondered about him," added Mrs. Goulding.

"Oh, yes! His eyes are shifty. He cannot be trusted!" exclaimed Mrs. Phillips.

Charlotte wanted to correct them and say that one lazy eye did not make a man untrustworthy, but she refrained. "It was not Mr. Saunderson. He is not charming enough to be a seducer, do you not agree?"

They looked thoughtful, considering her statement.

"I suppose it could be Captain Carter. He is a handsome one," said Mrs. Phillips.

"Oh yes!" cried Mrs. Long. "My nieces have said as much many a time."

"Yes, is it Captain Carter?"

"No, for he is rarely at the gaming tables when we have parties. Or has he changed since I left?" clarified Charlotte.

Mrs. Goulding shook her head vigorously. "No, you are right. He has no head for cards. I remember him telling me he did not gamble as a rule. How could I have forgotten?"

"It must be Mr. Denny!" cried Mrs. Phillips triumphantly. "He is always at the gaming tables, and he can be charming when he wishes to be."

"True," said Charlotte thoughtfully. "I heard nothing about him specifically, but I agree he should be watched carefully. He keeps unsavory company."

"Unsavory!" cried Lady Lucas. "Whatever can you mean, Charlotte?"

"Why, I speak of Mr. Wickham, of course."

The room erupted. She was thankful she had had the foresight to eliminate a few of the officers before she told them his name as they were now trying to say it could be anyone but him, for he was so very charming and affable.

"Do not seducers and rakes find charm to be their greatest weapon?" she said sagely before hiding behind her teacup.

Mrs. Long looked stricken, and Mrs. Phillips was red and spluttering.

"Come now, we must know all," demanded Mrs. Goulding. "What do you know?"

"I know that what Mr. Wickham told us about the living Mr. Darcy owed him was all a lie. He refused the living, never took orders, and was offered three thousand pounds in lieu of the preferment. He even signed papers to that effect."

Lady Lucas gasped. "No!"

"Yes. He was also given a thousand-pound legacy from old Mr. Darcy. After he spent the four thousand pounds he was granted—a single man with no home or family to support—he returned to ask Mr. Darcy for the living. I think we could all agree that Mr. Darcy was well within his rights to refuse to give it to him."

Mrs. Long was fanning herself vigorously now. "Oh dear! How very distressing!" She continued to mumble incoherently as the other ladies seconded her disbelief.

Mrs. Goulding looked at Charlotte with sharp eyes. "How have you come by this information, Mrs. Collins? We must know the facts before we condemn the man."

"Of course. I'm sure you required the same of Mr. Wickham when he was slandering Mr. Darcy."

Spinster Charlotte never would have said such a thing, but Charlotte Collins was certain of her position and had no patience for tomfoolery.

"I had it from more than one source. Colonel Fitzwilliam was the first. He is the nephew of Lady Catherine de Bourgh, son of the Earl of Blackburn, and a colonel in His Majesty's army. He is also Mr. Darcy's cousin and was an executor of his father's will. He has known Mr. Wickham since childhood and is a kind, intelligent, trustworthy man."

Mrs. Goulding did not like looking the fool, so she asked, "And how are you certain of that? We would have said much the same about Mr. Wickham yesterday."

"Colonel Fitzwilliam offered to have papers brought from the solicitor's office that prove the whole of it. Has Mr. Wickham offered any such proof?"

She sipped her tea calmly as the ladies looked back and forth at each other, doubt clouding their expressions.

"It was all seconded by Mr. Darcy, of course, who has direct knowledge of all of their dealings. He has become a friend." She looked significantly at her mother. Surely that woman would see that being friends with Mr. Darcy was much more advantageous than being friends with Mr. Wickham. "And of course Lady Catherine could tell you a dozen stories of Mr. Wickham's misdeeds." Those stories were more about how he had broken the glass in her carriage window while playing by the stables as a boy, but she *could* tell them, so Charlotte had not told a falsehood.

"He did spread a personal story rather freely," said Mrs. Long uncomfortably.

"Yes, and he conveniently waited for Mr. Darcy to leave before he did so," added Mrs. Goulding, now convinced and ready to throw her considerable moral weight against Mr. Wickham.

"Oh, what are we to do?" cried Mrs. Phillips.

"Well, to begin with, he should not be around any young ladies.

Think of his influence? I worry for Maria. What might he say to her? What might he attempt?" Charlotte widened her eyes dramatically and all the ladies nodded vigorously with her.

There was a chorus of exclamations and shocked half sentences before Mrs. Phillips jumped up and said, "I must go to my sister Mrs. Bennet! My nieces! Oh, they are so fond of the officers." She wrung her hands and said her goodbyes quickly before hurrying out the door.

"I must go as well. My nieces must be told to stay away from Mr. Wickham and anyone he associates with. Can you imagine? The immorality!" Mrs. Long bustled out behind her friend.

Mrs. Goulding took her leave more slowly, stopping to say to Charlotte, "I thank you for the information, Mrs. Collins. It is well we know when there is a sheep among the wolves."

Charlotte looked bemused, then chose not to correct the older lady. "Of course, Mrs. Goulding. I am happy to assist."

As their parlor emptied and Lady Lucas went to find her husband and inform him of the news, Charlotte caught her reflection in the mirror above the mantle. She smiled at herself and said, "Not badly done, Mrs. Collins. Not bad at all."

WICKHAM DID NOT UNDERSTAND why everything had changed. He had expected an invitation to Mrs. Phillips for dinner that week, but he had received nothing. He had seen her on the street and before he could approach her, she had ducked into the dressmaker's shop. He could not follow her inside without looking a fool, so he had put the incident out of his mind, though it was strange.

Then the publican had refused him credit when he wished to drink with the other officers. Wickham could not imagine why, and when he tried to cajole the man into giving him what he wished, he was unceremoniously declined. The publican had gone a step further and told Wickham he expected to begin seeing payment on the credit he had already been extended, and he would not be given any drinks, even for ready money, until Wickham had paid at least two shillings towards his debt.

Wickham was more than a little surprised by the man's heated response, but he supposed his account had run rather high—it was likely time to move on to another location.

He had tried to steal a kiss from Millie, the butcher's daughter, but she would not even meet his eye when last week she been more than happy to flirt brazenly with him.

Everywhere he went, he was met with averted gazes and unhappy shopkeepers. What the devil was going on?

"Wickham!"

He jumped and turned around outside his quarters. Saunderson approached him with a serious expression. "Do you have my money?" he asked gruffly.

Wickham tried not to blanch. Saunderson was a tall, gangly man with little charm and even less patience. He was younger than Wickham and often at the gaming tables, and Wickham had both won and lost to him many times now. He had never been concerned about his debts of honor before.

"Well? Do you have it?"

Wickham laughed nervously. "You know we are not paid until the end of the month."

Saunderson looked at him shrewdly. "Aye, but I hear you won against Chamberlayne last night."

Wickham backed away a step. "I did, but I have just come from the tavern. I had to pay there first, you understand."

Saunderson looked like he thought Wickham was lying, and he was not fooled by it for a second. He was not a particularly strong man, but he was an excellent shot and a good horseman. He was also known to be scrupulous with money.

He continued to stare at Wickham, unimpressed by the man's excuses.

"Perhaps I have a little put by."

Saunderson looked at him shrewdly. "Perhaps you do."

Wickham slipped into his room and drew out the small coin purse that held his winnings from the evening before. It was not much, but it was enough to get to London and disappear for a little while. Or he could pay Saunderson and have enough left to pay the publican, but then he would still owe three other officers and a handful of tradesmen. If they heard he had paid Saunderson, they would expect to be paid as well.

Feeling a rivulet of sweat making its way down his back, he swiftly hid his winnings inside his small clothes and stepped into the hall with a shilling between his thumb and forefinger.

"This will have to do for now, Saunderson."

The tall man took the coin and placed it in his pocket, looking at Wickham like he was a spider he had inadvertently stepped on. "I'll be back for the rest."

Wickham laughed nervously and smiled, attempting to be charming and failing miserably. "It won't be long now."

Saunderson glared at him and walked away, and Wickham breathed a sigh of relief. He must get out of Meryton. Tonight. He would wait until dark and sneak away, walking the five miles to the next town. A stage ran there regularly enough he should be able to catch it and disappear into London. Yes, it would work. He only needed to avoid the officers he owed money to for another few hours.

Shortly after midnight, Wickham shimmied out of the window with a small bag of his belongings. He dropped to the ground with a light thud and stood straight to dust himself off. He stayed in the shadows and had nearly made it beyond Meryton when he heard a voice say his name.

"Wickham. Where are you going?" Saunderson stepped out of the shadows and into Wickham's path.

"Oh, nowhere special," said Wickham as he backed away. "Just off for a spell. I shall return in a few days."

"Is that right? Does Colonel Forster know you are leaving the regiment?"

"Leaving the regiment!" Wickham laughed uneasily. He took another step back, darting his eyes to the side to see where he could successfully run to. "I would hardly call it leaving. More like taking a short break. I will be back before you notice I am gone. There is nothing to be concerned with."

"Oh, there isn't?"

A deep voice behind Wickham made him look over his shoulder.

"Denny!" he cried in relief. "I am glad to see you. Tell Saunderson I am only going away for a few days and that all will be well. There is nothing to be worried over."

Denny glared at him. "Your room is cleaned out. Looks like you plan to be gone longer than a few days."

Wickham scrambled for something to say. "I, well, that is, I had thought to return some things to my uncle in Town. I will bring back what is needed."

"You told me you had no family," said Denny darkly.

Saunderson spit in the dirt, leaning leisurely against a building in the moonlight. "Seems you are having a bit of trouble keeping your stories straight, Wickham. I stopped by the tavern. Publican says you haven't paid him a farthing." He spit again, the relaxed posture as he leaned against the brick only making Wickham more nervous.

He looked over his shoulder, only to see three more officers, two of them on horseback, waiting to take him back to camp.

"You know desertion is a crime, do you not?" said one of the men on a horse.

"You'd be surprised at what he does not know," said Denny with dark amusement.

"Now, wait just a moment! I am not deserting. Going to Town for a few days is hardly deserting your post!"

"Colonel Forster does not agree."

Wickham's eyes bulged as he turned to face Saunderson, who was now only a few feet behind him.

"Come along, Wickham. Don't make this worse than it needs to be." Denny took his arm firmly and propelled him through the dark streets of Meryton.

Wickham was in a blind panic, wondering how he would escape this mess. They were in a war. Desertion in a time of war was punishable by death!

He looked around desperately, searching for a way to escape or a savior to rescue him. The shops were dark, their doors bolted shut, and most of the rooms above were darkened as well. He saw a curtain flicker in one of the lit windows and a face pull back from the glass.

Any hope he had had that he would somehow escape this unscathed vanished like smoke. Mrs. Phillips would make sure the entire town knew of his humiliation by dinner tomorrow.

21

FRIDAYS ARE FOR GARDENS

Bingley's idea of going to Kew Gardens was agreeable to all, and soon they arranged a large party. Mr. Darcy's landau would convey Elizabeth, Miss Darcy, Lady Clara, and Mrs. Annesley, Miss Darcy's companion. Bingley would drive his curricle with Jane, and Mr. Darcy and Colonel Fitzwilliam would ride alongside.

Elizabeth was delighted with the opportunity to get to know Georgiana and Lady Clara better. Darcy had originally asked if she would like to ride along in the curricle with him, and while she found it delightful, she thought it important that she come to know his sister, so she declined. He was disappointed but heartened by her reason.

They were not ten minutes away from Gracechurch Street before Elizabeth knew she would have an uphill climb in befriending Georgiana. The poor girl was so shy she could barely utter a word. She sat next to Lady Clara, nodding along to whatever that lady said, and looking about at the scenery. Elizabeth asked her about the countryside, whether she had been to Kew Gardens before, and whether she preferred town or country. To each of her inquiries she received the shortest answer possible and eventually, she decided to speak with Lady Clara instead. She was just as in need of a friend, but far more

217

ready to converse. Perhaps Georgiana was like her brother and preferred to observe. Mayhap she would speak once she felt she knew Elizabeth better.

They reached the gardens without incident and before they could walk five steps, Lady Clara had taken Elizabeth's arm and pulled her ahead of the others.

"Lady Clara, what is it?"

"Miss Elizabeth, I must ask for your assistance in a personal matter."

"Of course, I will help however I can. What do you require?"

"Would you help me walk with Colonel Fitzwilliam? I know you have seen that I enjoy his company. If I orchestrate something—"

"You will look like you are scheming."

"Exactly. But if you do it…"

"It will appear I am scheming," teased Elizabeth.

"I am sorry to put you in this position. If it is too awkward, pray forget I said anything at all."

"I am only teasing, Lady Clara. Of course I shall help you. Only, I know for a fact Colonel Fitzwilliam must marry with fortune in mind…" She hesitated and looked inquiringly at Lady Clara.

"Oh, that is of no concern. My dowry is forty thousand pounds."

Elizabeth's eyes grew wide. "It is a wonder you are not yet married."

Lady Clara looked at her pleadingly.

"Right, this is not the time for that discussion."

"Thank you."

"Join him with Georgiana and I will call her away shortly."

Clara squeezed her arm and smiled brightly. "Thank you, Miss Elizabeth. I will not forget your kindness!"

Elizabeth smiled and pressed her arm, then moved to join Mr. Darcy where he was watching them rather quizzically.

"Do I want to know what you are up to with my cousin, Elizabeth? You have a glint in your eye that is quite frightening."

"Frightening! You do exaggerate, Mr. Darcy. What could possibly be frightening about me?" She smiled teasingly at him and he pulled her a little closer.

"You are positively terrifying when you choose to be, and you know it."

She laughed gaily. "I am no such thing! I can hardly be held responsible if a great man such as yourself is frightened of harmless ladies."

"Where are these harmless ladies you speak of?"

Elizabeth laughed again and leaned into his arm. "You are delightful when you tease, Fitzwilliam. I do hope you will continue to practice."

"I intend to, my love."

A few minutes later, she said, "Do you think Miss Darcy would like to walk with us?"

"I do not imagine she would object. Did you speak much on the ride?"

Elizabeth sighed. "No, we did not. I had thought she was merely shy, but perhaps you are correct and I have frightened her."

Darcy looked at her with a frown. "Are you teasing, Elizabeth? You know I cannot always ascertain your intentions."

"Only a little. We did not speak much, that is true. I eventually thought she might prefer to get to know me as you did—by watching instead of speaking. So I spoke with Lady Clara and she seemed to listen attentively. Perhaps when there are fewer women about she will speak more."

"Perhaps," he said thoughtfully. He looked over his shoulder and said, "Excuse me, my dear," and trotted off to join his sister and cousins.

Soon he was back with Georgiana on his arm. He offered Elizabeth the other and she smiled brightly at him.

Darcy then proceeded to surprise Elizabeth in the most pleasant way. He spoke. He talked of the flowers and plants they were seeing, the peacocks visible under a tree nearby, and the geography of the river that ran beside them. He spoke to Georgiana and herself in turn, eliciting more than one enthusiastic response from the young girl. He was very nearly charming! To add to the joy of the day, Mr. Bingley had fallen so far behind with Jane they could barely be seen, and Lady Clara looked exceedingly pleased with her position on Colonel Fitzwilliam's arm.

Elizabeth was enjoying the company of her beau and his sister and feeling quite proud of the assistance she had given Lady Clara when there was a rise of voices behind them. She stopped to look over her shoulder.

"Who is that?" she asked.

"I do not know. The gentleman looks vaguely familiar," responded Darcy.

A gentleman roughly Darcy's age and a woman with her back to them were talking to Colonel Fitzwilliam and Lady Clara. Colonel Fitzwilliam looked delighted; Lady Clara appeared mildly ill.

"Darcy!" The colonel waved them over. "You remember Jonathon Covington and his sister, do you not?"

Darcy looked at his cousin suspiciously, but he greeted the newcomers politely. Everyone was introduced, and the Covingtons were invited to join their party. They walked along as one large group for a time, but eventually Georgiana fell back to walk with Mrs. Annesley, who had been keeping to the outskirts of the group. Mr. Darcy and Mr. Covington seemed to be discussing some sort of horse race, and Miss Covington walked at her brother's side. Lady Clara was beside Darcy, looking disappointed.

Colonel Fitzwilliam looked around to make sure everyone was distracted, then grasped Elizabeth's elbow and led her to the side of the path.

"I need your help, Miss Elizabeth."

"What is going on? You look like you've been caught sneaking into the larder."

He gave her an eloquent look that said she was not far off. "I wish you to befriend Miss Covington."

"Me?"

"Yes."

"Why?"

"I cannot explain now, but I am asking you, as my friend, to do this for me. I would not suggest it if I did not think highly of her." His eyes locked on hers, blue meeting brown, and she nodded.

"Of course, Fitz. You have done a great deal more for me. I am happy to help." She had her suspicions, but she would keep them to herself—for now.

He squeezed her arm and smiled. "I will be calling you Lizzy soon enough, I'm sure." He ignored her look of surprise and added, "Thank you. I promise I will explain all in due time."

She nodded and made her way around the group, thinking how best to handle the situation. Hoping she was doing the right thing, she approached Mrs. Annesley.

"May I ask a favor?"

"Of course, Miss Elizabeth."

"Would you walk with Lady Clara? She is in need of companionship today," she said quietly. "I hope I may trust in your discretion?"

"Of course," said Mrs. Annesley with a nod. She and Georgiana quickly made their way toward the opposite side of the group.

Elizabeth sidled up beside Miss Covington.

"Have you been to Kew Gardens before, Miss Covington?"

"Yes, but not in some time," she answered quietly.

"I have always been partial to gardens myself. I could attend such an outing every week and never grow tired of it."

"I quite agree. My mother has always had a partiality for gardens. Her rose garden was quite extraordinary."

"It sounds lovely. My aunt is similar. Her garden is not large, but it is one of my favorite places in Town."

"Do you live in London, then?"

"No, I live in Hertfordshire on my father's estate. I am in Town visiting my uncle and aunt with my sister." She nodded behind her toward the two shadows that were Jane and Bingley. "She is the one strolling as slow as treacle with her besotted suitor."

Emma followed Elizabeth's gaze and smiled. "There are worse places for a romantic stroll."

"That is very true. Now, since my own suitor is glaring at me for abandoning him, I must insist you tell me all the interesting things about yourself and half the dull ones so that when I return to him, I will be able to say I was well and truly coming to know Miss Covington."

Emma Covington laughed and began to speak as Elizabeth looped her arm through her new friend's and pulled them ahead of the group.

"WHAT ARE YOU UP TO?" growled Darcy at Fitzwilliam.

"Whatever do you mean?" said Fitz innocently.

"I saw you take Elizabeth aside and speak to her, right before she suddenly began walking with Miss Covington, a lady she has never seen before in her life and whom she has no reason to seek out. *Your* Miss Covington. Confess, Cousin. What is going on?"

"Very well," said Colonel Fitzwilliam testily. "I asked Miss Elizabeth to assist me in making Miss Covington feel welcome."

"Because?"

"Because after I spoke with you the other day, and seeing how my mother has taken to Miss Elizabeth, I thought things might not be as hopeless as I had thought they were."

"So you arranged for them to meet us here?"

"I mentioned to her brother that we would be here today and that I would like to see them."

"You are certain you wish to pursue this? You will not raise her hopes and change your mind?"

"Of course not! What do you take me for? I am not cruel!"

"I know," said Darcy with a shake of his head, "but be certain you know what you are about, Fitz. You are doing things that cannot be undone."

"Darcy," said Fitzwilliam with the patience of a man who had seen more in war than he would like to remember, "kindly refrain from explaining to me about things that cannot be undone."

Darcy looked down. "Forgive me, Cousin. Of course you are correct. I misspoke."

Fitzwilliam clapped him on the shoulder. "In the three years since I met her, I have not met a single lady whose company I have enjoyed more than Miss Covington's. I believe it is time to act on that."

"Have you seen her much the last two years?"

Fitzwilliam glared at him.

Darcy raised his hands up. "I am not trying to discourage you. Merely ascertaining if you have learned her character as it is now."

"I doubt she has changed overmuch."

"Tragedy can change people rather quickly," Darcy said grimly.

"Well, as it happens, I have seen her from time to time the last two years—her brother is a friend, after all. And she has been as delightful as ever. A little saddened by all that has happened of late, but that is to be expected. In essentials, she is what she ever was."

"Then I wish you well, Cousin."

A tinkling laugh ahead of them drew their attention.

"Elizabeth seems to like her," said Darcy.

"I am glad of it." Fitzwilliam looked shrewdly at his cousin and said, "When will you propose to Miss Elizabeth?"

"When the time is right."

"And when will that be?"

Darcy exhaled heavily. "Why are you so invested in my marriage plans? Keep your attention on your own."

Fitzwilliam laughed. "I cannot! If you marry Miss Elizabeth, all the attention will be on you and I may slip off quietly to tend to my own plans."

"And what are those?"

"I hardly know yet, Cousin, but I thought I would start with seeing if the lady returns my interest."

Darcy clapped him on the shoulder. "A wise plan, Fitz."

BY THE TIME they stopped for refreshments, the stragglers had caught up to the rest of the group. Lady Clara still looked put out over Colonel Fitzwilliam's defection and then Elizabeth's seeming abandonment, but she seemed at least somewhat mollified by the attentions of Jonathon Covington, who was listening with rapt attention as she told him about the puppy she was training.

Elizabeth smiled and shook her head, glad Lady Clara was not too upset, and sought out her sister. Jane was smiling ethereally and all of Bingley's teeth were visible. Elizabeth approached Jane and whispered in her ear.

"Is there something you wish to tell me, Sister?"

"Oh, Lizzy! Why cannot everyone be as happy?"

"Mr. Bingley has proposed?"

"Yes! And I have accepted."

Elizabeth embraced her sister. "I am so very happy for you, Jane. Do you want to tell everyone else or wait until we return?"

"It may be too late for that," she answered with a fond smile and a nod toward Bingley.

He was standing between Darcy and Colonel Fitzwilliam and they were alternately congratulating him and slapping his back. Soon, the entire party knew of the engagement and Jane received their warm wishes as only she could.

Darcy watched Elizabeth with a pleasant feeling of contentment. He knew it would not be long until they were receiving congratulations on their own engagement. They had suffered a setback or two, but they were headed in the right direction—finally, and he felt that the difficulties had bonded them further, if such a thing were possible.

Lady Clara had tried to stay near Colonel Fitzwilliam as they clustered under the trees, but watching him dance attention on Miss Covington turned out to be an undesirable pastime and she moved to sit alone, preferring her own company over the ebullient effusions for Miss Bennet and Mr. Bingley's engagement. She was soon joined on her side of the tree by Jonathon Covington. He seemed determined to speak to her, and he appeared to be a kind and unassuming man. He was a friend of Colonel Fitzwilliam's, and though she was smarting from having been thrown over by him only a half hour ago, she did trust his judgement. And she was not completely against receiving a little attention of her own.

Soon, they continued their walk through the gardens and Lady Clara walked on the arm of Mr. Covington, now in the position of listener as he told her about the estate he was bringing back to its former glory. He had inherited it from an uncle and it was small and in disrepair, but with patience and diligence, it could be a lovely home. She nodded and smiled and commented where necessary, asking the occasional question. It never occurred to her to wonder why he was speaking to her of such a topic, or why he was not paying attention to anyone else in the party.

She walked happily along, only occasionally glaring at Colonel Fitzwilliam and the back of Miss Covington's bonnet.

SEEING everyone else was distracted and Georgiana was with Mrs. Annesley, Darcy felt no compunction in pulling Elizabeth slightly ahead of the party so they might converse privately.

"You arranged that rather conveniently, Mr. Darcy," said Elizabeth.

"I do not know what you mean," he replied.

"It has worked out rather well for your cousin."

She glanced over her shoulder and smiled fondly at the group comprised of their friends and relations. The ladies were clustered around Jane, questioning and congratulating her, and Bingley was somehow in the middle of them all, smiling like a fool and looking more than a little dazed. Colonel Fitzwilliam was on the outskirts of the group, trying to pull Miss Covington from the crowd.

"What is Colonel Fitzwilliam up to?" asked Elizabeth as they pulled farther away from the group.

"What do you mean?"

"He is paying a great deal of attention to Miss Covington, and none whatsoever to Lady Clara."

"Lady Clara? Why would he pay her special attention?"

Elizabeth rolled her eyes. "He needs a wife with a fortune, and she is in possession of one. They are both kind people and they are both connected to you. It is not an outlandish idea to think they would enjoy one another's company and possibly come to an understanding."

He looked at her incredulously.

"What?"

"You make it sound so simple."

She shrugged. "Sometimes it is."

His face expressed his doubt. "You would not behave so yourself. You know you would not."

She shrugged again. "I am not Lady Clara."

"You certainly are not." He leaned down to whisper in her ear, "You are much prettier."

Elizabeth blushed, more from the feel of his breath on her ear than his words.

"So your cousin is not at all interested in Lady Clara?" she asked, her voice a trifle unsteady.

Darcy smiled to see he had affected her and said, "No, he is not."

"Oh, dear."

"What is it?"

She looked at him with a guilty expression and bit her lip.

"Elizabeth?" He drew her name out, in what she thought would be the tone he would always use when she had done something she probably should not have.

She looked adorably sheepish as she said, "Lady Clara asked me to assist her in spending time with Colonel Fitzwilliam today. I saw no reason to refuse."

Darcy's lips tightened for a moment and he looked away, blowing out a breath. "Well, it is no one's fault but his own."

"What do you mean?"

"We did not run into the Covingtons by accident. Fitz invited them here."

"He has an interest in Miss Covington?"

"Yes, of long duration."

"I suspected as much, but I did not want to assume. Is it serious?"

"Serious enough. He is ascertaining the lady's feeling on the matter."

"Ah." Elizabeth turned to watch Colonel Fitzwilliam walking with Miss Covington. "She seems to return his regard, at least in part."

"How can you tell?" asked Darcy, looking at the couple in question with interest.

"Look at how she holds his arm. She is making no effort to distance herself. And see how she leans her head towards him when he speaks?"

"She could be merely trying to hear him better," Darcy reasoned.

"If she did not like him, she would not care what he had to say."

Darcy's face lit in understanding.

"And she would not have allowed him to lead her from the group, not when her brother is there to offer a rescue, as well as Mrs. Annesley and myself."

Darcy nodded.

"Poor Lady Clara," sighed Elizabeth.

"Why do you say so?"

"She is in her third season with no suitors on the horizon. I believe she truly liked your cousin."

"It is unfortunate it will not work out with Fitz, but she is hardly without suitors. I know of at least two men who would gladly take her to wife."

She looked as if she had swallowed a lemon. "Fitzwilliam, you have missed the point entirely. Lady Clara does not want to be 'taken to wife' as you so romantically put it. She wishes to be cherished by her husband. It is not so unreasonable a request."

He placed his free hand over hers on his arm and pulled her slightly closer. "No, it is not, my love. Forgive me. I spoke without thinking. A worthy woman should always be cherished."

She smiled at him sweetly and briefly laid her head on his shoulder. "You should not say such things, my dear. I cannot kiss you in public."

Now Darcy's cheeks flamed and he pulled her as close as he

possibly could, looking around frantically for a secluded nook to hide in while he kissed his beloved senseless. Alas, they were in a relatively open portion of the garden with their own party not far behind them and another group only a short distance ahead.

"Elizabeth. You are a minx."

She looked up at him in confusion for a moment before seeing the look on his face. Her cheeks darkened to match his and she swallowed heavily. "Forgive me, Fitzwilliam. I was not thinking."

He drew her hand to his mouth and kissed her knuckles. "Never apologize for expressing your heart to me, Elizabeth. I always wish to know your feelings."

She raised one brow and said, "Always?"

"Well, most of the time."

She laughed delightedly. "Well said, my love."

She looked forward and walked on, not having noticed her own words. Darcy could only stare blankly ahead of him, wondering if he had heard her correctly.

2 2

SWEET SATURDAY

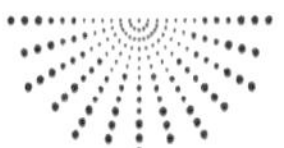

Darcy, Colonel Fitzwilliam, and Bingley arrived at Gracechurch Street as early as was polite. Mr. Gardiner had given Bingley permission to wed Jane, though she did not truly need it as she was of age, and he had brought the settlement for Mr. Gardiner to peruse. He had had it drawn up the day after he called on Jane in London for the first time and had been eagerly awaiting the opportunity to use it.

While Mr. Bingley was closeted with their uncle, Jane and Elizabeth took the other two gentlemen for a walk. To everyone's surprise, once they were out the door, Elizabeth took Colonel Fitzwilliam's arm, leaving Darcy standing rather stupefied next to an equally confused Jane.

"Jane, do you mind keeping Mr. Darcy company while I discuss something with Colonel Fitzwilliam?"

"Of course, Lizzy."

Elizabeth thanked her and moved swiftly down the walk, pulling Colonel Fitzwilliam alongside her.

He chuckled lightly. "Why are you in such a hurry?"

"I do not want Darcy or my sister to hear me."

His expression immediately became serious. "Is anything amiss? Are you well?"

229

"Perfectly so, thank you, but something is amiss. Are you going to tell me what yesterday was all about?"

Fitzwilliam looked away guiltily.

"Out with it, Colonel."

He sighed. "Very well. Some time ago, I became… let us say enamored, of Miss Covington."

"Go on."

"Her family fell on hard times, and she was soon after in mourning for her father, so the flirtation never had an opportunity to develop into something more."

"And now you wish to see if it will?"

"Yes, but I am more serious than you make me out to be."

"Forgive me, but I did not think Miss Covington was in possession of a large fortune. Do you not need a well-dowered wife?"

Colonel Fitzwilliam made a noncommittal noise. "I do, though…"

"You would not require it for the right lady."

"Just so."

"I see. So you are more than enamored of Miss Covington."

He flushed. "We have only recently begun to see each other regularly again."

She nodded. "But you think you would like to marry her?"

"She is my first choice, yes."

"First? Or only?"

"At the moment, only."

Elizabeth nodded but said nothing.

"I tried to forget her two years ago. I paid attention to the daughter of one of my mother's friends and thought we might make a go of it, but I could never fully forget Miss Covington. Every woman I met, I compared to her."

"Let me guess. They all fell short?"

"Precisely."

"Oh dear, I believe I should call you Fitz regularly now."

He looked at her in confusion.

"You have just confessed to being in love with Miss Covington. Such a statement demands a more informal address, don't you think?"

He looked surprised for a moment, then smiled and said, "I would be pleased for you to call me Fitz. Even though my dolt of a cousin has yet to work up his courage and propose to you."

It was Elizabeth's turn to flush. "I do not think it is courage he lacks."

"You do not?"

She shook her head. "I asked him to give me time to become accustomed to the idea. After all, it was barely over a fortnight ago that I would not have even considered him a friend."

"But you have spent a great deal of time with him since then. Much more than you would if you had seen one another at a few dinners and balls."

"You are not incorrect."

"So it is you who lacks the courage?" he asked softly.

She tilted her head and sighed. "It is not courage I lack, but conviction."

"You are still unsure of him?"

"Do not look at me like that. You have had a lifetime of knowing his character, seeing him in every situation, watching how he reacts to difficulties. I have had a fortnight. Under the circumstances, I think I have come a rather long way."

"Forgive me, you are correct of course. I know Darcy to be an exemplary man and I would be remiss if I did not tell you that you could do far worse in a husband."

She gave him a look he could not interpret, but he thought it was a cross of exasperation and interest.

"Not only would he be a good husband to anyone lucky enough to marry him, but he will be especially good to you, for he is desperately in love with you."

She could not help the smile that formed at such a pronouncement. "I have come to the same conclusion."

"So what are you waiting for, Lizzy?"

She looked at him in surprise, seeing the stern expression she would expect of any self-respecting elder brother. "Nothing, I suppose."

He smiled. "You should tell him that. The poor man is tied in knots."

She laughed. "I could. But I am enjoying this period of courtship. It is short, and it will only happen once. I want to savor it."

"That is understandable, but you may continue to court after you have accepted him."

"Hmm."

Fitzwilliam rolled his eyes.

Elizabeth laughed. "Very well. I relent!"

Fitzwilliam shook his head in exasperation as he smiled at her. "It is about time you came to your senses."

WHEN THEY ARRIVED at the park, Darcy quickly reclaimed Elizabeth.

"Dare I ask what you were discussing with my cousin?"

"I was asking him about Miss Covington."

"Oh?"

Elizabeth gasped and stopped suddenly. "I forgot to ask about him about Mr. Covington."

"Mr. Covington?"

"Yes. He paid a great deal of attention to Lady Clara and I wondered if Fitzwilliam organized it or if the gentleman did it of his own accord."

Darcy looked thoughtful. "Fitz has never been a matchmaker, but I suppose it is not outside the realm of possibility."

Elizabeth laughed at his turn of phrase. "I begin to think very little is outside the realm of possibility when it comes to your cousin."

"So you think Jonathon Covington is pursuing Lady Clara?"

"I cannot be certain—it was only one day. But he did walk with her the entire afternoon, and I saw them talking privately together each time we stopped."

"Hmm."

"Is he a good man?"

"I could not say. I know no ill of him. His care for his sister is commendable. I know he has done everything he could to rebuild her dowry after their father's mistakes. Not every man would have done so."

"No, they would not." She looked thoughtfully toward the trees. "He is a friend of the colonel's?"

"Yes, they have known one another some time."

"Do you think her parents would sanction the match if she were to choose him?"

"Why the sudden interest in my cousin's affairs?"

"Answer the question, Fitzwilliam."

"Very well. It would be an uphill battle. Mr. Covington is certainly not who they would have chosen for the only daughter of an earl. Her fortune is splendid."

"Yes, she told me. Forty thousand pounds is hard to overlook." She looked at Darcy searchingly. "Why do you suppose she is not yet married? She has a large dowry, good connections, and a pleasant personality. I do not understand."

"I know she was pursued heavily by more than one gentleman her first season, but her father found them all wanting."

"What was the problem? Were they lacking in connections?"

"One was too beneath the daughter of an earl. Another was too indebted and likely looking for a well-dowered bride to save him from his own mistakes. I cannot fault my uncle for refusing that one."

"Of course. So do you think other gentlemen have been reluctant to pursue her for fear her father will decline their suit?"

"That likely has some bearing on her prospects, though as her near family, I would hardly hear of it." Darcy looked about him uncomfortably and tugged on the cuff of his jacket. "We cannot ignore the matter of Lady Clara's relative plainness. She is kind and a worthy lady, but she is not handsome, and the gentlemen whom her father would approve of—"

"Rich and well connected," interjected Elizabeth.

"—are able to choose whom they wish."

"And they wish for a pretty wife."

"Just so. The less choosy gentlemen with less fortune or who are in need of connections would not meet the earl's approval."

"Even if they truly cared for her," said Elizabeth with sad finality.

"I am sorry to distress you."

Elizabeth sighed. "You have not, not truly. I hate that marriage is a business arrangement for so many, and that a lady may not simply choose the man she wishes to wed! Lady Clara has her own fortune. She could marry a younger son or a country gentleman with a small estate. They might be very happy together. But her father's ambitions will stand in her way."

"I cannot disagree with you. If Lord Hopewell continues as he has done, he will likely end up having to arrange a match for her in her fifth season when she is considered on the shelf."

Elizabeth huffed. "It is ludicrous that a woman can be a spinster at three and twenty, but a man can be well over thirty and still be considered a good catch."

"I shall refrain from commenting on that."

She glared playfully at him and took his arm as they continued walking. "What would happen if Lady Clara accepted a man her father did not approve of?"

"She is not of age. She cannot legally wed without his consent unless she elopes to Scotland."

"Of course. Do you know when she will be one and twenty?"

"This autumn, in September I believe, though I do not remember exactly."

Elizabeth looked thoughtfully at the trees again.

"While we are speaking of gaining one's majority, when is your birthday? You have never told me. You are twenty, are you not?"

"Yes, I am, though not for much longer. I shall attain my majority next month."

His eyes brightened. "I shall have to think of a way to celebrate."

She smiled. "Nothing extravagant!"

"I make no promises."

She shook her head at him.

"Is there anything in particular you would like?"

"As a gift?"

"Yes."

"I do not know. I have been planning to get a new pair of walking boots."

Darcy rolled his eyes. "Only you would think walking boots a suitable gift from a lover."

"What would you prefer to get me?" she retorted.

He turned to face her and gently placed his hand along her neck. "Something shiny and delicate, to hang just here." He traced the skin just above her neckline. "Or perhaps here." He raised her hand to his lips and kissed the inside of her wrist. "Something as lovely as you are."

Her breath quickened and she looked at him with a promise in her eyes. "Fitzwilliam."

Realizing he had started something he could not continue in a public park, he turned and began walking toward the pond with a determined stride.

"Mr. Gardiner tells me he is considering sending your cousin to school next year, though they may wait a year. What is your opinion on the matter?"

Elizabeth smiled to herself and answered accordingly, thinking that Colonel Fitzwilliam was right. It was time to relent.

23

A SIMPLE SUNDAY AND AN
EVENTFUL MONDAY

Elizabeth had expected to spend Sunday afternoon quietly at home with the Gardiners, but she had received an invitation to spend the afternoon with Lady Clara. A Hopewell carriage picked her up in grand style, and soon she was having tea in a small parlor at the back of the large house.

"This is a lovely room."

"Thank you. It is my favorite room in the house. I redecorated it last year. Mother said it would be a good way to practice being a wife, but in truth I think she could not be bothered with it. She has never enjoyed decorating."

"Well," said Elizabeth with an appreciative look around the room, "you have done a wonderful job. Everything flows together delightfully."

"I am glad you think so. I cannot abide a garish color scheme."

After several more comments on the striped paper and the patterned fabric covering a new chair, Elizabeth noticed Lady Clara seemed uncomfortable. She was fidgeting with the fringe on a nearby pillow, and she plucked at the skirt of her dress. Her forehead was often wrinkled in thought and she had started several sentences that she did not finish.

"Pardon me, Lady Clara, but is something on your mind? You seem distracted."

"Oh, forgive me, Miss Elizabeth. Actually," she hesitated and looked around the room nervously. "I was wondering if you might give me a bit of advice."

"Oh?"

"Mr. Covington came to call on me yesterday."

"Did he?"

"Yes. My mother was on her way out, so she had my aunt sit with us. She arrived in Town Thursday last and is half deaf and rather nearsighted."

"An ideal chaperone then."

Lady Clara smiled uneasily. "Yes, well, he was attentive. Do you suppose—do you think he might…"

"Do I think what, my lady?"

"Do you think he truly likes me? Or is he only in need of money?"

Elizabeth looked at Clara sympathetically and moved to sit near her on the sofa. She placed her hand over Lady Clara's on the cushion and squeezed. "I do not know him personally, but Colonel Fitzwilliam is well acquainted with him. I will ask for you and find out as much as I can."

Lady Clara's face lit up in relief. "Oh, thank you, Miss Elizabeth! That is very kind of you."

"It is the least I can do. I will tell you that I know Mr. Covington's family fell on hard times recently and he was forced to sell the estate to remain solvent. He was able to partially replace his sister's dowry and his mother's settlement, so they are not entirely destitute. I believe he has inherited a small estate from an uncle."

"Yes, he told me of it. It is in York. I have been there once before—it is a lovely county."

Elizabeth looked at her seriously. "Do you like Mr. Covington?"

"I believe I do. He seems kind and he has so many interesting things to say. He speaks of more than gossip and the weather." She suddenly looked more animated. "Yesterday, we spoke for a half hour on the current campaign on the peninsula. I have never had such a conversation with a man, well, other than…"

"Colonel Fitzwilliam. Yes, of course." Elizabeth tried to sound cheerful and supportive without giving her false hope in case it were to come to nothing. "It sounds as if you have at least made a new friend, even if nothing romantic comes of it."

"Yes. He told me he had known me before. I danced with him my first season, more than once he says, though I do not recall it. But then I do not recall most of that season. I was entirely focused on… you know."

"Yes, the good colonel has the effect on some people." She smiled brightly. "But Mr. Covington has found his way back to you and it is a good sign that he remembers you two years later, is it not?"

"Do you think so?" The hope in her voice was heartbreaking.

"I do. I shall ask Colonel Fitzwilliam as soon as possible and insist that he tell me everything he has ever heard about Mr. Covington. You have my word."

Lady Clara smiled broadly and clasped Elizabeth's hand in her own. "Thank you!"

~

Mr. Darcy,

Our newfound pastime of matchmaking requires attention. Do you know anything of Mr. Jonathon Covington? I have been tasked by a relation of yours to find out everything I may. I understand the Good Colonel has been his friend for some time. Might you pass on my request for information to him?

I eagerly look forward to our outing tomorrow. I have a new gown that Aunt assures me is perfect for the theater. If you do not recognize me in the lobby, I will be the one in the blue gown cut so fashionably you will think I am someone else entirely. Truly, I hardly recognize myself in it.

Will Miss Darcy accompany us? You had not decided when I saw you last.

I cannot wait to see you. Has it only been a day? I am ridiculous. I should not miss you after only a day.

Until tomorrow, my heart.

Yours,
Elizabeth

Dear Elizabeth,

I have passed on your request to Fitz and he is taking the matter as seriously as he does everything else—that is to say, not at all.

The writing changed drastically and in a larger hand was written:

Do not listen to a thing he says, Miss Elizabeth. Just because I am not sour-faced does not mean I do not know how to answer a question seriously. JC is a good man—I would go into battle with him, which is the highest commendation I could give. More to the point, I have known him several years now and have never seen or heard anything to cause me concern over his character. He does not gamble or drink to excess, and he is scrupulous and conscientious. He is also a terrific bowler, if you are ever in the mood for a game.

CRF

The writing changed back to Mr. Darcy's neat hand.

. . .

PARDON *my cousin's rude interruption. He has been too long in the barracks. I have also heard no ill of Mr. C and seeing what my cousin wrote, I would say those are all good qualities in a husband. I assume that is why you are asking, though correct me if I am mistaken.*

G will not accompany us to the theater. She is still too shy for such an outing, though she has asked if you and Miss Bennet might come to tea later this week so that she might get to know you. Tell me when you may join her and I will send the carriage for you.

Now that I know the color of your gown, I will be sure to watch for a stunning woman in blue in the lobby of the theater, bearing a slight resemblance to my Elizabeth.

Truly, my love, do you not know how breathtaking you are? You were pretty when I first met you, then you became remarkably handsome. You have since moved past beautiful and are now firmly lodged in my heart as the most lovely, pleasing, perfect woman I have ever met.

How goes my first attempt at a love letter? Fitz stands behind me even now laughing uproariously over my efforts. You may laugh and smile when you read this, and I can imagine how your eyes will dance in the candlelight.

Regardless of my bumbling, I hope you know how dear you are to me. I look forward to tomorrow with great anticipation.

Yours,

FD

FITZWILLIAM,

THANK *the colonel for the information. I have relayed it to Lady C and can only hope it gives her some peace of mind. She is a dear girl and deserves happiness if it can be had.*

Your first attempt at a love letter was quite well received—so well received I have naught to say in response. My aunt has been teasing me relentlessly on my blushes since it was delivered.

I will await you at the theater with great anticipation.

· · ·

Yours,

Elizabeth

~

Darcy stood in the lobby of the theater with his heart in his eyes. This was the night he would publicly declare to all of the ton that he was well and truly taken by Elizabeth Bennet. A month ago, he would have been worried how she would be received. Would her relations embarrass him? Would he feel the scorn of society for his choice?

Now, he was nothing but proud of his choice. Well, proud and anxious. He was glad he had not asked her to marry him that wretched Thursday in Kent. If she had accepted him, he would not have come to value her as he did now. If she had refused him—it did not bear thinking about.

He looked towards the door, finally spotting Mr. and Mrs. Gardiner arm in arm. Jane was on her uncle's other side. He saw a dark head behind Mr. Gardiner he hoped was Elizabeth and made his way to them. Bingley arrived at the same time.

Bingley wished everyone a good evening while looking only at Jane—and standing annoyingly between Darcy and his lady. Soon Jane was on Bingley's arm instead of her uncle's. The Gardiners greeted him and finally Elizabeth stepped out from behind her uncle.

Darcy's jaw nearly dropped to the floor. She was incredibly fashionable, as she had said, but more than that, she was lovely in her own right. A well-made gown could not magnify beauty that was not there.

"Elizabeth. You are a vision."

She flushed and said quietly, "Thank you, Fitzwilliam."

Mr. Gardiner cleared his throat and they were reminded that they were in public and should probably not refer to each other so informally. Darcy could only nod and continue to stare at his love, his heart in his eyes.

By the time the first intermission arrived, Elizabeth was breathless. In a fit of magnanimity, the Gardiners had taken the seats in the front row. Their box was long and narrow, only three seats across and three rows deep. Bingley and Jane sat in the center seats while Darcy and Elizabeth had taken the ones in the back. Darcy had said he would sit in back due to his height, and the Gardiners had agreed, likely thinking it safer for it to be he and Elizabeth in such private seats, who were only courting, instead of Bingley and Jane who were engaged.

They were wrong.

Darcy began with merely holding Elizabeth's hand. Their joined hands rested on her knee and all was perfectly innocent. Until he had tugged her glove off, one finger at a time, then slowly kissed each fingertip in turn, nibbling a little for good measure.

Elizabeth had squirmed in her chair, resisting the urge to audibly sigh, and eventually settled for resting her hand on Mr. Darcy's thigh, just above his knee. She could not know how such a simple gesture would inflame him.

In retaliation, he drew circles on the back of her hand with his fingertips.

She drew them on his knee.

He reached across the back of her chair and played with the curls hanging down her neck.

She shifted in her seat until her entire left side was pressed against him.

He moved his right leg behind her ankles where they were daintily crossed in front of her. Her eyes widened as he moved his foot in a rhythmic motion along the backs of her feet.

She turned to face him, her eyes reflecting the sparse candlelight the only thing he could see, and her expression was more than any mortal man could be expected to resist. He leaned across the tiny space and closed the distance between her mouth and his.

Elizabeth reacted by placing her hands in his hair, running her bare fingers through his locks until his eyes crossed in pleasure.

Just before the lights came up for intermission, Darcy said he would fetch them refreshment and exited the box. Elizabeth patted her hair, feeling that it was thankfully in place, and slipped her glove back on just before her aunt and uncle turned around in their seats to ask how everyone was enjoying the performance. She stayed in the shadows near the corner, grateful her seat was at the very end, and told herself to behave with more decorum after the interval.

She did not.

By the time Darcy escorted them home to Gracechurch Street, she was a mass of longing and need, wanting nothing more than to continue her activities from the theater with Darcy.

She had heard of it, and read of it, but she had never before experienced it so potently.

Desire.

"May I take a turn in the garden with Miss Elizabeth?" asked Darcy as he escorted them to the door.

Mr. and Mrs. Gardiner looked at each other, then nodded their permission.

Darcy followed Elizabeth into the darkened garden, barely noticing the fragrance of the flowers or the sound of the wind in the trees.

He reached for Elizabeth's hand and tugged her to him. "Elizabeth," he growled. "Come here."

She came willingly and nestled herself against him in a way he found positively delightful. "Yes, Fitzwilliam?"

She looked up at him and he said, "You have the most beautiful eyes."

"They are a simple brown. Yours are a remarkable shade of blue. Like the sky after a storm has cleared out all the clouds."

"Yours are the perfect shade of brown. Brown like Scotch whisky, and they make me equally lightheaded."

She smiled. "You say the most delightful things sometimes, Mr. Darcy."

He smiled roguishly and pulled her deeper into the garden, looking for a bench he remembered seeing there. Finally, he found it beneath a willow in the back corner and pulled Elizabeth down to his lap.

She gasped as she landed on his thighs, then settled her weight more comfortably and leaned against him. He loved the way she sank into him so easily, so filled with trust. He could not believe she was his —after all the longing and the denial and the difficulty, she was happily sitting on his lap in the garden.

Her neck was in a perfect position to be kissed and he could not resist. She let out a little sigh of contentment and whispered his name. He could hold back no longer.

"Elizabeth, my love, my heart, marry me. Please marry me and be my wife." He kissed her cheek and then her mouth, slowly, sweetly. "I love you so, my darling." He kissed her lips. "Marry me." He kissed her again. "Marry me." His lips dragged back along her neck. "Marry me, my love." He suckled gently at the place where her shoulder met her neck, causing her to gasp in pleasure. "Marry me and let me love you always."

She sighed, her heart light and happy. "Fitzwilliam, yes, I will marry you. Yes, my love."

He continued kissing her neck and worked his way back to her mouth where he kissed her deeply before pulling back and looking straight into her eyes. "You did say yes?"

She nodded.

"I did not imagine it?"

She shook her head with a dreamy grin.

"You will marry me?" he asked again, a tentative joy overtaking his features.

She smiled brightly now. "Yes. I will marry you!"

He crushed her to him so swiftly she nearly lost her breath. "My love. I will make you so happy, I promise. You will not regret it."

She smiled and rested her forehead against his, a feeling of contentment settling over her. "I'm certain I will not, my dear."

"Elizabeth, I have not the words to tell you how happy you have made me." He sighed, a surge of emotion threatening to bowl him over.

She stroked his cheek, saying softly, "I love you so, Fitzwilliam. I cannot wait to marry you."

He sat up straight, nearly unseating Elizabeth in the process. "What did you say?"

"I said I cannot wait to marry you."

"Before that."

"Oh." She smiled shyly. "I said I love you so, Fitzwilliam."

He smiled more broadly than she had ever seen him do. "My very heart."

"Darcy, I have excellent news! You must congratulate me."

Darcy looked up as Colonel Fitzwilliam burst into his study late Monday night.

"What is it, Fitz?" He sounded disinterested and uncaring, but he could not be bothered about that. He could only think of Elizabeth. The smell of her hair, the feel of her lips on his face, the touch of her fingers on his chest.

"Darcy!"

"What?"

"I called your name half a dozen times."

"Oh. Forgive me, Fitz. My mind wandered."

"Judging by the look on your face, I can guess where it wandered to."

He ducked as Darcy lobbed a pillow at him.

"What is this news you were crowing about?" asked Darcy.

"I spoke with Mother. I told her I had met a lady I would like to court and wed, but that I could only do so if I knew I could provide for her after the wedding. She agreed to talk to Father."

"Was he amenable?" asked Darcy, suddenly all attention.

"He said that as long as the lady is not embarrassing or awful, his words, not mine, he would give me the estate and wish us well."

Darcy leapt up and slapped his cousin's back while vigorously shaking his hand. "That is wonderful news! Have you decided on Miss Covington then?"

"I have called on Miss Covington twice now. I am certain she returns my interest, and my regard is as strong as it ever was."

Darcy smiled broadly, moving to pour them a glass of brandy from the decanter. "This calls for a celebration. My cousin, the perpetual bachelor, has finally been caught."

"You are one to talk! I at least have made myself useful in the army while waiting to wed. You have been lolling about for no good reason at all!"

Darcy laughed. "Only you would consider running an estate to be lolling about."

They toasted Fitzwilliam's future happiness, his new estate where he would be free to loll about to his heart's content, and the ladies they had rather shockingly fallen madly in love with.

"You are different," said Fitzwilliam.

"What do you mean?"

"I do not know. There is something about your face—you seem lighter somehow."

"Are you saying my face usually looks heavy?"

"Oh for heaven's sake, Darcy! Tell me what it is. You look like the cat who got the canary."

"I proposed to Elizabeth," he said simply, a contented smile on his face.

"And?"

"She accepted."

Colonel Fitzwilliam whooped and leapt out of his chair. "It is about time you came to the point. When is the wedding?"

"We have not decided yet. I must speak to her father first. But we had thought we might join Bingley and Miss Bennet in a double ceremony."

Colonel Fitzwilliam shook his head, a wide grin on his face. "I wish you happy, Darcy. Truly. Miss Elizabeth is the perfect match for you."

"Thank you. I hope you will stand up with me when the time comes."

"Of course! I wouldn't dream of missing it. And you must return the favor for me."

"You would not wish for one of your brothers to be your witness?"

Fitzwilliam guffawed. "My brothers are either too young and naïve or too old and cynical."

"And I am just the right age?"

"It is more that you are just the right combination of innocent and cynical."

Darcy threw another pillow at him.

"Can you believe it?" said Fitzwilliam, leaning back to stare at the ceiling. "In a few months' time, we will both be married men."

"I cannot believe it. I spent so many months wishing for Elizabeth, I have had to assure myself more than once that I am not dreaming."

"I can assure you that you are not dreaming. Unless you were with someone else who would leave a love bite on your neck." He pointed and Darcy clapped a hand over the offending mark. Fitzwilliam laughed uproariously. "It is a good sign, Darcy. Wear it as a badge of honor."

Darcy grumbled.

"Do you know how many men wish their wives would leave such a mark on them? You are fortunate that you will have a wife who loves you and can abide your person."

Darcy was looking dreamily at the fireplace again, and Fitzwilliam rolled his eyes and rose from his chair.

"I shall go to bed now. Enjoy your dreams, Darcy."

He was nearly to the door when the pillow hit the back of his head.

24

A FINE THURSDAY IN JUNE

The banns had been read, the wedding clothes ordered, the breakfast prepared, and the church decorated. All was in readiness for the grandest wedding Meryton had ever seen.

Mrs. Bennet was all aflutter. Her two eldest daughters—the most deserving and the most troublesome—were marrying rich men today. They would be so very grand. Such carriages! Such jewels! Such pin money! She would go distracted if she thought on it too much.

"Come, my dear. We will be late for the church," said Mr. Bennet drily.

"Oh, Mr. Bennet! Two daughters married!"

"Yes, yes, it is all well and good, but they will not be married if we do not get them to the church."

"Mary! Kitty! Lydia!" she screeched.

Mr. Bennet placed a hand over his ear.

"Get in the carriage, girls!"

Mr. Bennet shooed them out the door and into the Bennet carriage. Mr. Darcy had generously sent over one of his carriages to deliver Jane, Elizabeth, and Mr. Bennet to the church.

"I cannot believe we will be married today!" said Jane as she entered the entrance hall. She was a vision in pale green silk, her expression radiant and her eyes glowing softly.

"Are you ready, girls?" asked Mr. Bennet, his voice choked.

Elizabeth smiled softly at him and stepped to his side. "We are ready, Papa."

They rode to the church in silence. Elizabeth opted to sit beside her father, his calloused hand clasped between both of hers. When they pulled in front of the old stone building, he stepped out and helped Jane down first, then Elizabeth. She stopped in front of the church, the sun shining brightly behind her father, the air filled with the scent of blossoms.

"I hear there is a wonderful library at Pemberley," she said softly. "We could explore it together."

He cleared his throat. "You must do that with your young man. He has earned the privilege. But I reserve the right to come and visit—likely when you least expect it."

"Shall I have a bed moved into the library for you?"

"That is an excellent idea, Lizzy."

They laughed together in front of the church, then Mr. Bennet sighed and looked back and forth between his daughters—the one he had loved first and the one he had loved most.

"It is bittersweet, giving away one's daughters."

They smiled sweetly at him and each took an arm.

"I could not have parted with you for gentlemen any less worthy."

Jane sniffled and kissed his cheek, and Elizabeth followed suit.

Mr. Bennet straightened his spine and lifted his chest. "Enough of that now. Let us get you two married."

After a short ceremony and an interminable wedding breakfast, Darcy was out of patience. The breakfast was held at Netherfield and he and Elizabeth would be staying the night there, along with Jane and Bingley, before leaving for Pemberley four days later. It had seemed a good plan when they first arranged it, but now he wondered at his stupidity.

If *they* did not need to leave the breakfast, how would they make the guests leave?

He was certain Mr. Bennet knew of his predicament for the old man had looked at him and laughed several times when Darcy was feeling particularly frustrated. Mr. Bennet could have ended it all by thanking all of the guests and wishing the newlyweds well. But he would never turn down an opportunity for sport, and Darcy was making it entirely too easy on the old man.

"Fitzwilliam, be careful or you will chip a tooth."

He turned to his new wife—his wife!—and attempted to rein in his irritation. It was not her fault, after all.

"Do you know how much longer this will go on?" he asked as politely as he could.

She made a sympathetic face and looked around at the room full of people. They were still eating and drinking and the staff continued to bring out more food. "I'm afraid it will be some time yet."

He took a deep breath, trying not to groan aloud. He disliked parties at the best of times, but when he was the center of attention, it was exceedingly uncomfortable. Add his desire to be alone with his wife and it was positively torturous.

"I have an idea," Elizabeth whispered in his ear. He raised a brow in question and she said, "Say goodbye to your family, then meet me by the staircase in fifteen minutes."

He did not know what she had planned, but he very much liked the sound of fifteen minutes and Elizabeth going upstairs in the same sentence.

He found his great uncle, Sir Daniel, first. The older man wished him well and promised a visit to Pemberley soon. Darcy said goodbye to Lord and Lady Blackburn and his cousin Harry. Fitzwilliam was nowhere to be found, and Darcy thought he had probably escaped to the garden with Miss Covington. She had come with her brother and would leave first thing in the morning, hopefully while Darcy was still sound asleep. In bed. With his bride.

He found his sister and told her to be a good houseguest for his aunt and that he would see her at Pemberley next month when she travelled north with the Bingleys and Mrs. Annesley. Finally, he caught Bingley's eye across the room and waved. Bingley smiled broadly and nodded, not surprised in the least to see his friend escaping his own wedding breakfast early.

Elizabeth did something similar. She said a quick goodnight to Jane, who she would be seeing soon, said the same to each of her sisters, and had a short chat with Charlotte. Charlotte was smug and proud of her romantic deduction in the best possible sense. She wished Elizabeth a wonderful evening and made her promise to call before she left for Pemberley. Elizabeth kissed the Gardiners on each cheek and thanked them for all their assistance during her courtship. Then she asked them for one last favor: to tell her mother she had left after she had had plenty of time to escape.

Mr. Gardiner laughed—he knew his sister well—and promised he would do as he was bid. Mrs. Gardiner was pleased to help, so long as Elizabeth would promise to take her around the grounds of Pemberley in a light open carriage when they came to visit in August.

"Anything for you, Aunt." With one last embrace, and Mrs. Gardiner's parting words of "all will be well," Elizabeth snuck off to the stairs to meet her husband.

Her father caught her just as she was leaving the drawing room.

"Leaving early, Elizabeth?"

She sighed. "Papa. Do not tease me now. It is unkind."

He had the grace to look sheepish, then smiled again with the glint in his eye she had long learned to recognize. It gave her an idea.

"Have you met Sir Daniel yet?"

Mr. Bennet rolled his eyes. "There are so many titles in this house I cannot keep them straight."

"You will like this one. He is a retired high court judge."

Mr. Bennet's brows rose.

"He only arrived early this morning. I cannot believe I forgot to introduce you before." She grabbed her father's arm and towed him to the other side of the room.

"Sir Daniel, may I present my father, Mr. Thomas Bennet of Longbourn?"

They exchanged courtesies and Elizabeth said, "My father thinks all the prisoners should be conscripted to the army in order to make use of them and save on cell space." She smiled mischievously between the two of them. "Discuss." With a cheeky grin and a wink, she skipped off towards the door.

She made it to the staircase ten minutes late to find her new husband pacing across the hall.

"There you are!"

"I am sorry, my love. My father was attempting to be funny, so I took him to Sir Daniel."

"That was clever of you."

"Thank you." She smiled cheekily and began moving up the stairs. She looked over her shoulder at Darcy. "Hurry! We do not know when we will next be interrupted."

He got a look in his eyes that her feet understood before her mind did. She sprinted up the steps, Darcy hot on her heels.

It had only taken three weeks of courtship, a month-long engagement, and an interminable wedding breakfast to finally get him to chase her.

THE END

Want more *Pride and Prejudice*? Type the link into your browser to get a free copy of *Meryton Vignettes*, a collection of 6 short stories.

https://bookhip.com/TFKCFLF

Or find all of Elizabeth's books on Amazon and Audible.

Elizabeth Adams is a book-loving, tango-dancing, Austen enthusiast. She loves old houses and thinks birthdays should be celebrated with trips—as should most occasions. She can often be found by a sunny window with a cup of hot tea and a book in her hand.

She writes romantic comedy and comedic tragedy in both historic and modern settings.

You can find more information, short stories, and outtakes at EAdamsWrites.com